TEETH IN A PICKLE JAR

by H. B. Milligan

Hand-in-Hand Publishing

To Carol,

Best wishes
Helena

Praise for Teeth in a Pickle Jar

A love story rooted in real life!

"Spunky and upbeat, a terrific piece of work. I was laughing out loud. I could visualize the characters and was amazed at how much I became wrapped up in their lives. I even had tears in my eyes at the end. What more can you ask for?"

Christina Ferrari, former editor, Teen People Magazine

"An intelligent, humorous and well-written story. The characterizations sparkle, the dialogue has 'zing' to it, and the plot gleefully defies expectations."

Cheryl Jeffries, Heartstrings Reviews

"The book is filled with laughter, love, sweetness and hope. A good, solid, enjoyable read with very human characters to which many of us can relate."

BellaOnline, "The Voice of Women"

"Very smooth and very human. The author brings the characters to life so well, you feel you know them."

Times-Standard, Eureka CA

"A great read. I could hardly put it down until I finished the last page. Wonderful character development. I felt as if I had made new friends by the end of the book."

Paula Murray, editor, U Magazine

"H.B. Milligan has a fantastic way with words. I read this book in one day. I couldn't put it down until I found out what happened at the end."

Internationalwoman. net

"It's a delightful story, a fun read."

News at Noon, WWSB-TV (ABC affiliate)

What readers are saying:

“I LOVED the book! I finished it at 2:30 am and didn’t want it to end. It was so engaging and insightful, drawing you into the characters. Thank you for such a wonderful book.”

Michelle McCaffrey, Beachbums Book Club, Sarasota FL

“This novel is very readable, engaging, witty and light-hearted. The plot moves along nicely.”

Cathy Nolan, journalist, Paris, France

“An absolutely lovely story. I love the humor throughout; it’s very on, very quick, and fun to read.”

Elizabeth Z, Convent Station, NJ

“A great read, inspiring and uplifting. I didn’t want it to end. One instantly becomes part of Megan’s world. Waiting for more from this talented writer.”

Susan H, Sonoma CA

“A story of romance and passion for life; about taking a chance and finding happiness in unexpected places. It’s a great read, funny and compelling till the end.”

Mary H, Kingston PA

“Just had to tell you how enjoyable this novel is. I had to keep turning the pages for two days. Looking forward to another book, hopefully in ther near future.”

Sara G, Winter Haven, FL

“Loved the book, had many a good laugh.”

Muriel S, Boston MA

“A wonderfully entertaining novel, fun and a pleasure to read.”

Marlene B, Vancouver, Canada

Teeth in a Pickle Jar

ISBN 0-9768994-0-X

Hand-in-Hand Publishing, Bradenton, FL 34209

The Hand-in-Hand Publishing World Wide Web site address is
http://www.handinhandpub.com

Publisher's Cataloging-in-Publication
(Provided by Quality Books, Inc.)

Milligan, H. B.
Teeth in a pickle jar / H.B. Milligan.
p. cm.
ISBN 0-9768994-0-X
LCCN 2005933297

1. Man-woman relationships--Fiction. 2. Parent and adult child--Fiction. 3. Mothers and daughters--Fiction. 4. Critically ill--Family relationships--Fiction. 5. New York (N.Y.)--Fiction. 6. Love stories. I. Title.

PS3613.I5627T44 2005 813'.6
QBI05-600141

Printed in U.S.A.

Visit ***Teeth in a Pickle Jar*** on the web:
http://www.teethinapicklejar.com

Acknowledgments

A big thank you to:

My husband, Bob, who supported and encouraged me during the upheavals of writing this novel, and who laughed in all the right places.

My friends on both sides of the Atlantic, who swore they would buy this book as soon as it is published, and who will now keep this promise.

Most of all, to my father, Joseph, who kept telling me for many years that I should write a book, and to my mother, Faina, who kept telling him to stop nagging.

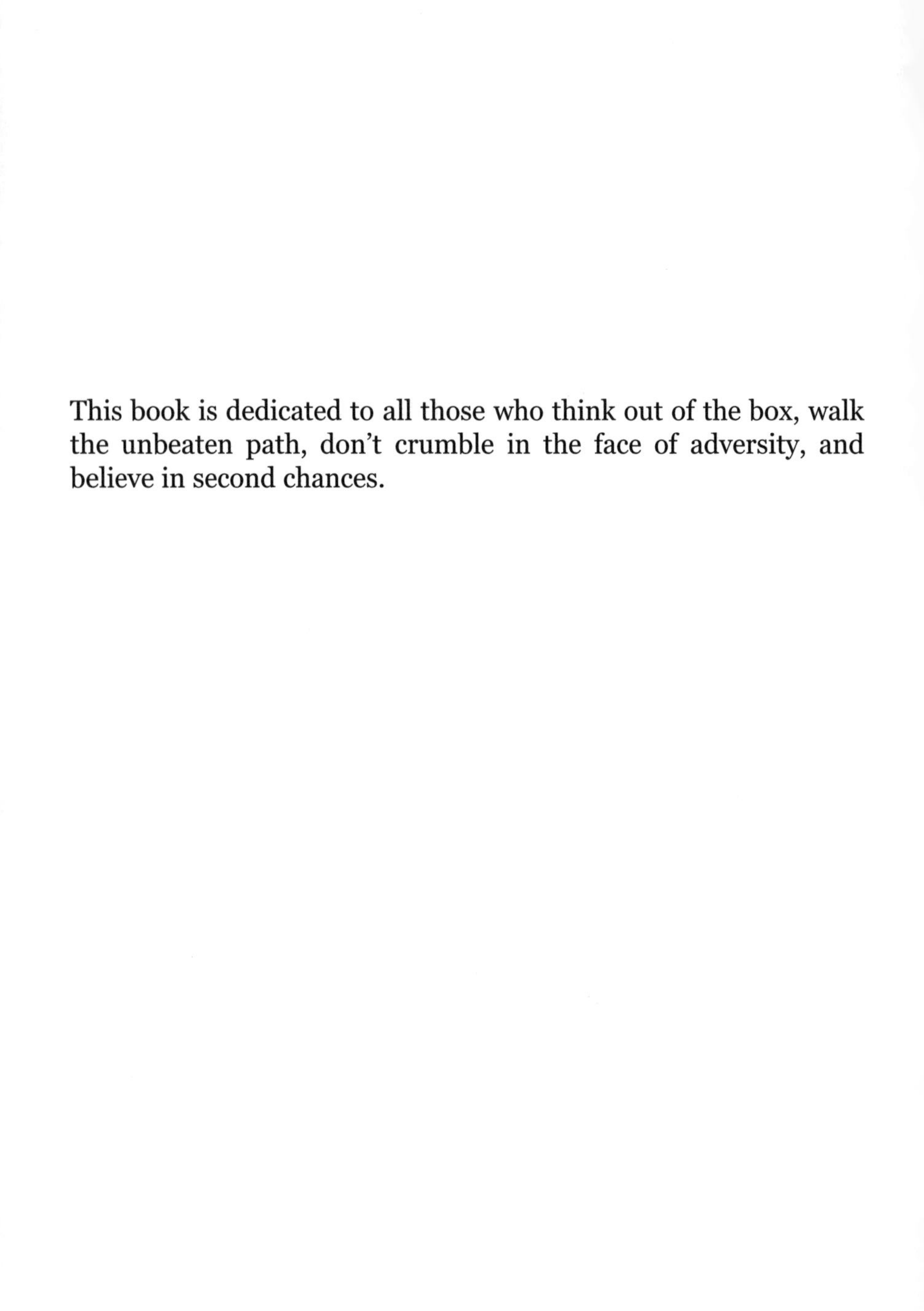

This book is dedicated to all those who think out of the box, walk the unbeaten path, don't crumble in the face of adversity, and believe in second chances.

“Every journalist has a novel in him, which is an excellent place for it.”

J. Russel Lynes

Prologue

I sit crossed-legged on the sand and peer at the faraway line where the sea mingles with the sky. Any minute now the bright orange ball on the horizon will dip into the water and shroud the beach in darkness.

Seagulls and pelicans hover noisily overhead, scavenging for fish that washed ashore. Shivering, I zip the windbreaker all the way up to my chin and shove my hands into my pockets for warmth. My fingers touch an envelope in the right pocket, the unopened letter from Mamma.

The letter arrived this morning. I saw an envelope with the familiar slanted, slightly lopsided handwriting and my heartbeat accelerated. I leaned against the kitchen counter and held the envelope in my hand, hesitating whether to open it right away. What kind of emotions would it unleash? Would the letter rehash old conflicts and reignite not-yet-quite-buried frustrations, or would it offer a glimmer of hope, a reconciliatory olive branch? This envelope was my Pandora's Box, and, as I stood in my bright, sun-washed kitchen, I knew that I couldn't bring myself to open it. No, not yet.

"I'll read it tonight, at the beach," I murmured as I slid the envelope into the windbreaker's pocket.

The beach has been my sanctuary, my haven of peace. During the warm months I walked barefoot along the shore, shifting grainy sand and tiny shell particles with my toes. In cooler weather I sit huddled under a palm tree and watch the changing colors on the water's surface. I sense that whatever emotional upheaval Mamma's letter might cause will be soothed by the soft sounds and breezes of the sea.

The wind blows salty air and whiffs of seaweed and fish at me. I take a slow, deep breath and fill my nostrils with tangy smells of the sea.

Only half of the fiery ball is now blazing over the horizon, poised for the final descent. I narrow my eyes and sit very still, trying not to blink. One...two...three. I silently count the seconds until the sea, bathed in an orange glow, swallows the entire ball.

"Wow," I whisper, gazing at the now barren horizon. "That was magnificent."

The red sky turns grey and the beach grows quiet. The palm trees, which only moments ago ruffled my hair and whipped the windbreaker into a balloon-like shape, emit only timid breezes now. The birds' noisy cacophony mellows into a melodic chirping. And the foamy waves that pounded against the shore are now softly lapping the sand. It is as though all the forces of nature have winded down with the vanishing sun, preparing for the respite of nightfall.

I close my eyes and listen to the flutters and whispers of nature. Odd, how our lives follow the cycles of the sun. The restlessness and tumult give way to serenity just like the sunset's dramatic crescendo wanes into calmness. And then the sun rises over the horizon again, lighting up the darkness in our souls with vibrant hues of yellow.

What about sunsets and sunrises, the ebbs and tides of my own life? I think about the still-new love that suddenly, unexpectedly crashed into me like a powerful wave. The love that lit up the darkest corners of my heart and filled me with the greatest joy I have ever known.

"Megan, old girl," I whisper, "at long last, life is sweet."

I open my eyes, look up and see the still fuzzy outline of the crescent moon. Quickly, before the dusk turns to starry blackness I reach into my pocket and retrieve the envelope. It is made of recycled paper, grainy and thick, and I smile at Mamma's thriftiness. I imagine her going into an outlet store and buying the cheapest stationery in bulk just so she could write one letter.

I open the envelope, take out the folded sheet of paper and, as my heart beats faster and louder, read it in the breeze.

Chapter One

"I'll break every goddamn bone in my body," I muttered as I slowly made my way up a narrow stairway. "They'll have to scrape me off the floor."

I had just come in carrying two heavy, rain-soaked grocery bags and found a "sorry, out of order" sign posted on the elevator door. Damn, the new super we got last month was slacking already.

I balanced the bags against my chest and went through the side door marked "Emergency stairs. Use in case of fire." I chugged upstairs to the fifth floor wheezing and snorting like a steam locomotive, my soggy sneakers squishing on the cement steps. By the third landing my drenched sweater and jeans clung to my body like Saran wrap, and my hair was plastered to my scalp and clammy forehead. I smiled at the thought that I probably looked as fetching as a wet scarecrow.

Just as I reached my door I saw the elevator button light up, followed by the lurching noise of a moving elevator. "Oh, thank you very much, Mr. Super," I mouthed. "What great timing."

I put the bags on the floor, took the keys out of my pocket, and let myself in.

The phone started to ring just as I reached the kitchen. Before I could put the groceries on the counter and grab the receiver the wet bags ripped and their contents scattered noisily onto the floor. A can of soup bounced off the sink, rolled into the living room, and landed under the coffee table. A jar of gravy and six fruit yogurts splattered all over the kitchen floor, and Twinkies, crushed by the falling can, crumbled at my feet. Oh, no, not the *Twinkies*!"

"Damn!" I angrily grabbed a roll of paper towels from the counter, knelt, and scooped the unappetizing, gooey puddle off the linoleum and into the garbage.

"Sixty bucks of Food Emporium groceries gone to waste!" I screamed over the shrill ringing of the phone. "I schlep the bags up five flights of dingy stairs for *this*? That's just terrific!"

The ringing stopped and the answering machine came on.

"Hi, Mom" Hayley's voice said breathlessly. "Just wanted to tell you that I'll be coming home Tuesday after class. I can leave Syracuse, let's see...say around noon, so I'll be there, well, whenever, depends on traffic. So anyway, see you soon, okay? Love you."

"Sorry, sweetheart," I shouted, as though Hayley could hear me. "Your mother, the klutz, can't come to the phone because she's on her hands and knees wiping her week's dinner off the floor. I reckon we'll have to hire a maid, what do you think? "

I stood up and tossed the roll of paper towels back on the counter. It bounced off the wall and landed at my feet. I kicked it like a soccer ball.

The lost groceries and the messy, sticky floor were the last straw to a long day of teaching, battling rush hour crowds, standing in a long line at the store, getting soaked, and carrying the heavy bags up five flights of stairs. And now my comfort Twinkies were *gone*.

I glanced at my watch - thank goodness it was waterproof - and saw that it was five already. Ohmigod, I thought, Mamma would be here in an hour. I'd better get out of the soggy clothes and put on a happy face.

I showered, changed into a dry T-shirt and sweatpants, and went to the kitchen to wait for Mamma. I poured that morning's coffee from the pot into a mug and nuked it in the microwave. The stale, brown liquid looked more like dishwater than java, but I was too tired from walking up five flights and managing the ensuing cataclysm in my kitchen to brew a fresh pot.

I brought the mug to my lips and took a sip.

"Ugh," I grimaced. I spit the acrid coffee back into the cup and flung the mug's contents towards the sink. "That was god-awful!"

I filled a glass with tap water and drank it in one go. The coffee's bitter after-taste still lingered in my mouth, but it wasn't as strong.

I looked at my watch. Almost six, Mamma would be here any

minute, I thought. I tried to remember when the weekly dinners started. Was it three years ago, when Hayley left for Syracuse University? Yes, it was. The day after Hayley drove upstate, her little Ford Focus filled to the brim with boxes and cartons, Mamma had showed up at my doorstep with a pasta casserole.

"You gotta eat, eh," she had said, as she unceremoniously pushed her way in. "Now that Hayley gone, you no cook no more."

"Mamma," I said, as she scurried from the hallway to the kitchen, "I *never* cooked, remember? So it's not as though I'll suddenly starve."

From then on the dinner followed one of two scenarios: Either I went to Mamma's apartment in Queens, or else she prepared an Italian dish ahead of time and brought it over to my place on West 77th Street. The thought of Mamma transporting casseroles and baking dishes filled with food to Manhattan on the New York City subway brought out occasional pangs of remorse in me.

"Why don't we eat out?" I once asked.

"Eat *out?*" Mamma's voice was a mixture of indignation and disgust, as though I had suggested something atrocious, like eating locusts for dinner. "You think food in restaurants better than mine, eh?"

"No, of course not," I quickly said. "I just thought it would be more convenient."

"*Convenient*?" You know what they do to food in restaurants, eh?"

"Serve it?" I asked, although I sensed that a logical retort was not what Mamma expected.

"Sure they serve it. But before they serve it they *spit* into it."

"Who spits into it?" I wanted to laugh but I didn't want to antagonize Mamma.

"Who? Everybody, eh, whole kitchen staff, cook, busboys, waiters. *Everybody.*"

"Oh, Mamma, where did you hear this nonsense?"

"It ain't no nonsense. Everybody know it."

I suspected that Mamma had heard this rumor from customers at Francesco's Italian Grocery, where she had been working for the past forty years. Like Mamma, the customers were Italian immigrants, and, like her, they thrived on gossip. Mamma never paused to verify or even consider the veracity of any particular rumor; to her all gossip, no matter how absurd or outlandish, was the absolute truth.

"Mamma, believe me, it *is* nonsense. Just because someone told you this doesn't make it true."

"Why you argue with me, eh?" Her voice went up a few octaves to an unpleasantly high pitch. "You *wanna* eat other people's spit, eh?

"No, Mamma," I sighed. "I sure don't want to eat other people's spit."

Damn, I thought, was there no way to reason with Mamma? Must I *always* surrender my own opinions, thoughts and desires, and pander to *her* idiosyncrasies?

The ringing doorbell jolted me back to the present and, with a sigh, I went to open the door. Six o'clock on the dot. Even the Swiss couldn't beat Mamma when it came to punctuality.

Chapter Two

"Weather awful," Mamma announced as she came in carrying a dripping umbrella in one hand and a Macy's bag in the other. She wore a pair of dark green galoshes that looked at least two sizes too big, and a hooded plastic poncho that reminded me of the yellow slicker I wore in kindergarten.

"Mamma, where did you get those shoes?" I chuckled.

"I buy them on sale, seven bucks. This the only pair they have left. What's the matter, you no like them?"

Mamma placed the galoshes and the umbrella on a rubber mat by the door and hung the dripping poncho on the doorknob.

"Let's just say they look suitable for walking in manure," I said. "*And* they are big enough for an elephant."

I laughed at the image of an elephant trudging through cow dung in Mamma's galoshes.

She glared at me.

"You think it funny, eh? You think I should wear ballet slippers in rain?"

I wanted to laugh out loud at the mental picture of Mamma's thick, veiny legs jumping over puddles in dainty satin slippers, but I managed to keep a suitably respectful demeanor.

Mamma smoothed her hair and readjusted the bun tied at the nape of her neck. She had worn the same hairstyle ever since I could remember, but now her jet-black hair had streaks of silver in it.

Mamma brought the Macy's bag into the kitchen, put it on the counter and gently removed the aluminum foil covered baking dish from it.

"I made lasagna," she announced.

She picked up the dish and turned toward the oven.

"What, you no preheat?" she asked.

"Oops, sorry, Mamma, I... was rushing around and it slipped my mind."

"Like is so difficult to remember, eh?" she sniffed.

Mamma turned on the oven, took an apron out of her bag – she always brought her own, since I didn't own any – and tied it around her ample waist. She was short and heavyset, with a round face and dark eyes.

I often wondered why the laws of genetics were so unpredictable, for I looked nothing at all like Mamma. I was 5 foot 7, 130 pounds, and had dark blonde hair. The photographs of Papa that Mamma kept in a leather-bound album showed a tall, lanky, *dark*-haired man, so there was at least a slight resemblance from that side of the family.

Mamma slid the baking dish into the oven. I knew better than to suggest nuking the lasagna in the microwave. To Mamma everything, from cooking to scrubbing floors, had to be done the old-fashioned, slow, *laborious* way.

Contrary to Mamma, I avoided all but essential household chores. I wasn't exactly a slob in the strictest sense of the word, which I imagined meant breeding rats and roaches in one's kitchen. I occasionally threw a wet rag at a spider web hanging from the ceiling, or wiped off a thick layer of dust. But I never *consciously* engaged in the actual act of cleaning. Those mindless chores were for Mamma, not for me.

I wanted to distance myself from the drudgery and inanity of Mamma's life. Hers was filled with boring and meaningless tasks and I was afraid that if I behaved like Mamma I would end up just like her: scrubbing the floor on hands and knees, spending every evening hunched over the stove, peeling, chopping, slicing, mixing, stirring, weighing, measuring, blanching, oiling, frying, baking, basting, and stirring.

I actually believed that my aversion to domesticity was a *good* thing, for it meant that I was above such menial tasks and could therefore channel my time and energy into more lofty, intellectual pursuits: reading, for example, or watching educational programs on PBS. Mamma was interested in neither and she used to scoff at the pile of *New Yorkers* stashed under my bed.

"Like this is gonna help you get husband, eh?" she sniffed. "Better learn how to cook."

Contrary to what Mamma expected, these comments actually made me feel good, for they meant that I had successfully detached myself from the torturous pattern of Mamma's life.

So as an adult I filled my fridge and kitchen cabinets with an array of canned and frozen foods, and poor Hayley grew up thinking that a can of Chef Boyardee ravioli constituted a perfectly good alternative to the food pyramid. Mamma used to look at the contents of my cabinets and shake her head in disbelief.

"Macaroni and cheese from *box*? What the hell is *that*? And look at this," she took a jar of tomato sauce from the kitchen shelf and waved it at me. "*Salsa pomodoro* from jar! Like making sauce from *real* tomatoes is so hard, eh?"

She used to come over laden with groceries and cook up a week's supply of lasagna, chicken Marsala, or, Hayley's favorite, tiny, hand-molded meatballs smothered in her homemade tomato sauce. Hayley watched wide-eyed as Mamma stood sweating over a boiling pot, vigorously stirring its contents.

Once, when Hayley was six or seven, she asked why I couldn't cook like grandma, whom she called Nonna, or, for that matter, like her friends' mothers. I was about to plead some lifelong illness, possibly a stove allergy, but I quickly decided that if I had to lie to my daughter I'd better stay as close to the truth as possible.

"Well, darling, not *all* mommies cook," I made this answer up on the spot and hoped that it would not lead to further questioning.

"Yes, they *do*," she nodded her head.

"No, they *don*'t. *Some* mommies cook, yes, but others don't. It's perfectly normal for mommies *not* to cook. As long, of course, as their children don't go hungry."

Hayley pondered this answer for a moment.

"I'm not hungry," she said. "So I guess it's okay."

"So what's new with you?" I asked Mamma as I was setting the table. She stood at the sink washing lettuce.

"Vincenzo, one of Francesco customers, fell off horse and broke hip, knee and arm," she breathlessly reported. "He come to store on crutches and I look at him and tell him, old man like you gallop on horse through Flushing Meadows Park like bat out of hell? *Ché pazzo,* eh!"

Mamma blotted the lettuce leaves with a paper towel, put the salad into a bowl and tossed it vigorously with olive oil and vinegar.

"So anyway, I tell him that and you know what he say to me? He say, Angelina, you stay out of my business, okay? And I say, eh, *stupido*, I still have my two legs and two arms, and you, you stumble into my shop bandaged like Egyptian mummy."

Mamma put the salad bowl on the table and took the piping hot lasagna dish from the oven.

"Eat," she commanded.

I took a bite. The fresh, hot, gooey lasagna melted wonderfully in my mouth.

"This is delicious, Mamma," I said. "I didn't realize how hungry I was."

Mamma's face flinched and I sensed that she was displeased with me. Goodness, all I did was compliment her on the lasagna.

"Look at you!" she snorted. "You forty-four-years-old and you still talk with mouth full, eh?"

"Sorry, Mamma," I said, swallowing.

"You know what happen if you talk with food in your mouth, eh?"

I smiled.

"I won't be invited to eat with the Queen of England?"

"What kinda *stupido* comment is that, eh?" Mamma put down her fork and took a sip of water. "What can happen is that muscles in throat tighten," she circled her hand around her neck and jerked her head backwards. "You can't breathe no more and you can *die*! All because you talk with your mouth full, eh?"

Oh, Mamma, this is ludicrous, I thought, but I didn't tell her that. Pointing out the fallacies behind Mamma's comments was useless. I had decided long ago that placating her by agreeing to whatever absurd theory or rumor she happened to advance at the moment – and she advanced many – was the only foolproof way of staving off an argument.

"Yes, Mamma," I sighed. "I'll keep it in mind."

Mamma picked up her fork, which I took to mean that I had been sufficiently chastised and reprimanded, and that it was now safe for me to resume eating.

"Did I tell you about Silvia?" she asked after what I thought was an enjoyable moment of silence.

"Silvia who?"

"Silvia, my new neighbor."

"No," I said, and cringed.

She wiped her lips and put down her fork and knife. Her eyes were bright and her cheeks red, a sure sign that she was about to deliver a choice morsel of gossip.

"She pregnant with triplets."

"Really? That's a handful."

"You know why she pregnant with triplets?"

"Three eggs were fertilized instead of one?"

I knew, of course, given Mamma's long record of warped logic, that she was not expecting an anatomically correct answer.

"You don't know what you talk about!" she exclaimed, inching closer to me and lowering her voice as though my kitchen walls had ears.

"Silvia have triplets," she said in a hushed tone, "because she eat too much cabbage."

"Really?" I said, trying to keep a straight face. "That much cabbage, huh?"

"Yes," she nodded. "She eat three cabbage a day. That much cabbage can give triplets."

"Well, let's hope she knew not to talk with her mouth full while she was eating all that cabbage. She could have choked before she even had the triplets," I said, and immediately regretted it. "Sorry, Mamma, but this story sounds, well, *crazy*."

"What, you no believe me?" The chummy camaraderie in Mamma's voice was gone. Her tone was now sharper, with a hint of outrage. "You think I... *lying*?"

"No, of course not," I sighed.

Somewhat mollified Mamma got up, retrieved yellow rubber gloves from her bag, put them on and started gathering plates, forks, and glasses. I knew better than to suggest putting the whole lot in the dishwasher. Just as she eschewed microwaves and other labor-saving gadgets, she didn't like, nor had she ever owned, dishwashers.

"So how is your job, eh?" she asked. "Making any money?

She stood hunched over the sink, vigorously scrubbing dishes and cutlery. I took a towel and started drying.

"Could be better," I sighed. "I placed an ad online last night for someone to design a website for me. Maybe it'll attract some more clients."

Mamma shook her head.

"I always tell you, teaching French don't bring no money, eh." She rinsed the last plate, and handed it to me for drying. "Look at me, I speak Italian. You see *me* rolling in money?"

"Maybe not. But if you didn't speak Italian you wouldn't be working at Francesco's. And just *think* of all the gossip you'd miss."

"You need husband," she sighed. "*He* deal with your fresh mouth."

"Really?" I chuckled. "And how would he do *that?*"

Mamma took off the rubber gloves and the apron, and put them into the Macy's bag.

"I go now," she said, and went to the hallway. She put on her galoshes and poncho, took the umbrella, picked up the bag, and opened the door.

I walked with her to the elevator and pushed the button.

"You know that teaching French was not my first choice."

"I don't know what you talking about," she said, her eyes fixed on the elevator door.

"Peace Corps," I said. "Remember?"

Mamma didn't answer. The doors opened and she stepped inside.

"Bye," she said, not looking at me. The doors closed and the elevator slid downwards.

I went back inside. I filled an electric kettle with water, switched it on, and leaned against the kitchen counter waiting for it to boil. Is it possible, I wondered, that Mamma really forgot the Peace Corps incident? *I* certainly didn't. I closed my eyes and remembered...

I was in my senior year at Queens College majoring in liberal arts, the limbo-land that prepared me for everything and for nothing. I had thought that liberal arts was general enough to encompass a variety of disciplines and give me an array of career choices. But Mamma could not understand how anyone could study at a university for four years and not become a rocket scientist.

At first, she thought that being a liberal arts major meant I would become an impoverished abstract painter like her cousin Guido. To hear Mamma say it, Guido had never earned a single lira and was supported by his hard-working wife, Paola, who put in double shifts at a village bakery while Guido sat in front of his easel in a black beret, blissfully producing worthless scrawls.

I had to promise Mamma that I was not thinking of following in Guido's footsteps.

"One crazy liberal artist in family is enough," she said. "*Basta*!"

"Yes, Mamma."

"So what kind of money can you make in liberal arts, eh?" she kept asking.

Poor Mamma. I didn't have the heart to tell her.

A few days before Easter I saw a notice on the campus bill-board. It was about the Peace Corps. I read it carefully and I suddenly knew, as though by a divine revelation, that this was what I was destined to do. I took the brochure home and pored over it, reading and re-reading the fine print. The more I read, the more excited I became. I imagined helping impoverished children read and write and, in my spare time, traipsing through Africa in a safari outfit. The thought of doing something meaningful, *and* far away from Queens and Mamma's reach, filled me, for the first time in my life, with heart-pumping exhilaration. Was this what happiness felt like, I wondered?

Of course, I still had to tell Mamma. I was awake several nights in a row thinking of how to break this news to her gently and diplomatically. I wanted to convince Mamma that this was a great idea, not some far-fetched, half-hatched plan. But how? In the end I decided to tell her simply and quickly. I just wanted to get it out.

Mamma sat hunched over the kitchen table painting Easter eggs for the church bazaar.

I cleared my throat and swallowed.

"I want to join the Peace Corps," I told her, my heart pounding. I was very nervous for I had never before delivered such potentially earth-shattering news to Mamma.

Her hands started to shake and she carefully placed the egg she was holding on the table. Then she turned to me and screamed.

"You wanna join WHAT?"

I thought of sitting down next to her but decided to stand by the kitchen door. By putting some distance between us, even if it was a mere four feet, I hoped to stave off her wrath.

"Peace Corps," I replied. I felt the beads of perspiration forming on my neck, face and forehead. "I'd be working in developing countries. Probably in Africa."

Mamma took a deep breath and shut her eyes. She always did that, ostensibly to calm her nerves, but this technique never seemed to work. If anything, it only served to agitate her further.

"Africa!" she yelled and banged her fist on the table. "You know they still eat people there, eh? And what about diseases? Your uncle Pietro, Papa's cousin, may he rest in peace, he was missionary in Africa. He die there from some horrible sickness he catch from eating bananas."

"Mamma, I promise not to eat bananas," I sighed. I sensed, by then, that this conversation was not going the way I had hoped it might, but I wasn't yet ready to give up the only inkling of happiness I had ever felt.

"And what about wild animals, eh? What if giraffe bite you?"

I opened my mouth to tell her that giraffes ate the thorny leaves of the acacia trees, not people, but I knew that Mamma had no interest whatsoever in zoology.

Mamma turned back to the table, reached for the egg and resumed painting. To me this signaled that our conversation was now over. Tears welled in my eyes and I felt an overwhelming sadness, grief almost, as though something inside of me had died.

"You not gonna go to Africa," she said. Her voice was calmer now as she focused on painting little, perfectly shaped red dots on the egg's blue shell. "You stay here, find good job and decent husband, eh."

For a moment, in my desolation, I considered defying Mamma. I would join the Corps, train, get assigned and *then* tell her.

No, this would never work, I thought, as hot tears streamed down my cheeks. I couldn't stand up to Mamma, I just couldn't. For an Italian I was feeling an unhealthy dose of Jewish guilt.

I wiped the tears away with my sleeve, went into my room and quietly closed the door. I sat on the bed and stared at the wall in front. The thought of being forever confined to this tiny bedroom was so stifling, I actually felt as though I were choking. For an instant, the briefest moment, I hated Mamma. And then I was overwhelmed by guilt for allowing myself to have such thoughts.

Chapter Three

I put a tea bag into a mug, poured the boiling water over it and waited for it to seep. I liked my tea very dark and bitter, with just a sprinkling of sweetener and a dash of lemon.

I took the mug into the living room. Before I sat down at the computer desk, I noticed that a leg of my coffee table was scratched. I placed the mug on the desk, lit a lamp, and knelt down to inspect the damage. The curved leg was dented in several places. Shit! My beautiful, almost brand new teak table that Hayley and I had bought three months ago at a Pier Imports clearance sale was chipped now. We carried it home fifteen blocks with nary a scratch, but one knock of a soup can and look what happened.

Oh what a pity, I thought, as I surveyed the living room. That table was by far the nicest piece among my nondescript hodge-podge of furniture that lacked any discernible color scheme or style. The worn–out, formerly green but now drab grey sofa still had stains from Hayley's baby formula, and the threadbare rug under it could only be described as antiquated shabby-chic. Well, much more shabby than chic, actually.

I sat down at the desk and turned on the computer. A few moments later an unfamiliar name popped up on my IM box.

FloridaBrent: Megan?

MeganM: Yes. Who are you?

FloridaBrent: Brent Newman. You e-mailed me the other day about possibly designing your website. You gave me your screen name so I could get in touch. Remember?

MeganM: Yes. Hi.

FloridaBrent: Hi. So, any decision yet?

MeganM: To tell you the truth, I haven't given it any thought yet. I mean, I know that I need a professional-looking website. I'm giving French courses at the YMCA right now, but I would like to attract private clients, especially business people who need to learn basic French. Anyway, I narrowed the search down to three candidates, but I didn't go beyond that.

FloridaBrent: Am I one of the three?

MeganM: Yes.

FloridaBrent: Great. How can I eliminate the other two? Peacefully, of course.

MeganM: Well, you're the first one to show up on my IM box. So right now you're ahead of the others! But I have to be upfront with you: I can't afford an elaborate website. I need something effective but simple. By simple I mean inexpensive.

FloridaBrent: How did the price I quoted you grab you?

MeganM: If I didn't eat for a week I might possibly be able to pay you.

FloridaBrent: I see that teaching French is not as lucrative as it sounds.

MeganM: Yeah, right...Seriously though, if you could go a bit lower, say, 20% lower, we might have a deal.

FloridaBrent: As my ad says, no job is too small for me. So I agree to your terms and let's have a virtual handshake on that!

MeganM: That's great, thank you. How do we begin?

FloridaBrent: Will you be back on the IM tomorrow evening?

MeganM: Yes, I can do that.

FloridaBrent: Good, we can talk about it then. Right now I have to finish another project but as of tomorrow I'll be all yours.

MeganM: By the way, where in Florida are you?

FloridaBrent: Bradenton, on the Gulf coast. Sandwiched between St. Petersburg and Sarasota.

MeganM: Nice. What's the weather down there?

FloridaBrent: Glorious sunshine, mid -70s. Wonderful.

MeganM: Figures.

FloridaBrent: What's the weather up north?

MeganM: Raining, windy, cold, slush lining the sidewalks of Manhattan.

FloridaBrent: Figures.

MeganM: So I'll see you on here tomorrow evening, yes?

FloridaBrent: Absolutely. Bye for now.

MeganM: Bye.

I leaned back in the chair and chuckled. This guy thought that teaching French was *lucrative*? Ha, if he only knew that my so-called job barely paid for my groceries and utilities.

"Good thing I don't care much about fashion," I said, as I glanced down at my washed-out pale yellow sweat suit. I often talked to myself just so that I could hear the sound of a human voice resounding in my ears. "Or home decorating. Or *eating,* for that matter."

Suddenly a feeling of sadness came over me.

"Who are you kidding, kiddo?" I sighed. "You have a *shitty* life. Except for weekly visits with your neurotic mother, you are all alone in a shoebox of an apartment. Your life *sucks*."

I sniffled, turned off the computer, switched off the lights, and went to my bedroom. I curled up in bed, pulled the blanket up to my chin and closed my eyes. And then memories came flooding back.

Chapter Four

I met Joe Moseley at a pre-graduation party in early May, about a month after Mamma nixed my idea of joining the Corps. I was still trying to decide what to do with my life. The get-together was at my friend Joyce's house on Long Island; Joe was her next-door neighbor. The Island was an enclave of the wealthy and Joe's family was no different. Before Joyce – whose banker father was not exactly a pauper either – introduced us, she whispered to me that Joe was a scion of a very rich family that traced its origins to the Mayflower. They lunched at a country club, vacationed in the Hamptons and owned prized racehorses. The only horse my family ever owned was an old grey mare my grandfather used for plowing the fields. I saw its photograph once in Mamma's album – a dejected looking, skinny animal with a bag of oats over its muzzle. Of course, I wasn't about to tell Joe *that*.

Joe was not what I, or anyone else for that matter, would call handsome. He was skinny, pale, balding, and wore wire-rimmed glasses. As we were sitting side by side on Joyce's living room sofa, he told me that he was twenty-four and about to graduate from Harvard Business School. He already had a job lined up in his father's company, which manufactured components for the aviation industry. Joe was telling all this to me in a flat, monotonous voice while staring at the carpet. I started to wonder whether he had a speech impediment, or was he really as boring as a piece of wood?

"How do you and Joyce know each other?" he asked.

"We met at the Fifth Avenue library," I said. "We both wanted to borrow the same book, so we flipped a coin and I won. We've been friends since."

I didn't tell Joe that Joyce was the *only* friend I had. The other girls, my classmates, seemed very standoffish and aloof. Joyce, as I had learned, was as much of a loner as I was. That, and the fact that we were both avid readers, created a bond between us.

An uncomfortable silence followed as Joe fidgeted with his watch.

"Mother's family is listed in the Burke's Peerage," he finally muttered.

"Burke's *what*?"

"Uh, it's a genealogical lineage of Great Britain's titled families."

Oh, great, I thought. Was I supposed to bow or curtsy?

I was about to disengage myself from Joe and find someone more plebeian to talk to, but as I started to stand up I heard him mumble.

"Did you say something?"

"Um, I...I just asked whether you'd like to...go out sometimes." He didn't even look up at me; his eyes were still firmly fixed on the carpet.

Joe's request took me by surprise. It was obvious that we had nothing in common. When I thought of the ideal boyfriend – and I thought of him often – I imagined someone gregarious, funny and at least somewhat presentable. Joe was none of the above.

Still, I decided that, what the heck, I had nothing to lose by going out with him. Nothing to gain either, but what was the harm in a date or two. After all, guys were not pounding on my door. If they were, Mamma would undoubtedly scare them off.

Truth was, I was getting desperate for some male company. I had not dated at all because every time I went to Manhattan Mamma worried that I'd be hit by a car, a bus or a taxi. And, of course, going out on a date had its own potentially grave consequences. Mamma would cite some far-fetched example of a customer's cousin back in Italy who was "disrespected" by a boy and left lying in a dark alley, fodder for beggars and stray dogs. Needless to say, after the girl recovered from the ordeal she could no longer find a decent husband, and spent the rest of her life as a spinster, shunned by all the villagers.

Maybe I was still smarting from not being able to join the Corps. Or perhaps I was just fed up with being the only twenty–two–year–old virgin on campus. Whatever it was, I told

Joe that I would go out with him.

Joyce tried to dissuade me.

"If you date him you'll have to contend with Annabelle, his mother. Believe me, I wouldn't wish *that* on anybody."

"Joyce, dealing with a crazy mother has been my life's work," I replied. "Besides, Joe mentioned that his is listed in some kind of a book for blue-bloods, so I assume that at least she has some class."

"Megan, Joe is still tied to his mother with an umbilical cord. She smothers him beyond belief and keeps him in line with never-ending warnings of floozies stalking him on every corner, waiting to trap him into marriage. He's so scared of angering his darling Mommy that he just obediently follows her every whim and command. He has never been on a date, I swear."

"Well, neither have I."

The more I listened to Joyce, the more I became convinced that Joe and I were not that different after all. We may not have been kindred spirits, but we did have at least one thing in common: we were both virgins. We were both virgins because we didn't dare to upset our mothers and cause trauma in our respective households.

Joe and I met in Manhattan a couple of times. We sat over tasteless cups of coffee and talked. Or rather, I talked and Joe stared into his cup, occasionally grunting an answer. Was it possible, I wondered, that this person who rarely uttered anything other than a monosyllabic retort graduated from Harvard? I thought that if I persevered, Joe's pathological – and pathetic – timidity would eventually dissipate and a nice guy might emerge from underneath the gawkiness. Mamma, of course, knew nothing of my dates. I scheduled them while she was at work so that I wouldn't have to explain where I was going and with whom.

But my reasons for continuing to see Joe were not totally selfless. I started to see my virginity as the symbol of the hold Mamma had on me. I thought that having sex – even for all the wrong reasons – would allow me, at least briefly, to take control of my own life. The mere idea of rebelling behind Mamma's back – and without actually hurting her – was very thrilling.

So, by our second date, as we were drinking cappuccinos in the Village, I decided – unilaterally at that point – to take our "relationship" to the next illogical level: sex. I thought that the way my life was going, or rather not going, I might not have another opportunity like this for a long time.

My chance came sooner than I expected. On our next date Joe and I went to visit his former college roommate, Chris. He had an apartment on the Upper East Side. Actually, it was his parents' pied-à-terre, but they were spending the weekend visiting Chris's sister and her newborn baby in Atlanta. Chris had the place to himself and invited some friends over.

We sat, drank and talked for a couple of hours. When the last guest had departed Chris announced that he was getting hungry and would go get something to eat. As we were standing up to leave with him, he turned to us and nodded toward a red velvet couch.

"No need for you guys to go yet; there is no hurry," he said. "I'll be gone a while, so why don't you stay and, uh, make yourselves comfortable."

With that he quickly grabbed his keys and left.

At first I thought that Joe had pre-arranged this but he seemed to be as surprised by Chris's hasty departure as I was. He sat down on the couch and stared at the floor. I realized that if I didn't make the first move nothing would happen. And that, of course, would be a terrible waste of an empty apartment. I also had just finished my period so I knew, from reading *Cosmopolitan*, that this was a safe time of the month.

So I sat down next to Joe and took his hand. I was very nervous; my throat was dry and my heart rate accelerated by the second. I sensed that if we were to have sex I'd have to be the one to initiate it, but I had no idea what to do next. So we just sat holding clammy hands, not saying a word, not even looking at each other. Finally I turned toward him.

"Joe," I said, my heart pounding, "do you want to have sex?"

There. I couldn't believe how easily, how nonchalantly, these words slipped out.

Joe didn't respond or even budge. For a minute or two he sat staring at the floor and gave no indication that he had heard me. I felt my eyes stinging. Oh, God, how could I embarrass myself like this?

I was about to tell Joe to forget it, that it was just a silly joke. But before I could tell him that he slowly turned to face me and, as though we had done it countless times before, we both leaned forward and our lips met in the middle.

We started – at first slowly and hesitatingly, and then faster and with more urgency – fumbling with buttons and zippers, our discarded clothing and shoes forming a small pile at the foot of the couch. Then we sat side by side, two red-faced virgins, with no clue what to do next. I suddenly wished that I had read those *Cosmos* more thoroughly. From the corner of my eye I saw sweat beads forming on Joe's forehead. I knew that I had to do something, pronto, to lighten up the mood. But what? Another *Cosmo* tidbit jumped to mind: humor.

"Hey, Joe," I said in a falsely upbeat voice, "did you hear the one about two virgins sitting naked on a sofa, not knowing what to do?"

"Er, no," he muttered, not looking at me.

"Neither did I."

Well, I thought, so much for humor. Clearly, Joe didn't read the same magazines as I did. I decided that if nothing would happen within the next five minutes I would dress, leave, and crawl into the nearest hole.

Again, I extended my hand and took Joe's. I gently pulled him toward me and we kissed.

"I'm as clueless about this as you are," I whispered. "Let's just...improvise?"

We lied down and clumsily did what should have come naturally, but didn't. As Joe propped himself on top of me I shut my eyes to block the image of his red and sweaty face over mine. I clenched my fists at the discomfort of being pinned under him, and winced at the burning feeling between my thighs. A few thrusts and grunts later Joe groaned and fell on me like a lifeless bird.

Shit, I thought as I stared at the ceiling, what the hell had I done? I instantly regretted this totally emotionless, joyless and uncomfortable experience. I also felt some psychological discomfort – which is just a fancy name for guilt – at having sex on somebody else's velvet sofa. These were probably not the thoughts one was supposed to have after losing one's virginity, but that was what I was thinking. I had no way of knowing what was on Joe's mind because when it was over and we got our bodies off the couch, he didn't say anything. Not a word.

Without looking at me he stood up, fished his underwear and trousers out of the pile on the floor, and put them on. Then he knelt in front of the couch, fumbling between the cushions in search of his eyeglasses.

I quickly put on my jeans and blouse, ran fingers through my hair, and stood in the middle of the living room watching as Joe assiduously cleaned his glasses with a monogrammed handkerchief. He didn't look at me.

"Hey, Joe, are you okay?" I asked cheerily. I didn't feel even remotely cheerful, which was probably why my voice sounded like a falsetto.

He didn't look up or stop polishing his glasses.

"Yeah, yeah, I'm fine," he mumbled.

I sat down on the sofa about a foot away from him. All kinds of thoughts dashed through my mind. Should I take his hand? Should I stay or quietly slip away? I wondered what the etiquette was for awkward post-coital interactions.

As I sat pondering my options, I heard a key turn in the lock and Chris calling, cautiously, from the hallway.

"Are you guys decent?"

"Sure, Chris, come in," I called back.

He came into the living room and surveyed the scene.

"So, did you have a good time?" he asked, a sly smile on his face.

I felt my face redden.

"Great," I croaked.

Truth was, I had serious pangs of regret. Since there was nothing loving, romantic, or even enjoyable about this encounter, I suspected that it was just a misunderstanding borne out of a desperate need to distance ourselves from our domineering mothers, and to assert our own identities.

That night Joe drove me home in silence. He held the wheel tightly and stared ahead without as much as a sideways glance. As he dropped me in front of my building, I kissed him on the cheek.

"See you soon?" I asked, although I wasn't sure, at that point, whether or not I wanted to see Joe ever again.

"Sure," he said, still not looking at me.

He drove off before I reached the front door.

I didn't hear from Joe after that night. I decided to erase all memory of him and of what had happened between us.

Easier said than done.

I tried to focus on my future now that the Peace Corps idea had bitten the dust. I was considering a grad school, preferably somewhere far away, when I started waking up in the morning feeling queasy and tired. After a week of morning malaise I decided to see our family physician, Dr. Marino. He was a cousin twice removed of Francesco's wife, Vittoria.

"How long have you been feeling this way?" Marino asked, peering at me from above his glasses.

"About a week, maybe more."

He scribbled down the information.

"And your last period was when?" he asked, still writing.

I tried to think. Six weeks? More?

Oh, my God. OH – MY – GOD!

The realization that I might be pregnant sent electrical jolts through my body; powerful tremors that brought on the worst nausea and dizziness I had ever experienced. I shut my eyes and thought. How could this have happened? Joe and I had sex right after my period.

Marino took one look at my ashen face and rang his nurse.

"Please bring Miss Gigliardi a glass of water," he said over the intercom. "And then give her a pregnancy test."

I sat on a green plastic chair in the waiting room, sipping water from a paper cup. I was numb; my arms and legs felt as though they were made of lead. My heart was beating very fast and I was having difficulty breathing.

After about half an hour the nurse led me back to Marino's office.

"Sit down, Megan, sit down," he said, leafing through my chart. "Feeling any better?"

"Not really," I whispered. I was still fighting off nausea and my limbs felt heavy.

Marino cleared his throat.

"The test is positive," he said, still looking at the chart.

So that was it. My future, my entire life, was now mapped out.

"Thank you," I muttered, suppressing the sobs that were fighting their way to the surface. I thought that maybe I was having a nightmare, and that I would soon wake up and realize that everything – Joe, sex, pregnancy – was just a frightening dream.

But of course it wasn't. This was real, and there was no way of escaping it. My chest tightened and I could no longer squelch my tears.

Marino closed the chart, leaned back in his swivel chair and took off his glasses.

"What are you going to do, Megan?"

I reached for the Kleenex box on his desk, took out a tissue, and dabbed at my eyes.

"I don't know what I'm going to do," I said in a hoarse voice that I didn't recognize as my own. "I need time to think."

"Of course. Think it through. Talk to your mother."

Shit. What was I going to tell Mamma?

I walked home in a daze. The thought that I was going to have a baby hadn't sunk in yet. I let myself into the apartment and went straight to my room. It was the size of a large closet, with a narrow bed, a small desk, a chair, and some shelves on the wall. Mamma slept on the pullout sofa in the living room and kept her clothes in a hall closet.

I lay down, closed my eyes and, as the realization of my condition started to make its way to my consciousness, I felt hot tears stream down my cheeks. I pulled the cover over my head and, in this woolly cocoon, cried until I fell asleep.

When I woke up I saw Mamma standing at the foot of the bed. I sat up and rubbed my eyes.

"Hi, Mamma," I said, still dazed from the nap. "What are you doing here?"

"I live here," she snapped. "And you, what *you* doing sleeping in middle of afternoon, eh?"

I opened my mouth to answer, but no sound came out. Instead, as I stared at Mamma, I felt tears welling up in my eyes again. I dried them with the back of my hand.

"What's the matter?" Mamma asked, her voice alarmed. "You sick or something?"

I was going to answer that nothing was wrong, nothing at all. The last thing I wanted to do was upset Mamma.

"I'm pregnant," I blurted out.

I heard Mamma's sharp intake of breath even before I saw her panicked face. I suddenly remembered the definition of the word "dumbstruck" I once saw in a dictionary: "Made silent by astonishment." No phrase could describe Mamma's reaction better.

Mamma stood still for a moment and then sat down on the edge of the bed. She put her head in her hands and sat like that, hunched, without moving, without saying a word, for what seemed like the longest time.

"*Dio mio*," she finally whispered. "Why you not tell me before, eh?"

"I just found out today, this afternoon."

"You not even tell me you have boyfriend!" she said, her voice rising.

"He wasn't really my boyfriend. I hardly knew him."

The words were out of my mouth before I realized what I had said. Thankfully, Mamma didn't catch on.

"So who is this boy?" she asked after another long silence.

"His name is Joe Moseley. He went to Harvard."

I thought that the mention of Harvard would somehow validate my pregnancy in Mamma's eyes.

"And he has degree in liberal arts too?"

"No, Mamma, Joe has a degree in business," I said.

"So this Joe, he is gonna marry you, eh?"

I hesitated. Should I tell Mamma the truth, or would it be better, at least for the time being, to appease her by telling her that Joe and I would be having a big white wedding and live happily ever after?

"Joe doesn't know," I sighed. "But I'm sure he won't be jumping for joy. He behaved like a jerk."

"You mean, he don't wanna do the right thing by you?" Mamma's voice was high-pitched again, indicating that her distress level was rising. "But what you gonna do, alone with baby? No husband. What we gonna tell people, eh?"

"I couldn't care less what people think," I said, fighting the onslaught of tears again.

Mamma continued to talk, to gesticulate, and to evoke the names of various Italian saints. After a while I didn't hear what she was saying. I didn't hear it because her words were muted by my sobbing.

The next day I sat down at my desk and wrote Joe a letter, informing him that I was pregnant. I told him that I didn't expect anything from him, financially or otherwise, but I thought he should know.

"His mother, Annabelle, will be furious," Joyce told me on the phone that evening.

"Who cares about *her*? How do you think Joe will react?"

"Difficult to say. He hardly shows any emotion. That's not to say that he doesn't have any; he is just not very good at expressing it."

"Oh, Joyce," I sobbed. "What am I going to do?"

"I don't know. What do you *want* to do?"

"What I want to do is turn back time and undo what I did. You know, like *not* have sex with Joe."

"I mean, what do you want to do, *realistically* speaking?"

I sighed.

"I have been thinking of nothing else. I wish I had a lot of options, but I only have one."

There was a long silence. I could hear Joyce's breathing and my own pounding heart.

"Well," she prodded, "are you going to tell me or not?"

"I can't have an abortion. I've always been pro–choice, but, until now, it was a hypothetical situation. When it becomes real and personal, you have an entirely different take on it. This baby is inside me now and I have to come to terms with it. Of course, I have no idea how I'm going to manage; I haven't given it much thought yet."

"You have to believe that things will work out, somehow. Just beware of Annabelle's antics."

"Oh, she is the least of my worries right now," I sighed.

Two days later the phone rang. It was Joe. Up until that moment I had thought that the sound of his voice would send me over the edge. In my mind he was a selfish and insensitive boob who hadn't called once in all these weeks. But now, as I held the receiver close to my ear, I realized that I had no feelings whatsoever toward Joe. No love, no hate. Nothing.

"I, uh, got your letter," he mumbled. "It was a surprise all right."

"Imagine how I felt. Not exactly something either of us had bargained for, huh?"

"You can say that again."

"It's not exactly something either of us had bargained for."

"What?"

"You said that I can say it again. So I did."

I wasn't sure where I was going with this flippancy. I wanted to lighten up the mood because I wasn't yet ready for heart-wrenching discussions about the implications of an unplanned child on both our futures. First I needed to figure it out by myself.

Joe must have sensed my reluctance to talk shop. Or perhaps he was relieved not to talk shop. I heard him clear his throat.

"Listen, Megan, I have to run."

That was the Joe I knew and disliked.

"Fine, thanks for calling," I said dryly. I felt as though I needed to add something else, but didn't know what.

"I'll talk to you soon, okay?"

"Whatever."

I hung up, but the phone rang again. I picked it up.

"May I speak with Miss Galardi, please?"

An unfamiliar voice, but the moment I heard it I sensed that the woman on the phone wasn't calling to tell me I had won the New York State Lottery.

"If you mean Miss *Gigliardi*, this is she."

"Miss Galardi, this is Annabelle Moseley," she said in a poised, cool voice, polished up, no doubt, at an expensive finishing school for blue-bloods. "Joe's mother."

I closed my eyes and, despite Joyce's warnings, decided not to be intimidated.

"How do you do, Mrs. Moseley," I answered in a calm voice honed – for free – at the Forest Hills High School.

"Miss Galardi," she went on, ignoring my question, "you may be wondering why I'm calling."

Actually, I wasn't. She was calling because her darling, well–bred boy knocked me up.

"I am calling to discuss your, er, condition," she continued, her voice starting to quiver just a tad. "And how we can best resolve this, um, *problem*."

So Joyce was right! Was Annabelle calling to convince me to get an abortion, or to offer me money to stay out of her son's life? If she only knew that I intended to stay away from him anyway.

I decided, right there and then, that I was not going to be bullied by Annabelle. I might have been unable to stand up to Mamma, but, by God, I was not going to allow Joe's mother to manipulate me.

"What is it about my condition that you would like to discuss, Mrs. Moseley?" I asked in a firm, steady voice.

"I believe, Miss Galardi, that such matters would be better discussed in person. Would you be available to meet, say, the day after tomorrow, at three?"

"I will, er, *shall* be delighted to meet with you, Mrs. Moseley," I said, determined to milk this moment for all its worth. "But please hold on a moment while I check my agenda."

I thought that I could hear her intake of breath, as though she were shocked I even owned an agenda. I didn't, of course, but what harm was there in making her believe that I had some class?

I brought a newspaper close to the receiver and started turning the pages. I wanted Annabelle to think that I was leafing through the pages of my agenda.

I picked up the receiver.

"Let's see," I said, still turning the pages. "The day after tomorrow, you say? At three? How about three-thirty? I see that I have an appointment with my obstetrician earlier that afternoon, so I won't be able to cab it into Manhattan before three-thirty."

I didn't have an appointment, but I thought that a mention of an OB would be a nice, albeit a sarcastic, touch. And, of course, I would be taking the subway, not a cab. But what was the harm in making Annabelle wait and, hopefully, wince?

"Very well," she said, curtly. "It actually suits me fine as that will give me ample time to run into Bergdorf Goodman to pick up a scarf I ordered. I propose that we meet at the courtyard café at the Plaza Hotel, facing the main entrance. I shall be sitting at my usual table, in the back. Ask the maître'd for me."

"I know where the café is," I answered, although, of course, I had no clue.

"Fine, it's settled then," Annabelle said. "Goodbye, Miss Galardi."

Click. Annabelle hung up the phone.

I decided not to tell Mamma about Joe's and Annabelle's calls, or about my foray to the Plaza's inner sanctum. I wasn't actually lying to Mamma; I was just withholding the information. Momentarily. Knowing Mamma, she would insist on coming along, so that she could chide Joe's mother about that no–good scoundrel son of hers.

I spent the next two days thinking about – fearing, actually – the meeting. What if Joyce was right? What if this woman was a real bitch? Would I be able to stand up to her and convey calmness and assertiveness that I didn't feel? Oh shit! What the hell did I get myself into?

On the day of the meeting I woke up frazzled. The first thought that entered my mind was that this kind of malaise was commonly referred to as butterflies in one's stomach.

"Butterflies?" I snickered. "I feel like a herd of elephants is having an orgy inside me."

A quick look at the contents of my tiny closet revealed that I had nothing to wear, certainly nothing dressy enough for the Plaza. To hell with it, I thought. I pulled out a pair of white slacks, a green T-shirt and a pair of open-toe sandals. My only concession to meeting Joe's aristocratic mother was brushing my hair. It was shoulder length and layered, and I usually just ran my fingers through it.

I sat on the Manhattan–bound R train smiling at the strange turn my life was taking. There I was, Megan Gigliardi, the daughter of impoverished Italian immigrants, going to meet with the upper echelons of Long Island society.

"There is something to be said for my lapse in judgment." I muttered under my breath. "One romp on a sofa and here I am, on my way to the Plaza."

I got off at the Fifth Avenue station and walked to the hotel. In front of the steps leading to the main entrance I paused and took a deep breath. I was nervous, but determined to stand up to Annabelle. I couldn't rebel against my own mother, but I could – and would – rebel against Joe's, to whom I was not shackled by love or blood.

I walked up to the hotel and entered.

I must have looked like someone's poor relative because a uniformed employee immediately materialized in front of me. Did these people have built-in antennas that started beeping whenever someone in a lower income bracket walked through the door?

"May I help you, Miss?" he asked haughtily. I thought he was going to direct me to the side entrance.

For a fraction of a moment I felt like turning back and running away. That would be the easiest, and probably the smartest, thing to do. But I didn't.

"I'm meeting someone at the café," I responded and walked past the lackey, as though the mere fact of having an appointment at the Plaza entitled me to talk down to him.

As I approached the courtyard café, I immediately spotted her. I had never seen her before but I just knew: Annabelle.

She sat at a small table by the wall, straight as a rod, a slim woman with a stern face. She had thin lips and a thin nose, and her blonde hair – no doubt bottle blond – was tied in a severe knot at the back of her head. She wore a sleeveless brown linen dress, which was drab and wrinkled but probably cost more than the GDP of a developing country, and a strand of pearls with matching studs in her ears.

As I neared the table she turned her head and looked straight at me. If looks could kill I would have died from hypothermia right there and then.

She looked me up and down and stared at my be–sandaled feet.

All of a sudden I felt an adrenaline rush. I realized that, stripped of her ancestry, social standing and the pearl choker, Annabelle would be nothing more than a stern-faced, middle-aged woman in a wrinkled dress. She breathed the same air as the rest of us. I decided that there was no reason, none whatsoever, why I should not feel her equal.

Feeling brashly assertive I stood in front of her, smiled, stretched out my hand and, in the sweetest of voices, said:

"Mrs. Moseley? I am Megan Gigliardi. It is a pleasure to meet you."

I hoped that she wouldn't notice, not immediately anyway, that my voice was dripping with sarcasm, not sincerity.

She took my hand but barely touched it, as though she were afraid she would contract leprosy.

"Please sit down, Miss Galardi." She pointed to a chair across the table from her.

"I hope I am not too late," I said. "My cab took forever."

"Never mind, I was a few minutes late myself. I lingered at Bergdorf's."

Shit. Annabelle: one. Megan: zero.

"So," Annabelle continued, "what would you like to drink? I have ordered a glass of sherry for myself, but you may prefer some tea."

I wasn't a big drinker – as a matter of fact I disliked alcoholic beverages – but at that particular moment I could have used a stiff drink. Still, I didn't want Annabelle to think of me as a boozing floozy. I was carrying her grandchild, so some sense of decorum was called for.

The idea of tea sounded nice but I knew – without ever setting foot in this hotel before – that I would not be getting a Lipton bag soaking in a chipped mug. No, I would be presented with an impossible choice of specialty teas and the sad truth was that I did not know the difference between your Lapsings and your Oolongs.

I suddenly recalled reading somewhere that the French drank sparkling water called Perrier. I had no idea what it tasted like, never having drank anything other than plain old club soda, but I was willing to go out on a limb.

"I would like some Perrier, please," I told the waiter who had magically appeared in front of us.

If Annabelle was surprised at my worldliness, she didn't show it. Instead she looked at me and cleared her throat.

"Tell me about yourself, Miss Galardi," she said.

I sensed that she had as much interest in me as a person as Mamma had in the Burke's Peerage. She probably was just ascertaining my suitability as the mother of her grandchild. Would she be able to introduce me to her blue-blooded friends, or would I be a skeleton in the family closet?

"I just graduated from Queens College," I said. "Liberal Arts. I'm still deciding what to do next."

"I see."

Her face was so harsh and tense, she looked like a witch.

"And what about your family, your parents?"

Great! Was I supposed to tell this woman that while her family was making history on Plymouth Rock, mine was plowing the fields with a skinny mare back on the old continent? Stop it, Megan, I thought to myself. There was nothing wrong with hard work.

"My parents came here from Italy in the late 1950s," I said, looking Annabelle straight in the eye. "My dad worked in a tire factory, but he died when I was little. Mom works in a grocery store in Queens."

There was a long, and undoubtedly uncomfortable – for Annabelle – silence.

"Joe tells me that you are about two months pregnant and that the baby is his," she finally said. "I assume this is accurate?"

I nodded.

"Have you thought about what you are going to do?"

"I'm going to have the baby. Naturally."

The waiter appeared with the sherry and the Perrier, set them down on the table and departed. Annabelle took a sip of her drink.

"And this decision is non-negotiable?" she asked, watching me from above the rim of her glass.

I started to really despise this woman.

I poured the fizzy water into my glass and drank some.

"What exactly are you suggesting, Mrs. Moseley"? I asked, trying to convey, in my tone, as much shock and horror as I could. "Surely not that I *not* have your son's baby?"

Annabelle's patrician features tightened up and she glared at me. It was a look of loathing. At least we had one thing in common, the witch and I: we were united in our mutual hatred for each other.

"Let's not beat around the bush, Miss Galardi," she said coldly. "If this is indeed Joe's child, and he assures me that it is, I shall be happy to welcome him into our family."

"I am delighted to hear it, Mrs. Moseley. A child needs to know his or her grandparents. I will make every effort to ensure that he or she visits you often."

Another sip of sherry. Another sip of Perrier.

"I am afraid you misunderstood, Miss Galardi," she said, staring into her glass. "Maybe I didn't make myself clear."

She put down her now empty glass.

"I meant to convey to you that Mr. Moseley – Joe's father – and I will be happy to take the child in and raise him as our own. The child will not want for anything. Of course, you will be remunerated generously."

A chill went through my body and I quivered. Annabelle and I stared at our respective glasses for a long moment. Finally I raised my eyes and looked at her.

"Does Joe know about this offer?" I asked.

"He does not, but I am certain he would approve. He would want his child to grow up with all the advantages that he himself has had. British nannies, riding lessons, sports, private schools."

I was speechless at the woman's audacity and just sat there, staring at her icy blue eyes and pale skin. She probably took my silence to mean that I was considering her offer and maybe even crunching some numbers.

"Do take your time and think it over, Miss Galardi, I am in no rush," she said, crossing her legs and leaning back in the chair. There was a smirk on her face, as though to say "Aha, I knew you could be bought!"

"I just did," I replied, and took a deep breath. "First of all, it's *Gigliardi*, not Galardi. I suggest that you learn to pronounce it, Mrs. Moseley, because this will be the name of your grandchild."

Annabelle's smirk disappeared. Instead, her mouth twitched, her facial muscles tensed up, and her already ashen skin became even paler. She looked like she was about to keel over.

"Secondly," I continued, in as calm and steady a voice as I could muster, "the child will grow up without pony rides and snotty nannies. He will be supported by my income, once I get one."

I stood up, picked up my bag, and slung it over my shoulder.

"Thank you ever so much, Mrs. Moseley, for the Perrier and for a very informative chat," I said.

Annabelle didn't respond. She didn't even look at me. I turned my back to her, held my head high, and left. I just hoped that I wouldn't stumble on my way out and ruin the triumphant exit.

I left the hotel feeling like, well, like a million bucks. Of course, unlike Annabelle, I didn't have a million bucks. I couldn't laugh all the way to the bank, but I did laugh all the way to the subway stop.

The next afternoon Joe called.

"Megan, we have to talk," he said. "How about if I pick you up in an hour?"

I waited for Joe downstairs, in exactly the same spot where he had unceremoniously dropped me off – or rather dumped me – two months ago.

I wasn't sure how I would feel seeing Joe after all this time. Even though I was certain that I was over him, I was a little afraid that being face to face with him would rehash the discomfort of our encounter and unleash all kinds of unpleasant sensations.

But standing in front of Joe was like being with a stranger. I felt nothing.

"How about a cold drink?" he asked.

We walked across the street to Al's Diner and ordered ice teas. We sat in a booth, the seat's vinyl cover sticking to the back of my legs. For a long moment we sat in silence, Joe playing with the salt and pepper shakers on the table.

"Megan, please hear me out," he finally said, not looking at me. "Don't interrupt; just let me have my say, okay?"

"Okay."

"First of all, I want to apologize for Mother's behavior. I had no prior knowledge of her plan."

"I know you didn't, Joe. But thanks for telling me."

"Also," he continued, "I did a lot of thinking these past few days. I, well, I, that is...I think..."

He turned away his face, looked out the window, and mumbled.

"Sorry, Joe, I didn't hear."

He looked at me and cleared his throat. I realized then how much he resembled his mother. Damn! Was this what my child would be condemned to? To look like Annabelle?

"I said, I think we should get married."

WHAT? Did I hear him right? Joe was proposing to me? If my thighs were not stuck to the vinyl, I would have fallen out of my seat.

"Did I hear you right? You are...proposing to me?"

Joe looked out the window again.

"Yes."

As screwed up as my life was at that moment, I instinctively knew that I couldn't, didn't want to marry Joe. Had I been prepared for his proposal I would have had an appropriate retort. But I wasn't and I hadn't.

"I really don't know what to say," I finally uttered after what seemed like an infinite silence. "This is so unexpected."

"Yes. The whole situation came out of the blue, didn't it?"

Yes, it did. It certainly did.

"But let me tell you something," he continued. "Father's company is opening a subsidiary in Paris. It will be their European marketing office. I will be running it."

Was Joe telling me that he – we – would be living in France? In Paris? That certainly put a new and fascinating spin on what just minutes ago seemed like a very grim future. I would have loved to live in Paris, which, I imagined, was totally different from Queens. I would have loved it even more than trekking through Africa. But, there was one problem.

"Joe, there is one problem," I said. "We are not in love. We don't even know each other very well. And I was very hurt at how you treated me after...you know, that time at Chris's."

Here we were, discussing marriage, and I couldn't even utter the word "sex." This did not presage a happy future, even *I* knew that.

Joe's face reddened and he looked down at the table. He reached for a napkin, crumbled it, shredded it into small pieces, and rolled each piece into a tiny ball.

"I understand," he said, still not looking at me. He piled all the little balls into a neat heap in the middle of the table. "I owe you an explanation for my, er, very rude behavior that night. I...I wish I could give you a satisfactory answer. That night, at Chris's, well, I felt terrible...inadequate and awkward."

Sweat beads formed on Joe's red face. He was now playing with his straw, flattening and bending it every which way. It looked like a grotesque abstract sculpture. Suddenly I felt sorry for him, for his obvious discomfort.

"Listen," I said. "I need time to think."

"I understand."

We got up and walked across the street to where Joe's car was parked. He got in, waved, and drove off. And I went into the house to ponder my future.

For the next three days I did little else. I knew that I had to bring closure to my life, but how? I had no feelings for Joe, that much was clear. I couldn't imagine spending the rest of my life with him and Annabelle. On the other hand, what could I, alone, offer my child? I had neither a job nor a prospect of one. I lived in a tiny one-bedroom apartment with an overbearing mother. Didn't my child deserve a better life? The more questions I mulled over, the fewer answers I had.

In the end, Mamma made the decision for me. We sat at the kitchen table eating dinner. More precisely, she ate and I pushed the food around the plate with my fork.

"You crazy, eh?" she yelled when I told her of my doubts. "You call him right now and tell him yes!"

"But Mamma, I don't love him," I whimpered. "I don't even like him all that much."

Mamma sniffed.

"Love, like, what the matter with you, eh? You wanna baby not have father? You wanna be poor? You wanna that people look at you in the street and whisper behind your back?"

"Mamma, nobody will whisper behind my back," I sighed. "This is not Italy in the 19th century."

"*Ché stupida bambina*! You may have fancy liberal arts degree but up here," she pointed to her forehead, "you have nothing, *niente*! You think your Papa come to America for this, so you be poor and alone with child?"

Bringing Papa back from the dead had always been Mama's trump card, the ultimate guilt trip she laid on me. Most of the time it worked. The mere thought of my father being displeased with me, even from his grave, was enough of a reprimand.

The gutsiness I showed the previous week in standing up to Annabelle had dissipated now that I was pressured by Mamma to do the "right thing." That night I dreamt of standing in a windy field, holding an infant. I started to walk up a narrow path, hugging the baby close to my chest to keep it warm. Suddenly Joe drove up, stopped the car and beckoned me to get in.

"Get the baby out of the cold," he said. "The car is nice and warm"

I hesitated for a fraction of a second, but got in. I sat in the back seat clutching the child as hot tears streamed down my face.

I woke up the next morning and I knew what to do: I had to marry Joe for my child's sake. At the very least, I thought, he was an honorable man, choosing to live up to his responsibilities rather than shirking them. That was one point in his favor.

Mamma was overjoyed. I had no way of knowing how Annabelle would react because Joe and I had decided not to tell her until *after* the fact. Had she known that I was about to become her daughter-in-law she might have slipped arsenic into my food.

The "wedding" took place the following week before the Queens City Clerk with Mamma and Joyce as witnesses. I went through the brief ceremony without any joy, trying to squelch the doubts and apprehensions that had been plaguing me for the past few days. Joe gave me a diamond–encrusted platinum wedding band, which was far too ostentatious for my taste and so heavy, it weighed my finger down.

After the ceremony the four of us went for lunch at a restaurant next door to Francesco's. Throughout the meal strangers kept coming to our table, hugged Mamma and me, and vigorously shook Joe's hand, all the while talking in rapid-fire Italian.

"Mamma," I finally asked after the umpteenth person bear-hugged me, "who are all these people?"

"Francesco customers," she said giddily.

I put down my fork and took a sip of water.

"Why are Francesco's customers here, and how do they know I just got married?"

"I tell them," she said cheerily, her cheeks flushed from too much Chianti. "I tell them my daughter, she marry man who go to Hayward, eh!"

Joyce brought a napkin to her mouth to stifle a chuckle. Joe winced.

"Mamma, how could you?"

I pushed my plate away. The revelation the Mamma had spread the news of my marriage like some kind of a crazed town crier spoiled my appetite.

Joe sat staring at his plate. I wondered whether he too had started to regret our hasty marriage. I wanted to get up and run; run as far away as I could from this restaurant, from Mamma and, most of all, from Joe.

But I knew that I couldn't. The deed was done, officially recorded at the County Clerk's office. I had no place to hide.

I excused myself from the table and went to the restroom. There I stood over a sink and cried, not even caring that the tears smudged my black mascara and stained the white blouse I was wearing.

I raised my head and looked at myself in the mirror. My eyes were puffy from crying and rivulets of mascara ran down my cheeks. I looked like a character from a horror show.

"Oh, Megan," I sobbed, "what have you done?"

Just then the door opened and Joyce came in.

"Hey, Megan..." she said, but stopped in mid-sentence when she saw my mascara-streaked face in the mirror. She came over to me and put her arms around my shoulders.

"Oh, Joyce, what was I thinking?" I wailed. "Why didn't I just wait? Maybe if I had given myself more time...maybe..."

Joyce took a hankie out of her purse and started dabbing at my face.

"Listen," she whispered, "the only thing you can do now is think positively. Who knows, maybe Joe will exceed your expectations and everything will...work out somehow."

"Joyce, this is not a fairy-tale," I whispered back. "This is real life. So the chance of this...thing having a happy ending is, well, slim to none."

"Still, there's no harm in being positive. I mean, a dash of optimism can't hurt."

"I wish it were that simple," I sighed. I was calmer now or maybe just more resigned to my fate.

I washed off the last mascara streaks from my face and dabbed at my blouse.

"This has got to be the worst wedding day ever," I said. "Usually the bride cries out of happiness, not out of despair."

Joyce smiled.

"Yeah, and you still have to drive to the Island and break the happy news to Joe's parents. If I were Jewish, I'd wish you a Mazel-Tov."

Despite the sadness in my heart, I chuckled.

"Thanks for reminding me. Just when I thought this day couldn't get any worse."

In the car Joe and I talked very little. He gripped the steering wheel tightly and gave monosyllabic answers to my questions regarding his parents.

"How do you think your Dad will react?" I asked.

"Uh, I can't say, really."

I closed my eyes and put my head against the seat's headrest. I was thinking – hoping actually – that at any moment now I would wake up and realize that everything – the pregnancy, marriage, and this drive to Long Island – had been a hellish nightmare.

But when I opened my eyes and saw the white mansion in front of us, I knew that the nightmare was real. And that it was only beginning.

The sight of Joe's house took my breath away. No, not because it was huge and surrounded by impeccably sculpted gardens, but because everything, from the marble columns to the statues of Greek gods flanking the main entrance, was absurdly exaggerated. The mansion stood as tangible proof that wealth and good taste did not always converge.

Goodness gracious, I thought, how could *anyone* live in this monstrosity?

We parked, walked up to the entrance, and Joe punched in the code at the security panel by the door. The enormous, carved oak portals opened with a screech, as though in a haunted mansion.

Inside the foyer we stood under a massive crystal chandelier. It reminded me of my new wedding band.

A small Filipino woman carrying a stack of folded towels approached and smiled.

"Good day, Mr. Joe," she said, bowing her head.

"Hello, Gloria. Do you know where my parents are?"

"They in library, Mr. Joe," she said and scurried off.

I followed Joe up the winding staircase, feeling more queasy and shaky with each step. I wondered whether it was because of the pregnancy, the parmesan chicken I had at lunch or the prospect of coming face–to–face with Annabelle, my new monster–in–law.

"This is where they are," Joe whispered reverently, pointing to the heavy oak door on the first floor. "They like to retire to the library after lunch."

Retire? Were these people speaking English?

Joe opened the door and I followed him inside. The room was large – was there anything in this house smaller than the state of Rhode Island? – and high ceilinged. An intricately carved bookcase stood against one wall; paintings of dogs and horses in ornate, gilded frames hung on the others. Heavy, fringed red velvet drapes blocked the sunlight from streaming through the tall windows. Matching velour settees, recliners and armchairs were placed along the walls. To me the room looked like a drawing of a Victorian brothel in my history book.

It took me a few moments to find my bearings in this epitome of bad taste. But once my eyes adjusted to the red velour that lined every inch of the room, I noticed Annabelle sitting on a sofa in the corner, staring at me wide-eyed. Next to her was Joe's father reading a newspaper.

Annabelle's intake of breath was so sharp, I thought that she was choking. Joe's father turned and followed her gaze to us.

"Mother. Father." Joe said in an irritatingly officious, I-am–kissing–your–ass voice. "This is Megan, my...um...wife."

Annabelle uttered what sounded like a small dog's yelp. Her face became contorted and deathly pale – or maybe it just looked that way against the garish red background – and her left eye started to twitch.

She turned to her husband.

"Stanford," she said in a slow, deliberate voice, "call the attorneys. Ask them about an annulment."

"Mother!" Joe said pleadingly. "You know that Megan is pregnant with my child."

After a long silence Joe's father folded the newspaper and stood up. He was a tall, lanky man with thinning grey hair and wire-rimmed glasses like Joe's.

"Well, then, this calls for a drink," he said.

He walked toward the carved, ornate monstrosity by the wall and opened its hinged top to reveal a well-stocked bar.

"Scotch?" he asked Joe.

"Yes, please, Father. On the rocks."

"And what about you, dear?" Stanford asked, peering at me through his thick-lensed glasses. His blue eyes looked grotesquely large.

"Nothing, thank you," I mumbled.

He filled three glasses with ice, poured scotch, and handed one glass to Joe and another to Annabelle. He took the third and raised it.

"Congratulations," he said. "This is, to say the least, a surprise, but here's to your happiness."

Stanford and Joe brought glasses to their lips. Annabelle's stood untouched on a small table in front of her. She sat pale and motionless, as though in a state of deep shock. Or possibly mourning.

Suddenly my head started to spin and I knew that if I didn't run for the bathroom I'd throw up all over the gaudy furniture. I bolted for the door and, once on the landing, looked around for the nearest bathroom. There were three doors to my right and four to my left. I ran downstairs as though Atlanta were still burning and headed for the main entrance. I hoped that, once a blast of fresh air hit me, I'd feel better. But the door was locked and the handle wouldn't budge.

All of a sudden Gloria the maid materialized in front of me like the Good Fairy.

"Where is the bathroom?" I shouted." Quick!"

"Bathroom there." She pointed to a long hallway on my right. "Third door."

I ran and reached it just in time. I had never been in such a luxurious bathroom before, much less thrown up in one. Afterwards I sat on the cool marble floor, fingering the plush monogrammed towels.

I wasn't sure what happened next. I woke up in a bed the following morning; Joe wasn't with me. I had spent my wedding night alone, in Annabelle's house.

Joe and I moved into a furnished two-bedroom apartment on East 72nd Street. His father's company owned it and the plan was to stay there until the birth. Then we would be going on to Paris for a year, where Joe would supervise the firm's European sales and marketing operations.

The thought of living in Paris kept me going through the loveless and joyless marriage. Joe and I didn't fight or argue. Since we spent very little time together the opportunities for conflicts were drastically reduced.

During the week Joe got up early and went to the office. Midmorning he called, inquired about my health, and then announced that he'd be having dinner with clients or associates and not to wait up for him. He came home late and – ostensibly so as not to wake me – he slept in the spare bedroom. On Friday nights Joe, still a pussyfooting, obedient mamma's boy, drove to Long Island for the weekend. Naturally, I was invited too, more, I was sure, out of courtesy than a genuine desire for my company, but why on earth would I subject myself to spending two hellish days under Annabelle's roof?

A few times Stanford called and asked me to come.

"We never see you, dear," he said.

He seemed to be a nice man who, I assumed, was dominated by Annabelle the same way Joe was. I suspected that the meek, soft-spoken Stanford was merely a figurehead, while the steel-willed, iron-hearted Annabelle was the money and the brains behind the company.

I thanked Stanford for the invitation and said something appropriately vague about trying to make it another time. I didn't tell him, of course, that I wouldn't be coming to the house because I couldn't stand being with his rottweiler of a wife.

I spent my days walking around Manhattan, going to movies and museums, and – now that I had unlimited funds – shopping for the baby. Focusing on the child became an obsession; cribs and baby clothes filled a terrible emptiness and dulled an ache inside me.

Mamma called every night, and I saw her once a week, but she knew nothing of my torment. Every time she asked how the marriage was going I replied that it was fine. This wasn't really a lie – after all, Joe and I weren't exactly at each other's throats – and it kept Mamma off my back.

Truth was, the thought of spending the rest of my life with Joe filled me with dread and anguish. But what could I do? In my desperation I decided to focus only on the positive aspects of my life: the baby and Paris. I told myself that as long as I channeled all my mental energy into those two shining lights, I would be fine.

One night ten days before the baby's due date I started to have contractions. It was a Friday, and naturally Joe wasn't home. The contractions weren't particularly uncomfortable and I decided to wait until morning. By then they became so powerful and painful, I picked up the phone to call Joe. Gloria informed me that he and his father were playing tennis. I hung up and called Mamma to tell her that I was taking a cab to the Lennox Hill Hospital.

"Keep your legs crossed so baby don't drop out in taxi," she shouted excitedly into the phone. "And don't sneeze!"

When I arrived at the hospital I couldn't even stand up straight, much less walk. And by the time I was brought upstairs I knew that the natural childbirth I had read about definitely wasn't for me.

"Give me something for the pain," I asked the nurse, as she was strapping me to a monitor.

"I'll call the doctor," she said and walked out.

The pain was so intense, it brought tears to my eyes. I panted, and the heavy, spasmodic breathing made me queasy.

"GIVE ME DRUGS!" I shrieked as soon as the door opened and a doctor walked in. "NOW!"

An epidural eased the pain and I could relax. I closed my eyes and tried to focus on Paris. I saw myself walking down the Champs-Elysées with my baby in the carriage and... oh, my God! I suddenly realized that not once during my entire pregnancy did Joe and I discuss any names. We had taken our lack of communication to ridiculous new lows.

I dozed off and dreamt about a huge bright comet blazing in the sky. I basked in its light and tried to catch its tail with my outstretched arms. I woke up with a powerful urge to push.

"I have to push," I hollered to no one in particular.

The epidural must have worn off because I was again in the throes of pain. In a matter of minutes I was surrounded by masked and gowned people telling me to push; push with all my might. Fifteen minutes later I heard my baby's wailing.

"It's a little girl," the doctor announced and held her up like a trophy.

A daughter! Tears of joy welled up in my eyes and were streaming down my face, but I was too sore and exhausted to wipe them off.

A flutter of activity followed as the baby was suctioned and toweled off, and her umbilical cord cut. She was then placed in my arms, a perfect little bundle with a duvet of fine blonde hair. I put my lips to her forehead; her skin was soft, warm and as smooth as velvet. The fact that I was holding my newborn daughter hadn't yet sunk in.

"What's her name?" a nurse asked.

My mind went blank and then I remembered my comet dream. There was something magical and ethereal about it.

"Hayley," I whispered. "Her name is Hayley."

"Ché *bella bambina, piccolina*!" Mamma exclaimed when she came to visit a couple of hours later. "*Bionda come un angelo*!"

Mamma always reverted to Italian when she became emotional. I had never heard her utter any endearments in English; come to think of it, I had never heard her utter any endearments at all.

"Why you name her Hayley, eh?" she asked after the first wave of oohs and aahs had subsided. "I can't pronounce it."

"We had no names picked out and I dreamt of a comet and, well, it just seemed so fitting...I wasn't sure of the spelling, so I figured H-a-y-l-e-y sounded pretty."

"I never heard of no such name," she said.

Joe didn't see his newborn daughter until later that evening.

"Sorry I wasn't here," he muttered after a perfunctory glance in the crib. "Father and I were playing in a tennis tournament."

This was all he said. He didn't comment on the name, or on how beautiful his daughter was. He just stood there motionless, as though bidding seconds before he could decently make his escape. Was it humanly possible, I wondered, that a man, even one as emotionally inept as Joe, could be so unmoved by his child's birth? Was Annabelle's genetic imprint so deep within him that he was incapable of showing any feelings?

The thought of spending the rest of my life with a robotic husband brought tears to my eyes. I fell asleep that night sobbing from despair.

Two days later we brought Hayley home and I laid her gently in her crib. Joe was hovering uncomfortably, not knowing what to say or do. I was sure that, given the choice, he'd rather be at home in Long Island where no emotional interactions were called for or expected.

Less than an hour after my homecoming the doorbell rang. Annabelle swept in haughtily, carrying a huge white box tied with a pink ribbon.

"You can exchange whatever doesn't fit," she said curtly as I unwrapped fluffy blankets, stuffed animals, and tiny pink smocked dresses. I imagined that she was deeply pained at having to be nice to me.

"Thank you," I said, trying to sound gracious. "They are beautiful."

The moment of civility was short-lived.

"Why in the world did you name the baby *Hayley*?" she asked in an accusatory tone. "And why wasn't Joe consulted?"

I tried with all my might to unclench my teeth.

"Joe was playing in a tennis tournament," I said, hoping that she could hear the sarcasm in my voice. "And Hayley was named after a comet."

A comet!" she hissed. "You named my granddaughter after a comet?"

"Yes," I said, smiling. "Isn't it original?"

"Maybe it was Joe's mistake for not informing you that in our family the children are named after relatives, not comets," she scoffed. "It's a longstanding tradition that has never been tampered with."

Oh, goody, I thought. I was the first to break the vicious circle!

"Well," I replied, with a smug smile on my lips. "I did consider calling her Angelina, after *my* mother."

Annabelle's and Joe's faces flinched in unison. Despite the emotional upheaval that Hayley's birth had unleashed in me, this turned out to be quite a good day.

Joe and I arrived in Paris when Hayley was just five weeks old. My enchantment with the City of Lights was immediate. I loved the sights, the smells, the people. I even loved the air I breathed.

While Joe worked long hours behind closed doors – for all he knew, or cared, he could have been living in Newark – I walked the streets and bridges of Paris pushing Hayley in her pram. After the first couple of weeks I stayed away from the tourist spots and started exploring the narrow side roads where the real Parisians lived, shopped and dined. Away from the crowds the city was quieter and more laid back, but everywhere I went it exuded an indescribable aroma, a certain *je-ne-sais-quoi.*

I made friends with our next-door neighbor, an elderly widow who didn't speak a word of English. Still, Madame Renaud and I managed to communicate with gestures, facial expressions, dictionaries, and my broken French. She proudly showed me her beautiful collection of old Sevres porcelain and family antiques. She also introduced me to her great-nephew, Alain, a student at Sorbonne, who gave me thrice-weekly French lessons. After several months of total linguistic and cultural immersion I started to speak it fairly fluently.

Joe knew none of this, nor did he express any interest in my daily activities. He left for the office early in the morning and came back late at night. On Fridays he brought home a stack of papers and spent the entire weekend behind the den's closed doors, emerging only to get food and drink. I was certain the people in his office didn't even know he had a wife and child.

In the beginning I tried to suppress my doubts about the future of our marriage. I was so taken by the novelty of my surroundings that I managed to relegate these misgivings to the back of my mind. But as time went by I could no longer quell my doubts.

Joe and I didn't just have a bad marriage; we had no marriage at all. We had no feelings for each other. We didn't spend any time together or share common interests. We didn't talk. There was no intimacy, no passion, and no sex.

Since the evening Hayley was conceived on Chris's couch, Joe and I hadn't slept a single night in the same bed. There had never been any discussion about this aspect of our relationship, or any subsequent decision to remain celibate. We just naturally drifted into this inertness. Since we were nothing more than two strangers thrown together by raging hormones and bound by legality, sex or affection didn't fit into the picture.

"I don't really mind," I told Joyce one evening during our twice-monthly phone calls.

"Megan, you don't know what you're missing. I can't imagine *not* having sex with Rick."

Rick was Joyce's new boyfriend and all she talked about. He was an investment banker with a family pedigree not unlike that of the Moseley's. I didn't know Rick, but, selfishly perhaps, I started to resent the fact that Joyce was so focused on her own happiness, she neglected to empathize with me.

"Well, I'm ecstatic for you," I said dryly. "I hope the two of you will be very happy together."

There was a long silence on the line.

"Are you, by any chance, jealous?" Her voice was as dry as mine.

"I'm not jealous of Rick, so you can relax," I said. I realized that my voice sounded catty now.

Was I telling Joyce the truth? *Wasn't* I envious of her love, her happiness? Well, maybe just a little...or a lot? I shut my eyes. Stop it Megan, I thought, Joyce is your best friend. She is your *only* friend.

Before I opened my mouth to tell her to forget it, to let's not fight, Joyce jumped in.

"Yes, you sound very convincing," she retorted, her sarcasm coming through loud and clear. "You are married to a total ass and you're not envious of me? Ha!"

Her deliberate dig hurt me so much, I didn't know what to say. I hung up the receiver.

Jesus, what was happening, I thought, as I stood in the living room staring at the phone. Was I losing Joyce? She had been my only support system. What was I going to do? I went to bed that night weeping. The next day the phone rang and it was Joyce.

"Megan, I'm so sorry. I don't know what got into me. Forgive me?"

"Of course. And you were right – I probably *am* envious. Of you, of anyone who has a chance at happiness."

"You have a chance at happiness too," Joyce said. "Maybe not with the moron you're married to now, but who knows what life has in store for you."

"I hope you're right," I sighed. "But right now I feel very empty."

I felt as though despair was filling every crevice of my soul.

How long would I be able to live this way? Being in Paris gave some meaning and a new perspective to my life, but what would happen, I wondered, once we returned to New York and there would be no diversions from my unhappiness?

One night about two weeks before we were due to fly back, I was in bed thinking about my future and I started to feel nauseous and dizzy. In a matter of seconds my heart palpitated and I had trouble breathing. I sat up and my head spun so much that I instinctively reached for the bed's wrought-iron headboard. I needed something solid to hold, but my fingers were too numb to grasp the railing.

"Dear God," I mouthed between bouts of dizziness. "Please, please don't let me die. *Please*. I don't want to leave Hayley."

I continued to silently pray until my breathing became steadier, and the palpitations and dizziness started to subside. I hugged my pillow and wrapped the blanket tightly around my body.

What happened to me? Did I have a panic attack? I recalled seeing a TV documentary once about how anxiety and stress could bring on these frightening symptoms. As I wiped the tears off with the edge of my blanket, I knew that this episode was a warning sign I couldn't ignore. My mind, my body were telling me that I couldn't continue to live like this. My marriage had to end.

The next evening I knocked on the den door.

"Joe, we have to talk," I called out.

He opened the door and peered at me. I felt like an intruder.

"What about?" he asked.

"Us."

His muscles tightened, his Adam's apple moved and his forehead broke out in a sweat. Talking was a foreign territory to Joe, a risky endeavor potentially fraught with emotionality that he wasn't capable of. And, of course, Mother dear wasn't there to guide him.

I felt uncomfortable discussing our marriage – or rather the end of it – standing in the doorway, so I went inside and sat down on the sofa. Joe stood in front of me with his hands in his pockets. He was staring at the floor.

I took a deep breath.

"Joe," I said slowly and calmly, although my voice started to quiver, "you must know as well as I do that our marriage is not working. So I think that once we get back to New York we should...file for divorce."

There. The moment the words were out of my mouth I felt better. Relieved.

Joe stood immobile, staring at the dark burgundy carpet, but his facial muscles twitched so I assumed that he had heard me. After a minute or so he raised his eyes and actually looked straight at me.

"What about Hayley?" he asked.

So he did know that he had a daughter!

"She will live with me, but you can see her anytime, whenever you want."

The scary thought of Hayley spending weekends in the Long Island mansion reared its ugly head, but I immediately banished it from my mind.

"Well, if that's what you want," he muttered. "I'll inform Mother."

Naturally.

I waited for him to say more, to express regret over our failed marriage, but he didn't. I took this to mean that Joe had spoken his last word and that I would soon be a free woman. I left the den, went into the bedroom, and sat on the edge of the bed. I felt tears streaming down my cheeks, but, oddly enough, the sadness and despair were gone.

I dried my tears and shut my eyes. That was the moment of epiphany for me; I sensed that from that instant on I would no longer be a meek and submissive Megan. I would command whatever hidden strengths were within me and be the mistress of my own destiny. For the first time in my life I felt empowered.

"Nobody, ever, is going to take that away from me," I whispered.

The return to New York was not as difficult for me as I had feared. Certainly, I was sad and sorry to leave Paris, but the mere knowledge that I was no longer sentenced to a life of misery brought a glimmer of hope to my life.

Mamma, of course, didn't take the news well.

"You crazy, or what?" she shrieked when I told her of the

impending divorce.

"Not anymore," I said. "I'm finally getting my sanity back. And I'm happy."

Needless to say, the notion of esoteric happiness was lost on Mamma.

"Happy, eh? You call Joe right now and tell him you sorry!"

"I will do no such thing."

"You think is easy for woman alone with child, eh?" she yelled.

"Maybe not," I answered quietly. I certainly didn't want to get into a shouting match with Mamma because I couldn't out scream her. "But believe me, my life wasn't exactly a bed of roses."

Mamma shook her head.

"You had husband, money, coulda have nice house, nice life. And you think it ain't no bed of roses?"

"Mamma, I'm twenty-three-years-old. I'm too young to be stuck in a loveless marriage."

"You shoulda think of this before! *Before* you get pregnant, eh!"

I didn't answer. Arguing with Mamma was pointless and exhausting.

"What you gonna do now, how you gonna live, eh?"

"I'll manage."

"And what about Hayley?"

"She'll manage too," I sighed. "Listen Mamma, I don't want to talk about this anymore right now, okay?"

Mamma always managed to destroy whatever inkling of joy was emerging within me at a given time. I decided right there that I would always nurture all of Hayley's manifestations of happiness. And, of course, I would never lay any guilt trips on her.

Predictably, the only person other than myself happy about the divorce was Annabelle.

"That's a very smart decision, dear," she told me on the phone.

The mere fact that Annabelle was calling me "dear" sounded alarms in my head. Besides, her voice was pseudo-friendly rather than outright spiteful. I started to wonder whether she was plotting to snatch Hayley and raise her in the monstrous mansion.

"Yes," I answered. "It is. For all of us."

"Of course, Hayley always has a home with us, a comfortable home," she said. Her unnaturally sugary voice grated on my nerves. "Think about it."

"Even though she is named after a comet?" I asked.

I couldn't help the little dig.

"What?"

"Oh, never mind," I sighed. "Thank you for calling, Annabelle."

The divorce was more amicable than the marriage. It was straightforward and quick. The only thing I requested, more for Hayley's sake than my own, was an accommodation and child support. Joe seemed relieved that his family's sizeable assets would remain intact.

He bought us a small two-bedroom apartment on West 77th Street where Hayley and I lived rent-free. The apartment was to be mine for as long as I wanted it; Joe even signed the ownership papers over to me.

Now that Hayley's future and comfort were taken care of, my immediate concern was how to earn *my* living. Every day I read the classified ads in the *Times*, but there weren't exactly hundreds of employers seeking a young mother with a liberal arts degree. Actually, there wasn't a single one.

Then, one day, as I pored over the classifieds, I saw an ad from the *Alliance Française* French Institute. I signed up for their advanced courses and, when I felt that my skills were sufficiently honed, I started giving beginner lessons to children and senior citizens at the "Y." It wasn't much money, but I managed.

No, teaching French definitely wasn't as lucrative as Brent believed. I squinted and peered at the bedside clock. Two a.m. I had been awake, reminiscing about my life, for the past several hours.

I yawned, stretched, and turned to face the wall. Sleep was the only luxury I had and I wasn't going to waste any more of it.

Chapter Five

The next evening I sat down in front of the computer, turned it on, and immediately saw Brent's name in my IM box. He started to type as soon as I logged on.

FloridaBrent: Hey, Megan.

MeganM: Hi.

FloridaBrent: How are you this evening? Ready to work?

MeganM: As ready as I'll ever be. Anything to do with computers is a foreign territory to me.

FloridaBrent: That's why you hired me, remember? I speak fluent computerese.

MeganM: Well, it's all Greek to me.

FloridaBrent: Let's forget Greek for the time being, shall we, and focus on French. Tell me, where did you learn it?

MeganM: In Paris. I lived there once, for a year. A long time ago.

FloridaBrent: Lucky you. Did you absolutely love Paris?

I hesitated. Should I tell this stranger about my year in Paris, about the end of my so-called marriage? No, I thought, I couldn't share such personal tidbits with someone I hardly knew.

MeganM: Let it suffice to say that Paris was wonderful. *Magnifique*. The history, the architecture, the people, the food. I loved it all.

I stopped typing, but something inside me, some force I couldn't fathom or control, brought my fingertips back to the keyboard again.

MeganM: It was the best of times and the worst of times. And not much wisdom, mostly just foolishness.

FloridaBrent: Hmm, sounds very Dickensian. What does the "Tale of Two Cities" have to do with your stay in Paris?

MeganM: The book per se, nothing. But I think of my time in Paris as a mix of good and bad, the best times of my life and the worst.

FloridaBrent: Should all this be included on your website?

MeganM: Goodness, no! I was just babbling, sorry.

FloridaBrent: No apologies needed. But what you just said makes me think of another great quote: "The web of our life is of a mingled yarn, good and ill together."

MeganM: Shakespeare, isn't it? From "All's Well That Ends Well."

FloridaBrent: You read Shakespeare?

MeganM: Yes. I have always been an avid reader.

FloridaBrent: I read a lot too. One of my all-time favorites is "The Little Prince." Know it?

MeganM: By Antoine de Saint-Exupéry? Of course.

FloridaBrent: I loved it. It's about love and loneliness, hope and the little inner child that lies dormant in all of us. And, it has a touch of sci-fi, just perfect for me.

MeganM: Tell me, how did a person with such a great literary insight end up designing websites?

FloridaBrent: Your question suggests that technology and literature don't mix. Not so. Creativity and imagination are two essential ingredients for web design. And, of course, nothing fosters creativity and imagination more than great literary works. So there you have it.

MeganM: I stand/sit corrected! And speaking of websites, we

haven't progressed much on mine, have we?

FloridaBrent: *Au contraire*. With my mind's eye – and by the way, why is there always just one? – I see your website: the city of Paris with Charles Dickens as the guide. What do you think? Strikes your fancy?

MeganM: Not really.

FloridaBrent: Just kidding. But listen, I'll send you something by tomorrow, okay? Have a look at it and tell me what you think.

MeganM. Fine. I'll be looking forward to seeing it. With both my eyes.

FloridaBrent: And I'll be looking forward to talking to you some more. I don't get to talk much about books with my customers. I imagine most of them don't give a rat's ass about Shakespeare!

MeganM: Well then, I'll talk to you tomorrow.

FloridaBrent: Yes. Goodbye, Megan.

MeganM: Bye, Brent.

Chapter Six

I heard a key turn in the lock.

"Hey, Mom!"

Hayley bounded into the living room, threw her backpack on the coffee table and gave me a bear hug.

"Hi, sweetheart," I said, holding her close. Her shoulder-length, naturally curly brown hair smelled of apples and cinnamon. "How was the drive?"

"The longest 250 miles *ever*!" she complained. "The traffic was really slow."

Hayley sat down on the sofa next to me and immediately averted her eyes. I sensed that something was troubling her. Was she sick? Did she get into any trouble? A chill went down my spine, a vague anxiety that rang alarm bells in my head.

"Hayley, is...anything wrong?" I asked, trying to keep my voice calm and casual.

She picked up a throw pillow, hugged it, and looked at some indefinable point in the distance. There was a long silence as Hayley fidgeted with the pillow's fringe. Finally she put it down, took a deep breath, and turned to me.

"Mom, I'm going to Central and South America next week," she said. "With some friends. I saved all the money Grandma Annabelle has been sending me. You remember Carrie, my old roommate? Her uncle is some kind of a diplomat in Guatemala. He offered to put us up. We'd go all over, and of, course we want to see the jungle and the Amazon."

I felt relief, but only for the briefest of moments. As Hayley's words began to sink in – next week... friends... the jungle... the Amazon – I felt that chill in my spine again.

"Goodness," I said, trying not to sound alarmed. "When did all this come about?"

"Well, Carrie and I have been talking about it for a while. Then a couple of other people said they'd like to go too. Now we're all fired up about it."

"I see." My heartbeat accelerated at the thought of my only child trekking through a mosquito-infested jungle, and walking knee-deep in a river ridden with man-eating crocodiles. "And when will you be back?"

Hayley diverted her gaze to the pillow. She started playing with the fringe again.

"Two months, maybe three," she said, still not looking at me. Two or three months. This meant Hayley would miss her final semester.

"What about school, honey?" I asked, although deep down inside I already suspected what her answer would be.

"I won't be going back next semester. But I *will* finish college and I *will* graduate after I get back. Promise!"

I noticed how she put emphasis on the *wills,* as though she wanted to reassure me – and herself? – that she was not dropping out.

"Mom, I'm *not* dropping out," she quickly added, as though she were a mind reader. "I'm just postponing the last semester, that's all."

I closed my eyes and thought about Hayley's announcement. My daughter would be taking a semester off to travel in South America. Was this *bad* news and, if so, *why* was it bad? Was it because she was leaving school, albeit temporarily, or because she would be away for several months traveling God knows where, with all the potential dangers such an undertaking posed?

"Hayley, sweetheart," I said, weighing every word. I certainly didn't want to alienate the most important person in my life. "I think your travel plans sound very interesting. Exciting. But why don't you postpone them until after you graduate? It's only a matter of six months."

"Mom, college will be there when I get back. But an opportunity like this may never come my way again."

I opened my mouth to tell Hayley that she was young, that there would be plenty of chances to travel. But as soon as these thoughts were formulated in my mind, I remembered my talk with

Mamma that Easter twenty-two years ago. I wanted so much to join the Peace Corps, to travel, to see the world, to experience things other than the daily drudgery of our modest lives. But I had to give up that dream for Mamma.

Suddenly I knew: As much as I wanted to keep Hayley close to me, I couldn't – I didn't want to – have the same obsessive hold on her as Mamma had on me.

"Well, as long as you promise that you *will* go back to college and finish the last semester..."

Hayley's arms were around my neck before I could finish the sentence.

"Oh, Mom, you're the greatest! I knew you'd understand," she exclaimed. "I *will* make up the semester, I promise."

"You must also promise me that you'll be very, very careful out there," I said. "I don't usually like to elicit promises under duress – that's Nonna's *modus operandi*, not mine, but I'm making an exception in this case."

"Of course, Mom. That goes without saying. I'll be very, very cautious."

I sighed.

"I guess that's what they – whoever the mysterious, often-quoted *they* are – say about one's children flying the coop. I am starting to feel the empty nest syndrome."

"Mom, I've been away at college for three–and–a–half years."

"Yes, but you were only a few hours away, and I got to see you once a month. Now you'll be thousands of miles away, in a totally different world, and I won't see you for three months."

I felt my throat muscles tighten and my eyes sting. *No*, I thought to myself, I will *not* be a crybaby. I will be brave and put a smile on my face for Hayley.

"I know, Mom, but it's not like I'm moving away *forever*. We'll be in touch. We'll talk as often as we do now. And, before you know it, I'll be back."

I couldn't help smiling at Hayley's exuberance.

"I hope so," I said in a mock Italian accent. "Just remember: your poor, suffering Mamma will be sitting by the phone every night waiting for your call... *Eh!*"

Hayley laughed.

"My goodness, you really *did* sound like Nonna just now. You're...scaring me."

"I'm scaring myself too."

Suddenly Hayley's expression grew serious and she glanced at her watch.

"Uh-ho," she sighed. "I still have to tell Dad. And Grandma. And Nonna."

Yes, I could see what she meant. Joe would not be happy to hear this news, and of course Annabelle would be livid. And I could imagine how Mamma would react.

"I'll tell you what, honey. Don't worry about breaking the news to Nonna. I will talk to her."

"Will you Mom?" There was relief on Hayley's face. "Thanks, you're the best."

She got up from the sofa and stretched.

"I guess there's no use postponing this," she said, more to herself than to me. "I'll go to Dad's office. I might as well tell him."

Hayley picked up her backpack from the table, opened it, took out a tube of lip gloss and spread the shiny pink gel on her lips. It reminded me of how, at five or six, she used to rummage in my purse for "Mommy treasures." She had found my lipstick and gleefully spread it all over her lips and cheeks.

"Am I pretty, Mommy"? she would ask, looking like a circus clown.

"Very pretty, darling," I would answer.

Hayley put the gloss back and slung the backpack over her shoulder.

"How do I look Mom?" she asked. "Is the lipstick smeared?"

I smiled.

"It's amazing how little you changed in the last fifteen years. You used to ask me the same question when you were little, after you smeared *my* lipstick all over your face."

"*Little*?" Hayley looked at me wide-eyed. "Mom, I used to be a chubby kid. I certainly hope I changed a *lot* in the past fifteen years."

I smiled at the memory of a cherub with tight, blonde curls framing her apple-cheeked face. Now Hayley's hair was brown and shoulder-length, her face more oval than round, and the chubby little body was slim and tall. Only her large, brown eyes were the same.

"Well, I'd like to think that you are a little more mature now. And," I looked at the carefully applied gloss, "your aim is better."

Hayley laughed and turned toward the door.

"Hasta la vista, Mom," she shouted from the hallway. "Keep your fingers crossed."

As soon as Hayley left, seeds of doubt and apprehension took hold of me. Was I right in agreeing to this trip so quickly, I wondered? Shouldn't we have talked about it more, discussed the details? Why didn't I try to dissuade her?

Sudden, bittersweet memories of Hayley as a toddler and a little girl started to fill my mind. Hayley jumping up and down in her playpen, laughing and clapping hands. Hayley with a clown's red nose and much-too-big shoes. And, of course, Tina and Freddie. They had been as much a part of Hayley's life as I had been.

I shut my eyes and, once more, let my thoughts drift back in time.

Chapter Seven

I met Tina on the day Hayley and I moved into the apartment. As I was unpacking cardboard boxes and Hayley screamed like a banshee in the playpen set up in the middle of the living room, I heard my bell ring.

I opened the door and saw a young, thirty-something couple standing on the doorstep. The woman was short and slim, with short spiked black hair and bright blue eyes. Dressed in cuffed jeans overalls, with a red bandana tied around her head, she was a dead-ringer for Rosie the Riveter. The man was very tall, his light hair tied in a ponytail. He wore an incongruous combination of plaid flannel slacks, a beige button-down shirt, and sandals.

"Hi," the woman said cheerily, "we are the Bronsons. Tina and Fred. We live right here." She pointed to the door next to mine.

"Oh," I said, "you must be bothered by all the noise. I've been lugging these boxes, and my daughter is crying... I'm so sorry. My mother will come soon to help with the baby and the unpacking, so...

"Oh, no," Tina said, "we're not here to complain. Freddie and I saw you struggling with all this stuff," she pointed to the boxes piled up in the hallway, "and thought you may need some help. So, here we are!"

"I'm the brains and she's the brawn," Freddie said, smiling. "So we figure that between the two of us, we can be useful. I'll entertain the baby and Tina here can help you carry and unpack."

I burst out laughing.

"*You'll* baby–sit and *she'll* do the heavy work?"

"Yes," Freddie said. "What's the matter? Don't you believe in role reversal?"

I stepped aside and motioned for them to come in.

"I like people who think out of the box," I said. "Especially if they're ready and willing to help me with this thankless task."

Tina and Freddie stepped inside, went into the living room, and cooed over Hayley. She immediately stopped crying and began laughing and gurgling.

"What a precious baby," Tina said, and reached inside the playpen to ruffle Hayley's blonde curls. "What's her name?"

"Her name is Hayley and she is thirteen months. And I, by the way, am Megan Moseley."

"Hayley! What a wonderful name," Freddie exclaimed. "Just like the comet."

"Yes," I said, "that was the idea, but nobody in my immediate family seemed to appreciate it."

"How could they not? Such a celestial name, so – if you forgive the pun – out of this world."

"Do you have children?" I asked.

"Alas, no," Tina said.

I immediately regretted asking the question. I sensed, from the inflection of Tina's voice, that their childlessness was not a matter of choice.

For the next two hours, as Freddie entertained Hayley with hilarious facial expressions and animal noises which made her laugh out loud and clap her hands, Tina and I unpacked the boxes. I learned that Freddie used to work as a mime and a clown in a traveling circus troupe, and now ran theatre workshops for children. Tina taught philosophy at NYU.

We talked about my experiences in Paris, and Tina's and Freddie's own travels to Asia, Africa and South America. When Mamma arrived at the end of the afternoon, my stuff was unpacked and put away, and Hayley was sleeping blissfully in her crib.

"What kind of job is clown, eh?" Mamma asked incredulously after Tina and Freddie had left.

"I imagine it's a wonderful job. To make people laugh; what a great thing that is!"

"You crazy?"

"Well, Freddie was certainly wonderful with Hayley. He took a fussy, cranky baby and turned her into a laughing, babbling one. He'll make one heck of a babysitter."

"Babysitter? You gonna leave Hayley with *clown*?" Mamma

shouted.

"Relax, Mamma," I said. "They are very nice people. They offered to baby–sit whenever their schedules permit. Hayley can only benefit from having two such happy–go–lucky people in her life."

"If Hayley see his red nose, she cry."

"Mamma, the red nose is a part of a clown's costume. They don't wear disguises like that every day."

Mamma pouted her lips.

"You prefer to leave Hayley with strange clown rather than with your own Mamma?"

I put my arm around Mamma's neck and kissed her on the cheek.

"They live next door, so it's very convenient. But don't worry, *you'll* always be Hayley's favorite babysitter."

Tina and I became very close and Hayley grew attached to both her and Freddie. Since they had no children of their own – Tina later confided to me that Freddie had become sterile as a result of a particularly bad case of mumps he contracted at the age of twenty – they became Hayley's honorary godparents. They spoiled her with gifts, trips to the zoo, rides at Coney Island, movies, and Broadway shows. And, of course, Freddie's clownery made Hayley laugh so much, it brought tears to her eyes.

Little by little I opened up to Tina and told her about my one romp on Chris's couch.

"That was the night Hayley was conceived," I said. "And, believe it or not, I haven't had sex since. Pathetic, isn't it?"

"Well, now, you're still very young. Give yourself time."

Once, when Freddie and Hayley went to see a show at the Radio City Music Hall, Tina and I sat sipping jasmine tea in her kitchen.

"Tell me, why don't you ever go out?" she asked.

"You mean on dates?"

"Yes, on dates."

I put down my cup and sat staring into the clear yellow liquid.

"I don't really know."

That wasn't totally true. As much as I craved companionship and intimacy, I was scared of getting involved in another relationship. I was still smarting from the way Joe had treated me.

"Well, you should definitely get out more often, now that you have two willing babysitters."

"I'd like to but...my track record is not exactly stellar. I mean, look what happened with Joe."

"It didn't work out, so what? It just happened once. Doesn't mean that it'll happen again, or that you have to spend the rest of your life in isolation and celibacy."

"Yes," I sighed. "I know."

"Don't you want to be with somebody?"

I picked up the cup again and brought it to my lips.

"Yes, I would like that. But I don't know anybody."

"Well," Tina said and refilled our cups, "*I* know somebody."

"Who?"

"My nephew, Stanley. He is a freelance writer, about your age. He just broke off a long-term relationship and is moping."

"Tina, I don't want to go out with a guy who's moping and possibly on the rebound."

"Oh, no, he's over her, believe me. Anyway, what have you got to lose? He is nice, smart, and has a great personality."

Stanley and I went on a few dates. We discovered that we shared an interest in Impressionist art — I had developed a fascination with it in Paris – and we spent many hours traipsing through the Met and other museums and galleries. After several pleasant outings and Stanley's timid references to sex, I decided to go on the Pill. I was a little nervous about having sex again – I imagined that I was the only near-virgin mother on the face of the earth – but my desire for sex overrode my apprehensions.

It wasn't that I was desperate to release any pent-up sexual tension; no, I just wanted to have one good, enjoyable experience to erase from my psyche the unpleasant and hurtful memory of my encounter with Joe.

Stanley knew nothing of my sexual inexperience. As much as I liked him, I sensed that the superficial nature of our relationship was not conducive to intimate heart-to-heart talks. Not yet, anyway.

On our next date we went to a Monet retrospective and afterwards to Stanley's studio apartment on West 58th. We sat on his bed and he kissed me. His mattress was much too soft and the spring box very noisy. There was also a strong smell of fried onions emanating from another apartment. I was acutely aware of these decidedly unromantic sounds and smells, and, for the briefest of moments, wanted to get up and leave. But despite my nervousness, which manifested itself by an accelerated heart rate and an embarrassingly clammy skin, I closed my eyes and kissed him back. As we lay down I realized that, in spite of my near-nakedness, my apprehensions had, miraculously, dissipated.

As I cabbed it home that night, I had a smug smile on my face. Granted, there wasn't any emotional intimacy between Stanley and me, but at least the sex itself was far more enjoyable than my previous experience.

Two days before our next date, a letter arrived. It was from Stanley. He wrote that he had unexpectedly reunited with his erstwhile girlfriend, that the two of them eloped to Las Vegas over the weekend and hence he could no longer see me. He apologized and asked for my forgiveness.

I was livid.

"That fucking nephew of yours is a real jerk!" I shouted at Tina, shoving the letter in her face. "And you said he was over her!"

Tina's face was ashen.

"Megan, I'm *so* sorry, I had no idea. I was really under the impression that he broke it off with her, for good."

I immediately regretted yelling at Tina. She had always been so supportive of me, so generous. I shut my eyes and took a deep breath.

"Please forgive me, Tina, for yelling. Of course, I know it's not your fault. It's nobody's fault really. And, if truth be told, I liked Stanley a lot, but there was nothing deeper than that. So the relationship would have petered out soon anyway."

"You'll meet someone else, you'll see. Just give it time."

A month later Tina knocked on my door.

"Do I have a guy for you!" she exclaimed.

"Let me guess. Another moping nephew?"

"No, no more family members, promise! This one is Freddie's acquaintance. He is a stagehand on Broadway. Okay, off, *off* Broadway, but he can get you in to see all the shows for free."

"Terrific. I'll be hanging backstage like some kind of a love struck groupie."

But I did go out with Harry. He turned out to be cute and funny, and he did get me in to see the shows for free.

"Don't get involve with him," Mamma warned when I offered

to get her tickets to one of Harry's shows.

"Why not?"

"He in show business, eh. All them people crazy."

Mamma was telling me to stay away from Harry because *he* was crazy?

After a few months Harry left town. He got a job on the West Coast, as a stage manager for a road production of "*Cats*."

Several weeks after Harry's departure, Tina brought Jacques over to my apartment. She had met him through a colleague of hers at the university, although I didn't quite understand the connection between the two of them. There was nothing even remotely scholarly about Jacques, who was more a rogue than an intellectual. He was French-Canadian and we spent our entire four-month relationship speaking French. But despite the common language I never understood what Jacques did for a living. Every time I asked, and I asked often, he replied that he was a "distributor."

Jacques was fun-loving and wild, and we had some great times together. He leased a Porsche and we used to drive it around Manhattan like a pair of crazed teenagers. There wasn't much intellectual stimulation with Jacques, but I enjoyed spending time with him nevertheless. It sure beat sitting alone in my apartment.

Our relationship came to an abrupt end when Jacques had mysteriously disappeared from his sublet on West 96th Street. I had no clue whatsoever what had happened to him until his upstairs neighbor, also a French-Canadian, explained to me in hushed tones that Jacques was living it up in New York on someone else's money. One day the cops came, asked for his papers, and discovered that Jacques was living in this country illegally. He had gone back to Canada, never to be heard from again.

As the years went by, I continued to date sporadically and infrequently, but I began to yearn for a deeper, more meaningful relationship, for – as corny as it sounded — a true meeting of hearts and minds.

"No more shallow relationships for me," I told Tina one night when she brought up yet another potential suitor. "I'm tired of these fly–by–night guys who transit through my life without leaving any meaningful mark. I want more. Please tell me I'm not being overly sentimental."

"You're not being overly sentimental," Tina said.

As Hayley grew from sweet babyhood and little girlhood into

the dreaded teenage phase, she became even closer to the Bronsons. By the time she turned sixteen Tina and Freddie were her best buddies, while I, her mother, was left on the outskirts of their close little circle. Hayley became broody and withdrawn, giving only brief, monosyllabic answers to my questions, and generally avoiding any contact or interaction with me.

Once, in the tenth grade, she went to a party with her classmates and didn't get home until past midnight. I had never felt the need to impose any curfews since, up to that point, Hayley hadn't given me any reason to. But as I paced the floor nervously waiting for Hayley's return, Tina tried to calm me down.

"Listen, she is trying to find her boundaries, to see how far she can go. This is a textbook case of teenage rebellion."

"Terrific! But how do I deal with it? I don't want to be too authoritarian; that's just not my style and it reminds me too much of Mamma's way of dealing with me. On the other hand, she needs to know what her limits are...what the heck *are* her limits?"

"Hey, I'm only an honorary aunt–slash–godmother so I get to enjoy Hayley without having to discipline her – ha!" Tina laughed. She sat on the floor cross–legged, an oversized sweater stretched out over her knees. "Seriously though, you must figure this all out yourself."

I sat down on the sofa and clasped my hands behind my neck.

"I'm not ready to be a mother of a teenage daughter," I sighed. "I want to be a cool, hip mom, not a nagging crone."

"If it's of any consolation to you, I remember my niece, Lizzie, Stanley's sister, when she was Hayley's age. Seemingly overnight she turned from a sweet cherub into a hellion. Fortunately, by her senior year Lizzie calmed down, wised up, and graduated at the top of her class, which certainly helped her to get into Columbia U. So, there *is* hope."

"Senior year? But Hayley's only a sophomore. By the time she turns seventeen I won't have any natural hair left on my head. I'll tear it all out in frustration."

"So, buy a wig." Tina laughed. "By the time Hayley gets out of this terrible phase and becomes her old lovable self again, your hair will grow back."

We were still laughing when I heard the key turn in the lock and Hayley came in. As she neared the middle of the living room where Tina and I were sitting, I smelled cigarettes. Hayley's hair and clothes reeked of smoke. My first thought was that Mamma would have yelled and demanded an explanation for the tardy return and the rancid smell. That's what Mamma would have done if I ever dared to come home after midnight. But I didn't want to give in to hysterics. If I had learned anything at all from Mamma, it was not to be like her.

So I looked up at Hayley standing in front of me, and smiled.

"Let me guess." I shut my eyes and sniffed the air, as though smelling an exquisite perfume. "Marlboro Lights, right?"

Hayley opened her mouth to say something but she was so visibly surprised by my nonchalance, that she just stood there, staring at Tina and me, not saying anything.

Finally she turned to me and glared.

"I don't have to explain anything to *you*," she hissed. "It's *my* life, and if I feel like smoking, I will. You can't make me stop!"

I took a deep breath.

"You're absolutely right, Hayley, it is your life," I replied, as calmly as I could under these trying circumstances. "But this happens to be my life also so while you may choose to emanate the obnoxious smell of cigarettes, please keep in mind that I don't wish to smell, breathe, or be otherwise inconvenienced by the acrid odor you seem to find so appealing."

"Whatever," she spat out.

Hayley turned around and walked out, slamming the door to her room behind her.

"Jesus!" I exclaimed. "And I thought the 'terrible twos' were bad."

"Listen, you handled it really well," Tina said. "But you have to be pro–active. You have to, diplomatically of course, make Hayley understand that smoking is just not cool."

"Yes? And how do you suggest I do that, huh?"

Tina sat quietly for a moment, her arms circling her knees. Then she looked up at me and smiled.

"I have an idea. A brilliant idea!" She jumped up and came to sit on the sofa beside me. "There's this funky shop in the Village, all sorts of novelty and party items. Freddie goes there sometimes to buy disguises for his workshop. Anyway, as gruesome as it sounds, they sell all kinds of fake body parts and organs. I'm pretty sure I remember seeing a black lung... How about we go there tomorrow, buy it, and spring it on Hayley. Hopefully, the sight of this ugly thing will scare the hell out of her."

"And that is your diplomatic idea?" I laughed. "I love it."

The next morning Tina and I took the subway to the Village, found the shop, and bought the blackened lung. It was the ugliest thing I had ever seen.

At home I took the disgusting fake lung out of the paper bag and set it in the middle of the kitchen table. The mere sight of it made me nauseous.

Hayley came back from school, dropped her bag on the floor and went, without saying a word, to her room. I knocked on her door.

"Yeah?" she grunted.

"Sweetheart, would you like some chocolate chip cookies? Tina brought them over earlier. They are yummy!"

Yummy? When did I ever use the word "yummy" before? Jesus, I thought, this teenage defiance phase was turning my brain to mush.

Hayley came out of her room, went into the kitchen and sat down at the table. She reached for the plate of cookies, but her hand stopped midway and she stared, horrified, at the fake lung. She grimaced and recoiled in disgust.

"Yuck, did you *cook*?" she asked.

"That's very funny, sweetheart, very funny, and probably not so far–fetched either." I sat next to her and brought the amorphous blob closer to us. "This here is what a smoker's lung looks like. Repugnant, isn't it?"

Hayley jumped up and glared at me.

"You think I'm some kind of an idiot?" she shouted. "You thought this stupid little ploy of yours would actually work?"

She ran to her room and slammed the door.

Terrific, I thought, just great. What was I going to do now?

As I was sitting at the table considering my options, Hayley came back. I could see that she had been crying.

She sat down next to me and stared at the table.

"Mom," she said, still not looking at me, "I don't really smoke. I just tried a few puffs because everyone else was doing it. But actually, I hated it. I couldn't see what was so great about it. But...I didn't want to be the only square one, you know?

I smiled and squeezed Hayley's hand.

"No, I don't know. At your age, or at any age for that matter,

I didn't rebel in any shape or form. I just intuitively knew that defiance was out of the question. Nonna ran a tight ship."

"Mom, if I promise not to smoke again, will you please get rid of this horrible, nasty thing in the middle of the table? I mean, it makes me think of what a pot roast of yours would look like if you ever made one."

I drew Hayley closer to me and planted a kiss on her cheek.

"It's a deal," I laughed. "And I promise to stick to my long-standing policy of not cooking. The only chef allowed in my kitchen will be Chef Boyardee."

After that incident Hayley became her old friendly self again, and she continued to keep in touch with the Bronsons even after she went away to college.

One evening two years ago I came back from the Y and saw a light flashing on my answering machine. I pressed the button and Tina's frantic voice came on.

"Freddie fell ill and was rushed by an ambulance to Columbia Presbyterian," she said. "I'm calling from the ER. I ...well, I'll try to call later."

I ran out of the building and hailed a cab. I found Tina sitting in a chair in the ER waiting room, a minister holding her hand and whispering something into her ear. She raised her head and looked at me. Her face was streaked with tears.

"Freddie is...dead," she said in a croaky whisper.

I immediately felt a shiver go down my spine. I couldn't believe it. Freddie, dead?

I sat on a chair beside Tina and stretched out my hand. She took it and clasped it tightly.

"What...what happened?" I asked.

Tina opened her mouth to answer but instead she started to sob uncontrollably. She turned to me and placed her tear-soaked face on my shoulder. I put my arms around her and held her tightly.

"Mr. Bronson died about an hour ago of a burst brain aneurysm," the minister told me softly.

"An aneurysm?" I choked out. "But how?"

My voice was breaking and I couldn't utter more than those four words.

"I'm afraid I'm in no position to answer that with any certainty," he said. "I'm just a hospital chaplain, not a doctor. It was most unfortunate. My sincere condolences."

The minister helped me put Tina into a cab and I took her home. I gave her the sedatives the ER doctor prescribed and put her to sleep in my bed. I spent the night, fully awake, on my living room sofa.

I reached Hayley in the dorm before she left for her morning classes. She arrived that afternoon and the three of us sat holding each other on Tina's settee. Tina clutched Freddie's tattered shirt to her chest.

"I love him so much," she sobbed. "He was my soul mate."

She wiped her tears with Freddie's shirt and rubbed it against her cheek.

"How will I ever live without him?" she wailed. "How?"

"I don't know, Tina," I said, and dried my own tears.

That night, as we put a sedated Tina into my bed again, Hayley and I went into her room and lay down on the narrow bed.

"I loved him too, Mom," she sobbed. "He was like a father to me."

"I know, sweetheart." I patted her hair and held her close. "I know it's difficult but we must be strong, for Tina. We have each other, but she has no one."

The only family Tina had in New York – beside her wayward nephew – was her niece, Lizzie. Her other relatives lived in Chicago.

After the memorial service and the funeral, Tina became listless and withdrawn. She took a semester off from teaching and grieved. Lizzie and I took turns providing meals and moral support.

After a couple of months of almost total isolation Tina resurfaced. Her cheerful and upbeat personality slowly re-emerged, and she started to go out to movies and museums with Joyce and me.

"I'll never get over Freddie's death," she told me one evening as we sat in my kitchen playing scrabble. "But I have to stay positive and go on living. Mourning is not going to bring Freddie back."

At that moment Tina and I were united by loneliness; she had lost her one true love, and I haven't yet found mine.

With Freddie's passing Hayley grew even closer to Tina. She confided in Tina and sought her advice on boyfriends and other matters. At times I felt left out of their little clique, but I instinctively knew that my daughter wasn't intentionally favoring Tina over me; she simply was trying to fill a void in Tina's life by making her feel important and needed. And, in her infinite sensitivity and wisdom, Tina never overstepped her boundaries. Many times she hugged Hayley and then gently told her, "Why don't you discuss this with your mother?"

I opened my eyes and saw that it was already dark outside. I thought about Hayley's announcement that afternoon and my promise to tell Mamma about the trip. No use postponing the inevitable, I thought. I got up, went to the kitchen and dialed Mamma's number. Then I leaned against the counter and sighed.

Chapter Eight

"WHAT?" Mamma shouted into the receiver. "And you *let* her?"

As I expected, she was not taking the news of Hayley's trip well.

"It's not a matter of *letting* her, Mamma," I said. "She is twenty-two. I can't *forbid* her to go."

"Of course you can!" Mamma yelled. Her shouts were so loud, I had to hold the receiver a good foot away from my ear. "You her mother. She must listen to you, eh."

"Mamma, I don't want to argue with you," I said. I just wanted to placate her and hang up the phone. "I wish you'd accept the fact that Hayley has a mind of her own. And taking a sabbatical to travel is not the worst thing that can happen."

I heard heavy breathing in the receiver, a sure sign that Mamma was nowhere near being appeased.

"What you mean, is not the worst thing that can happen, eh?" she yelled. "A lot can happen."

Before I could disengage myself from Mamma's grip, she breathlessly listed potential disasters that could befall poor Hayley.

"She can get sick from water, she can get lost in jungle, she can get attacked by animals, she..."

"Mamma, stop it! Nothing bad will happen to Hayley."

Was I trying to convince her, or myself, I wondered?

Mamma hung up before I had a chance to finish the sentence.

I sat down in front of the computer and typed "travel, South America" into the search engine. As much as I hated to admit that anything Mamma said had any impact on me, I wanted to make sure that Hayley was not facing any *real* danger.

There were many listings and as I strolled down the page, a by-now familiar name popped up on the screen.

FloridaBrent: Hi Megan.

MeganM: Hi Brent.

FloridaBrent: I'm almost ready with a proposal for your site.

MeganM: Terrific.

FloridaBrent: I have a couple of ideas floating around in my head. Well, maybe *floating* is not a good word. It makes you think that my brain is so empty, any ideas that emerge in there have plenty of space to float.

MeganM: I didn't think that at all, but thanks for clarifying.

FloridaBrent: So anyway, I have a couple of ideas *crowding* my head. Want to discuss?

MeganM: I'm eager to hear it, Brent, but do you mind if we postpone it a bit? I actually logged on to do some research on Central and South America.

FloridaBrent: Cool. What do you need to know? Maybe I can help.

MeganM: Okay, Mr. Know-It-All. What do you know about Central and South America?

FloridaBrent: They are south of the border.

MeganM: Thanks. I would have never figured it out myself.

FloridaBrent: Why are you asking? Thinking of learning Spanish?

MeganM: Not at this time. But my daughter is going there with some college classmates. I heard it could be risky.

FloridaBrent: Getting up in the morning could be risky. Taking a shower could be considered risky too because you could slip and hit your head. And going out of the house is definitely risky because a bus could hit you.

MeganM: And what exactly does all this have to do with South America?

FloridaBrent: With South America? Nothing. But my point is that life is full of dangers. Even when you're close to home. But you don't stay indoors your whole life, right?

MeganM: Right.

FloridaBrent: So that's my point.

MeganM: It's a point well taken, thank you. Of course, my mother is not seeing eye-to-eye with me on this. She can be very overbearing. She likes to call the shots.

FloridaBrent: A Jewish mother?

MeganM: An Italian one. Same thing.

FloridaBrent: You're Italian? "Megan" doesn't sound Italian.

MeganM: There's a story behind this. My parents were Italian immigrants. Mamma was always more traditional than my Dad, who, from what I heard, was a free spirit. Mamma wanted to name me Margherita Angelina Maria, after her own mother, grandmother and great-grandmother. Papa's sister, aunt Gioia, told me that he didn't want to burden me with old traditions and a very long name, so he suggested an Americanized form of Margherita. He thought that Megan would be easy to pronounce for both of them. Gioia told me that Mama and Papa fought about it for three days, but since Mama was brought up to respect her husband's wishes, she finally gave in.

FloridaBrent: So they gave you a Welsh / Gaelic name? That's hilarious!

MeganM: It would be even more hilarious if you knew Mamma. I mean, even though she has been living in this country for over forty years, she is still bound – no, shackled actually — by old traditions and socio-cultural mores. Obedience, propriety, respect for your elders. No buts or ifs. Whatever she said, no matter how illogical, irrational or unreasonable, I had to comply. At times – many times actually – it made my life very difficult.

I stopped typing. Goodness, why in the world was I telling all this to the guy I had hired to design my website? I never talked about Mamma to anyone except Tina and Joyce. Not even Joe knew the whole story. And yet, here I was, shooting the breeze with a man I hardly knew. What the hell was *wrong* with me?

I had to disengage myself immediately from the much-too-revealing chat before I spilled all my guts to this total stranger.

> MeganM: So sorry, Brent, I have to go now. Let's touch base and talk about the website tomorrow evening, okay?
>
> FloridaBrent: Sure. Bye for now, Megan.

I logged off.

"What the hell is the matter with you?" I shouted, in disgust. "Are you so lonely, so starved for attention, that you actually believe your life is of interest to anyone besides yourself?"

Slowly my anger morphed into a dull ache inside me, but before I could wallow in self-pity I heard the sound of my front door opening.

"Mom, I'm home," Hayley announced from the hallway.

I straightened up and forced a smile. I didn't want Hayley to walk into the living room and see desperation written all over my face.

"So," I called out in as cheery a voice as I could muster. "How did your meeting with Dad go?"

Hayley came into the living room, sat down on the sofa, and groaned.

"He tried to dissuade me from going. He said Grandma Annabelle wouldn't like it."

"Ha," I scoffed. "That *has* to be *the* understatement of the century!"

Hayley paused for a moment and her brow furrowed.

"Mom, what am I supposed to do?" she finally asked. "Am I supposed to do what other people expect of me, or should I follow my own gut feeling?"

I stood up from the computer chair and sat down next to Hayley.

"Sweetheart, did I ever tell you about wanting to join the Peace Corps?"

"Yes," she nodded.

"I didn't do it and I'll always wonder what it would have been like. Who knows, maybe I would have hated it, and rushed back home to Nonna with giraffe bites all over my body," I smiled. "But I will never know for sure whether I would have hated it or loved it. Either way, it would have been a helluva learning experience."

"Mom," Hayley grinned. "*Giraffe* bites?"

"That was Nonna's take on it. But the point is, I was twenty-two and had wings on my feet. Nonna clipped those wings before I had a chance to spread them. *You* are twenty–two with the wings on your feet as well. Although I would like, selfishly perhaps, to keep you close to me, I also want you to spread those wings as wide as you can, and to feel the wind beneath them."

I brought a finger to my eye and wiped an emerging tear.

"Gosh, that was mighty poetic, wasn't it?" I smiled. "I have no idea where *that* came from."

"You phrased it so beautifully, Mom," Hayley said, clearly touched. "Thank you for being on my side."

She stood up and slowly stretched out.

"I'll go to sleep now," she said and pecked me on the cheek. "Sweet dreams, Mom."

Hayley's words must have lingered in my subconscious because that night I dreamt of a little boy dressed in a prince's robe. He sang softly about love, loneliness and hope. He stretched out his hand to me and pulled me gently toward him.

"My name is Brent," he said in a soft voice.

When I woke up the next morning I immediately thought about Brent. I still felt embarrassed about opening up to him above and beyond the boundaries of a business relationship. But I wasn't as hard on myself in the bright morning daylight as I had been the previous night. It was as if the sun streaming through my window lightened my mood.

It felt oddly good, liberating even, to talk about Mamma. Brent came across as sympathetic, affable and bright, with no axe to grind, or any hidden agenda that I could discern. So why *couldn't* we have a noncommittal exchange of ideas and experiences, I thought, as I dressed for work. Should I banish a potentially friendly interaction with another person just because business was involved? I mulled over this question, turned it around in my head, but found no clear basis for cutting off personal chitchat. By the time I returned home from the "Y" that afternoon, I decided that if an opportunity for some more repartee between Brent and myself presented itself again, I would seize it.

Later that day I sat down at my desk, turned on the computer and logged on. I immediately saw Brent's screen name and smiled.

I started to type.

MeganM: Hi, it's me again.

FloridaBrent: Hi, me again.

MeganM: I'm ready to work.

FloridaBrent: Didn't you say tonight?

MeganM: I did. Am I too early?

FloridaBrent: If you want to talk about the website, yes. I'm not quite ready yet.

MeganM: Okay, I'll log on later.

FloridaBrent: Do you have to go?

MeganM: Not really. Why?

FloridaBrent: Keep me company. I've had my eyes glued to the computer screen and the nose to the grindstone – figuratively speaking, of course — since nine. I could use some diversion.

MeganM: What kind of diversion? A dog and pony show?

FloridaBrent: Nothing quite as fancy, but thanks for the thought. How about some conversation?

MeganM: Sure. What would you like to converse about?

FloridaBrent: Let's leave religion and politics out of it.

MeganM: Let's.

FloridaBrent: So that leaves us, let's see...quantum physics?

MeganM: Oh, c'mon, can't you come up with something more complex?

FloridaBrent: Okay, suggest something.

MeganM: Actually, I just wanted to apologize for logging off so abruptly last night. I hope I didn't appear rude.

FloridaBrent: Not at all. Did I, by any chance, overstep any boundaries? I don't want you to think that I somehow, though inadvertently, pushed you into talking about personal stuff. It's just that I'm an easy-going, laid-back kind of guy and I don't go for formalities or social conventions. Still, I didn't want to offend you.

MeganM: Rest assured, you didn't. I was the one who started to talk about Mamma. I hope I didn't make you uncomfortable.

FloridaBrent: Not at all. I was concerned that you were.

MeganM: I was upset with myself, not with you. But to tell you the truth, it felt good to talk about Mamma with a stranger, someone neutral and non-judgmental.

FloridaBrent: Hey, at times we all need to get things off our chests.

MeganM: Yes, especially since this is a taboo subject. Talking about Mamma in any tone other than a totally reverent one makes me feel disloyal.

FloridaBrent: You told me a little bit about your Mom. What about your Dad?

MeganM: I don't remember him, unfortunately. He is a shadowy figure from the photographs carefully arranged in Mamma's album. Papa worked a double shift at a tire factory. One day he had a heart attack and died. I was only five, Mamma was twenty–five. She spoke very little English, had no skills, but through the neighborhood grapevine she found a job at an Italian grocery store nearby. She knew all the gossip, who married whom, who died from what disease, who had scoundrel children. She worked long hours behind the counter and the cash register, and then she came home in the evenings and cleaned, cooked, darned socks, all that.

FloridaBrent: So far she sounds like a loving, hard-working mother.

MeganM: Yes, I'm sure she wanted only the best for me. And because of that she gave up her own chance at happiness. Or so I thought.

FloridaBrent: What do you mean?

MeganM: I have a particularly vivid memory of one evening when I was in third grade. Mamma and I were in the kitchen; she stood at the ironing board with a stack of clothes and I sat with crayons and a coloring book at the table. She started to talk about potential suitors she had turned down because she had decided to devote her life to me, her beloved *bambina*. So I decided to repay

Mamma's boundless sacrifice by not doing anything, ever, that might displease her. I realize, of course, that this was not a healthy way to live, but as of yet I haven't been able to deal with that part of my life.

FloridaBrent: What happened when you had your own daughter, when you became a mother yourself?

MeganM: I decided early on that Hayley would be brought up differently than I was. I had no specific child-rearing philosophy in mind other than to let her grow up without the burden of guilt, with the freedom of thought, movement and expression. I pretty much fudged and fumbled my way through motherhood, raising Hayley on a hunch and an instinct rather than on the advice of the so-called child rearing experts, or, God forbid, her grandmothers. I thought that teaching Hayley unconditional obedience was wrong. She had the right to question and challenge authority, especially when decisions passed on to her were unreasonable or downright idiotic. On rare occasions when I had dared to ask Mamma the reasons behind a particular directive, she just gave me a generic answer: "Because! I am your mother and you my child. That's why!" I could never understand the logic, or rather the illogic, behind this retort. Did the mere fact of being a mother, which required no qualifications other than having sex, entitle one to make, and enforce, dumb rules? To me it made no sense whatsoever and I knew that I couldn't perpetuate this injustice. So the only rule I wrote in stone, mostly because we lived in Manhattan, was that Hayley should never cross a street until the light turned green. Everything else was negotiable.

FloridaBrent: Sounds very reasonable to me.

MeganM: Yes, I let Hayley have all the freedoms I couldn't have, but for some reason, which I still haven't quite figured out, I just can't seem to shake Mamma's hold on me. Pathetic, ain't it?

FloridaBrent: Did you ever discuss any of this with her?

MeganM: That would be the logical thing to do. But it's not so easy with Mamma. She is a talker, not a listener. Every time I start to tell her something, something about myself, she immediately diverts it to someone else, or repeats some cockamamie piece of gossip she picked up at her grocery store. I think she built a wall around herself to keep deep, emotional issues at bay.

She may be doing this subconsciously, but she is doing it. There's no way to penetrate that wall.

FloridaBrent: Then I suppose you just have to accept it and make your peace with it.

MeganM: Oh, I have accepted it, long ago. As for making my peace with it...I don't know.

FloridaBrent: Well, I hope talking about it made you feel better.

MeganM: Actually, I still feel foolish. When we start talking on here, I seem to forget that you're supposed to be designing my website, not listening to the story of my life.

FloridaBrent: Hey, I don't mind. Lending an ear is part of my job description, didn't you know? Seriously though, would it make you feel less foolish if I told you about *my* mother?

MeganM: Please do.

FloridaBrent: Mom had a stroke and died when I was ten. My sister Andrea was fourteen. Dad, who was never around much anyway, started to drink heavily. He was seldom home and when he was, he was oblivious to us kids. He just staggered around the house with a bottle of scotch. Andrea and I basically took care of ourselves, cooked our own meals, did the laundry, and all that. Then Dad brought some woman home. I think her name was Sue. She lived with us maybe two, three months. One day he announced that he and Sue would be getting married and moving to Hawaii. A week later he was gone. No goodbye, no nothing, just two hundred dollar bills on the kitchen table.

MeganM: Oh, Brent, I'm so sorry.

FloridaBrent: Don't be. Things did get better for Andie and me. Aunt Louise, Mom's sister, took us in. We lived with her, Uncle Jim, and our cousins, Billy and Tara. Aside from some spats with the cousins – after all, we were encroaching on their territory and shaking up the status quo – we had a pretty good life. Louise and Jim treated us fairly. We lived there until we both left for college. Andie went to Penn State and I got a scholarship to the University of South Florida, where I majored in business administration.

MeganM: And how is your sister now?

FloridaBrent: She is married and has twin boys. After Mom died she got into the habit of bossing me around: Brent do this, Brent do that; or Brent don't do this, Brent don't do that. Come to think of it, she still does that. But, what can I say, I love her to bits.

MeganM: I'm glad it worked out for you.

A faint noise coming from the hallway startled me. I heard Hayley hovering on the other side of the front door, rummaging for her keys. I quickly decided that I wasn't yet ready to tell her about my online chats with Brent. I was her *mother*, for heaven's sake, someone she looked up to and respected. How could I tell her that I had been spending hours on the IM, talking to a stranger?

My fingertips furiously worked the keyboard.

MeganM: Brent, I have to log off.

FloridaBrent: But, we haven't even talked about the website.

MeganM: I know. Can we re-connect later?

FloridaBrent: Sure. How does 11 p.m. strike you? Or is it too late?

I peered at the clock on the screen. It was almost nine; by eleven Hayley would probably be asleep.

MeganM: Eleven it is. Talk to you later.

FloridaBrent: Yes, later.

I quickly logged off and, as Hayley came into the living room, I hoped that she wouldn't notice how red my face was.

"What have you been doing?" she asked. "Surfing the net?"

"Er, no," I quickly replied, feeling like an errant teenager trying to cover-up a secret rendezvous. "I've been...just sitting here."

"Oh yeah?" she grinned. "Is *that* why your face is the color of a ripe beet?"

I suppressed a chuckle.

"Young lady," I said in a stern voice, "watch how you talk to your mother. Otherwise you...you'll be sent to your room without any supper."

"What a funny threat, coming from *you*," Hayley laughed. "When did you *ever* cook supper?"

My phony poker face broke into a smile.

"Anyway," she continued. "I *know* you were surfing. I caught you red-handed, if not red-faced. You were looking up South America, weren't you, to make sure I wouldn't be eaten alive by giant gorillas. Don't worry, Mom, I'll be fine. Really."

With that Hayley kissed me on the cheek and went to her room.

"Sleep well, sweetheart," I called after her. I hoped the coast would be clear by eleven.

Chapter Nine

At precisely 11 o'clock, as Hayley slept in her room, I sat down in front of the computer again and flexed my fingers like a pianist prepping for a concert. At 11:02 I saw Brent logging on. I smiled.

FloridaBrent: So, shall we take up where we left off?

MeganM: You'll have to refresh my memory. Where did we leave off?

FloridaBrent: Well, we got diverted by our personal stories and didn't even talk about my ideas for the website. I feel very guilty.

MeganM: Don't. Feeling guilty is my turf, remember?

FloridaBrent: And I'll gladly leave that to you. But if I recall, one of the first times we talked on here you mentioned, in a wonderfully Dickensian manner, that living in Paris was the best of times and the worst.

MeganM: Yes, I did say that.

FloridaBrent: This actually inspired me to go to the library and re-read the book. I thoroughly enjoyed it.

MeganM: I only mentioned it because I had to make a very difficult decision in Paris. I had to decide whether to stay in a bad marriage or not. I decided to divorce.

FloridaBrent: I was married at twenty-two because Cindy, my girlfriend, got pregnant. It was a shotgun wedding – her father stood at the altar with a Bazooka...No, I 'm kidding. But we had to get married, not because we loved each other, or wanted to spend our lives together, but because we were having a baby. So we stuck it out for two years, for our son, Sean. He's eight now. Finally we decided that we couldn't spend the rest of our lives together in a loveless marriage. Actually, I think I would have stayed, for Sean's sake. I know what it's like to grow up without a father so I wanted to be there for him. But Cindy met someone else. She's now remarried and has a little girl, but I see Sean often.

MeganM: Same here. Brief, loveless marriage. Pregnant at twenty-two, divorced shortly afterwards.

FloridaBrent: Never remarried?

MeganM: No.

FloridaBrent: Any serious current relationships?

MeganM: No. You?

FloridaBrent: Negative. After Cindy I was never seriously interested in anyone. Anyway, let's fast forward to the present. And to the website. This is what I have in mind, but it's only an initial idea, so tell me if you don't like it.

MeganM: Shoot.

FloridaBrent: A light blue background with a watermark of the Eiffel Tower. Or, if you prefer, another Paris landmark, no problem. Then, some pertinent links, information about you, your courses, and anything else you might want. Then...

MeganM: Hold it. I don't know what a "watermark" is. I assume you don't mean the mark indicating the height to which the water has risen.

FloridaBrent: Indeed I don't. It is a faint outline in the background. Why don't I just send you what I have and we can discuss it.

MeganM: Okay.

FloridaBrent: So, that takes care of the business part. I must tell you, though, that I have thoroughly enjoyed our chats. And I hope this doesn't make you run, but I find you very easy to talk to.

MeganM: No, it doesn't make me run. As a matter of fact, after some initial angst over mixing business with pleasure, I'm enjoying the chitchat as well.

FloridaBrent: Great. So, let's chat.

MeganM: Okay. Read any good books lately?

FloridaBrent: That's very funny, Megan. She reads, speaks French, and has a sense of humor. Where have you been all my life?

MeganM: How old are you?

FloridaBrent: Thirty.

Thirty? I stopped typing and felt a sinking feeling in my stomach. Brent was *fourteen years younger than I*? Shit!

The sinking feeling, which I identified as disappointment, was not dissipating, but I decided not to let on. What was I going to tell him anyway? Sorry, Brent, I sort of felt something, but I'm not sure what. Curiosity? Intrigue? Definite interest? Longing?

I sighed and typed again.

MeganM: I'm forty-four, so let's see: when you were born I was already in junior high. And when you started kindergarten, by which time you undoubtedly read the complete works of Homer, I was in college, dreaming of great adventures I'm yet to have. Does this answer your question?

FloridaBrent: Somewhat. But I must correct your erroneous assumption. I did not start reading the "Iliad" or the "Odyssey" until junior high. So I wasn't as precocious as you think. Sorry to disappoint you.

MeganM: That late, huh?

FloridaBrent: Actually, it was a bit of a challenge. I wasn't allowed to read after lights–out, so I smuggled the books into my room and read them furtively under the covers, with a flashlight. One night Aunt Louise barged in and demanded an explanation. She thought I was sneaking *Playboy* into my room!

MeganM: And you were sneaking Homer.

FloridaBrent: Yes, and Hemingway, Tennessee Williams, Somerset Maugham, Steinbeck, Hugo, et al.

MeganM: You're an embarrassment to teenage boys everywhere.

FloridaBrent: Okay, so there *was* Henry Miller in that stack as well.

MeganM: Naturally.

FloridaBrent: Anyway, listen, as much as I'm enjoying this conversation, and I really do, I must sign off. I have an early meeting tomorrow and I have to prepare. But I hope we can re-connect tomorrow, around two?

MeganM: Yes, of course. Goodnight, Brent.

FloridaBrent: Goodnight.

I logged off and leaned back in the chair. Was it possible, I wondered, to feel so quickly and so thoroughly connected to another person? Our conversations were easy and flowing, not shallow and lifeless like the talks I attempted to have with Joe. Suddenly, the website became meaningless. Staying in touch with Brent, talking with him, sending our thoughts back and forth seamlessly across the miles, became of paramount importance to me.

I went into the hallway and knocked on Tina's door. I immediately heard the shuffling of her feet.

"Who is it?"

The voice was hoarse and didn't sound like Tina's.

"It's me, Megan."

I heard clicks of various locks and bolts – this was, after all, New York – and Tina opened the door. She wore a bathrobe and slippers; her face was gaunt.

As I came in I saw clothes scattered all over the floor and a pile of unwashed dishes in the kitchen sink. The last time I saw the usually meticulous Tina this untidy was two years ago when Freddie died.

"Tina, are you ill?" I asked.

"I've had this nasty stomach flu that I can't shake," she said.

"But why haven't you told me? I could have gone to the drugstore for you."

"Nah, it's just a bug." She coughed and took a few sips of water. "I just have to wait it out, is all."

I sat down on the sofa.

"Hayley is going to South America for three months," I announced. "She'll finish her last semester when she comes back."

"Wow."

"Is this all you're going to say, *wow*?"

"No, it was just the beginning of a longer sentence," Tina said. "I mean, wow, what exciting news!"

"My initial reaction was that she should wait until *after* the graduation. But she seems so hell–bent on going, I went along with it. Deep down inside I feel like I want to take her into my arms, keep her close to me and never let her go. Of course, I can't tell *her* that. She'll think I lost my mind. "

Tina nodded.

"You did the right thing. Education is not only purely academic, you know. She'll learn more by traveling and mingling with people of other cultures than from any college course. Trust me."

"And you think it's safe out there?"

"She'll be fine. She'll come back happy and much wiser."

"That's what I'm thinking too. But," I sighed, "I have this eerie feeling, like a presentiment, that something will happen to her over there. Please tell me I'm being silly."

"You're being silly." Tina sat down next to me and patted my hand. "These feelings are normal. You're her mother and you worry about her."

"Yes, I do. And of course the thought of not seeing her for three months...That's hard."

Tina started to cough again and took another sip of water.

"Make sure she tells me goodbye before she goes," she said.

I stood up and turned to leave.

"Do you need anything, Tina?" I asked. "Medications, groceries, whatever? Do you want me to help you clean up this stuff?"

"Looks like a pig sty, doesn't it?" she smiled. "Probably smells like one too. Nah, I'll do it tomorrow. I'm sure I'll be feeling better by then."

"Well, I'm on the other side of the wall. Call, ring, holler, whatever. I'm here if you need me."

I put my hand on the doorknob and started to turn it.

"Oh, by the way," I said, and turned back to Tina. "I've been talking to this guy, on the internet."

"Really?" Tina perked up. "Who is he? And how did you come across him?"

"I hired him to design a website. But we started joking around and talking, all kinds of personal stuff. And..." My voice trailed off.

"And *what*?"

"I'm not sure I know how to answer that." I paused and thought about the strange way Brent and I had connected. "I know it sounds weird and I can't really explain it, but something just 'clicked' between us. We started to talk about ourselves, our lives. I told him personal stuff and felt totally at ease about it. He's so easy to talk to, and he is funny and bright. Look at me, I sound like I'm talking about a real person."

"He *is* a real person. Isn't he?"

"Of course he is. What I mean is, he is *anonymous*, faceless. It's just words between us, and thoughts and ideas. I don't know what he looks like, what his voice sounds like, what the touch of his hand feels like. Am I crazy, or what?

"Hon, the way you talk about this... what's his name?

"Brent."

"Brent, the way your eyes lit up just now, I have never, in all the years I've known you, seen you get so emotionally charged about anyone. Of course, I fixed you up with total losers, didn't I?" Tina smiled.

"That you did. Stanley, Jacques. Names from my dreadful past."

"Listen, I *should* tell you to be careful, for you never know who is lurking out there in the virtual world. But, while you proceed with caution, don't give up."

"Tina," I sighed, "there can never be anything between us other than online chitchat." The moment I said it, I felt sad. "First of all, he lives in Florida. Secondly, he is thirty-years- old. "

"So?"

"So, he lives in Florida and he is thirty. Doesn't sound like anything can ever happen. Plus, I have no idea what his feelings are. For all I know, I may just be another customer to him, and he is just being kind to me."

"Well, you never know," Tina said. "That's one thing about life: it can exceed your expectations."

"Or," I said, as I opened the door and went out into the hallway, "it won't live up to them. So, I'm keeping my expectations very, very low."

"Oh, one more thing," I turned to Tina again. "I'm meeting

Joyce for coffee tomorrow. She is having problems with that arrogant SOB she's married to. Do you think you'll feel well enough to come along and help me cheer her up?"

"Probably not. You don't want me to puke all over you, do you?"

"Well," I chuckled, "if you put it *that* way, I'm withdrawing the invitation."

"Hug her for me, will you?" Tina shouted as I was leaving.

I closed the door behind me. When I got into my own apartment, I felt very low.

Chapter Ten

The next day, while I was turning on the computer for my "meeting" with Brent, the phone rang. It was Joe.

"Hayley came to see me," he said in a flat voice that hadn't changed over the years. "Why didn't you try to stop her?

"Why didn't *you* try?" I asked. "You're her father. You pay her tuition."

"I did, but she is determined to go. She thinks she'll never have another opportunity like this."

"Well, maybe she won't," I said, remembering the Peace Corps incident. "Who knows?"

"That's rubbish, Megan. She is just starting out in life. She'll have plenty of opportunities to travel. And besides, I'm not too crazy about letting her go to South America. It's not the safest place for a young woman."

"What is a safe place?" I asked, without really expecting an answer. "There is no such thing."

There was a long silence on the other end of the line.

"I don't know what you mean, Megan," Joe said. "Staying home, close to her family, would be infinitely safer."

"You mean that Hayley should never leave home for the fear that something might happen to her? What kind of life is that? And besides," snippets of my conversation with Brent came back to me, "bad things can happen even in our own homes. You know, we can slip in the shower and hit our heads."

"What in the world are you talking about?" Joe asked, incredulously. "Why should Hayley slip in the shower?"

"Never mind. All I'm trying to say is, let her go. She will be back in a couple of months and she'll return to school. Nothing bad will happen to her."

"Mother will not like this," he muttered and then hung up.

The minute I saw Brent's name on the IM, I started typing furiously. I felt as though an old friend – well, maybe more than merely a "friend" – had just shown up on my doorstep.

MeganM: Joe, Hayley's father, is mad at me for not stopping Hayley from leaving.

FloridaBrent: Don't worry; I'm on your side.

MeganM: Terrific. What a relief!

FloridaBrent: Do I detect a touch of sarcasm?

MeganM: Maybe just a little. I mean, what am I going to tell him? That the guy I hired to design my website is in favor of Hayley's trip?

I instantly regretted sending the message. Why was I snotty with Brent? Just yesterday I told Tina how much I liked him. Now I was being positively pissy.

I quickly started to type again. I realized that nothing was more important to me at that moment than making amends with Brent. There was an eerie urgency as my fingers frantically worked the keyboard.

MeganM: Sorry, Brent. I didn't mean this. My fingers typed before my brain jumped into action.

FloridaBrent: Hey, no need for apologies. My own brain is often slow in catching up too, so my foot often lands in my mouth. Maybe I have a chronic case of foot-and-mouth disease?

I laughed.

MeganM: I know you can't see it, so I'm telling you: I'm sitting in front of my computer screen, laughing. That was darn funny.

FloridaBrent: That elicited a chuckle of my own too. How about that, here we are a thousand or so miles apart, both laughing. Aren't computers wonderful?

MeganM: Yes and no. They do bring people together, albeit virtually, but they create a false sense of connection and intimacy. You feel as though, in some strange, unexplainable way, you're growing close to another person. But this is just an illusion, isn't it?

My fingers hovered nervously over the "send" button. I became concerned that the message was too revealing of my growing attachment to Brent. "Gosh, I hope I don't come across as a desperate wacko," I mumbled.

I hesitated a few more seconds and then clicked on "send."

I sat staring at the IM box, willing Brent to answer. Seconds passed, then almost a minute. Nothing. I felt my face, my scalp, even my eyeballs getting hotter.

"You fool!" I muttered. "Your silly innuendos scared him off."

Just as I was about to log off – I didn't know what else to do – a message popped up.

FloridaBrent: I know what you mean. And I'm not sure whether it's an illusion. It may very well be real. This is just another way of communicating, of getting to know another person, even of growing to like that person. Sure beats getting to know people while getting sloshed in a bar.

I smiled. Could Brent be feeling the connection too? "Tread gently, Megan," I whispered. "Tread gently."

MeganM: I agree.

FloridaBrent: Take us, for example.

Oh, God. Can this be real? My heart pounded as I typed.

MeganM: Yes?

FloridaBrent: Do you feel it too?

MeganM: If you mean the connection between us, yes. I feel it too.

FloridaBrent: Strange, isn't it? And somewhat scary.

MeganM: Yes, on both counts.

FloridaBrent: And it gets stranger.

MeganM: It does?

FloridaBrent: Yes. Listen to this — how would you like to have dinner with me?

Dinner with Brent? But he was in Florida! Was this a joke? Yes, I thought, it *had* to be a joke. I decided to play along.

MeganM: Okay, but I'd better warn you: I'm a terrible cook.

FloridaBrent: Fine, if I ever ask you to cook I'll bring my own supply of Pepto-Bismol. But I'm serious about it. Dinner. In a restaurant. In NYC.

My heart started to pound again.

MeganM. Oh? You are coming all this way just to eat with me?

FloridaBrent: I have to fly to NY on Friday to meet with some clients. I didn't know it until about half an hour ago. So I thought that afterwards you and I could meet and I would show you what I have in mind for your website.

MeganM: Sure beats the old "come up and see my stamp collection" line.

FloridaBrent: Geez, you see right through me! But seriously, how about it?

Did I want to have dinner with Brent? Of course I did. I felt as though any minute now I'd break into a happy song–and–dance routine, except that I didn't know how to do either.

MeganM: That would be great.

FloridaBrent: Oh good, I can exhale now. I'm so excited about this, I promise to be on my best behavior. And even use the cutlery.

MeganM. So, when and where?

FloridaBrent: I arrive at 10:15, rush to a lunch meeting in Manhattan and should be through, hopefully with contract in hand, by three. So let's say at four. Unfortunately, it'll have to be quick because I'm catching the last plane to Tampa, at 8:30. So, any idea where?

MeganM: How about in front of Dean and DeLuca coffee place near Rockefeller Center. Know it?

FloridaBrent: Yes, I think so.

MeganM: How will I know you?

FloridaBrent: I'll be the one in a loud Florida shirt, with palm trees and pink flamingos on it.

MeganM: Cute.

FloridaBrent; Seriously though, didn't I tell you? I'm tall, dark and handsome.

MeganM: I'd love to tell you that I look like Meg Ryan, but I'd be lying.

FloridaBrent: Well, I have a feeling that we'll spot each other.

MeganM. Yes, I have that feeling too.

FloridaBrent: Great then. Don't stand me up.

MeganM: I won't.

FloridaBrent: Friday then?

MeganM: Friday.

We both logged off at the same moment. I jumped out of my chair and flung my arms. "Yippee!" I shouted, as loud as I could. "YIPPEE!"

Chapter Eleven

Later that day, on my way out to meet Joyce, I posted a piece of paper on Tina's door. I didn't want to disturb her in case she was resting. "Great news," the note said. "Brent is coming to New York on Friday. I'll finally get to meet the mystery man. Keep your fingers crossed. P.S. Hope you're feeling better. Call me. M."

In the subway on my way downtown to the Village Delight Café on Bleecker Street, one of my favorite coffee places, I thought about Brent. Actually, I had thought about little else since I found out he'd be coming. My feelings ran a gamut from elation to fear. I was ecstatic about meeting Brent face–to–face, but at the same time I was afraid of disappointment. I had built him up so much in my mind – all based on just a few IM chats, for heaven's sake – and I was concerned that meeting him would be a major letdown.

"Stop it, Megan," I said, not realizing immediately that I was talking aloud and that people sitting next to me were giving me furtive glances. "It's just a dinner for heaven's sake, not a lifetime commitment. If he is a loser, you can just get up and leave."

A burly man turned to me.

"Lady, shut up, will you?" he grumbled. "I'm trying to read the paper."

Ohmigod, I thought, as I felt my face redden. These people must think I'm some kind of a wacko. I averted my eyes and stared at the floor. I sat like this, immobile and red-faced, until my stop.

Joyce was already at the cozy café sipping a frothy cappuccino. I winced at her appearance. She looked tired and haggard. Her blonde hair, which she always had professionally styled, hung limply to her shoulders. She wore no make-up and without it her light skin looked ashen. Even her lips looked thinner. Instead of the designer clothes she usually favored she wore a drab T-shit with a denim jacket over it. She dresses just like me now, I thought and inwardly chuckled.

I sat down across from her, and for the first time noticed wrinkles and crow's feet around her eyes and mouth. Goodness gracious, I thought, is this what *I* looked like up close?

Joyce glanced up from her cup with a self–deprecating smile.

"I know, I look like hell," she said. "This is the real me, in all my glory!"

"You look fine, Joyce," I lied. "Maybe just a little tired, is all."

She had told me on the phone about "problems" she and Rick were having, but did not elaborate. I surmised that Joyce's new, unkempt look was the result of domestic troubles.

Rick was handsome but very arrogant, looking down on anyone who didn't have as much wealth, power or connections as he did. Why Joyce, who was a genuinely nice and a down–to–earth person, married Rick was beyond me. I imagined – though she never told me this – that she was infatuated with him and mistook this emotion for love. Once they married – the same year Joe and I divorced – and had a son, Austin, shortly afterwards, she was stuck.

I ordered an *espresso* and turned to Joyce.

"So tell me," I said.

She looked at me and her blue eyes were pools of sadness.

"Rick is so demanding, so authoritarian," she said in an almost inaudible voice. "Nothing I do is ever good enough for him."

She paused and took a couple of sips from her cup.

"I arrange a dinner party for his business associates and he tells me I did a lousy job. The menu was crap, the wine was crap, and even the linen was unsuitable. So for the next party I hire the caterers and guess what. The caterers were crap, the food they prepared was crap, and so on." She took a crumpled tissue from her bag and dabbed at her eyes. "I just don't know anymore what to do."

"Joyce, how long has this been going on?"

She looked into her cup as though trying to figure out the duration of the abuse.

"I can't really say. It's not all the time. When Rick is in a good mood, he is fine. We have long stretches when he is civil with me. But when he is under stress at work, well, he becomes horrible."

"Do you *love* him?" I asked.

"I... don't really know."

"Why don't you file for divorce?"

Tears started to stream down Joyce's cheeks and she again dabbed them with a tissue.

"I can't do that," she silently sobbed. "What about Austin?"

"Hon, Austin is a sophomore in college. He is not a baby."

Joyce didn't respond. She continued to dab at her eyes and cheeks.

"Rick said if I ever leave him I wouldn't get a penny." She blew her nose and tossed the crumpled tissue into her bag. "I do have a small trust fund from my parents, but I couldn't support myself on that forever."

"Joyce, there are courts in this country. Rick can't unilaterally make these kinds of decisions."

"I wouldn't be so sure. He knows a lot of people, can pull a lot of strings. I just can't risk it."

I thought about my own divorce. I *could* have stayed with Joe and would be rolling in money by now. But if I did, I knew for sure that my soul would have died.

"Stop being a victim," I said. There was urgency in my voice, as though conveying this particular message was of utmost importance to both of us. "Stand up for yourself!"

"It's not that easy," she sighed. "I need to think about it."

We sat in silence for a while, sipping our coffees.

"So how are things with you?" she asked.

I hesitated. I wanted to tell Joyce about Brent but decided that the moment was not opportune.

"Hayley came home this week. She announced that she's going to South America with friends. She is leaving Sunday, for three months. She'll resume college when she gets back."

"How are you taking it?" Joyce asked.

"Of course, I want her to have a wonderful time. But," I sighed, "I have this nagging feeling inside me that maybe I should have tried harder to talk her out of it."

"You know kids will do what they want, regardless of what their parents tell them."

I chuckled.

"I disagree. When did *I* ever do *anything* against Mamma's wishes?"

"You did it behind her back, kiddo. Dated Joe, remember? *And* you divorced him against her wishes."

"Ah, you got me there," I laughed. "I plead guilty, but two offenses in the otherwise exemplary forty-four years of dutiful service are hardly worth mentioning. Of course, I haven't heard from Annabelle yet about Hayley plans. But I'm bracing myself for it."

"Don't worry about Annabelle. You know her bark is far worse than her bite."

"I know no such thing!" I exclaimed in mock horror. "As a matter of fact, I still have scabs and bite marks all over my body."

We both laughed, but a few moments later Joyce's expression turned serious again.

"Actually," she said, looking at me from above the cup's rim," I'm looking for a job."

"A job? That's fantastic! It will get you out of that big empty house of yours. I'm sure it will do you a world of good."

"I wish Rick felt this way too," she sighed. "But he said no wife of his was going to work."

"What an oppressive, controlling ass!" I exclaimed. "Listen, Joyce, you are a grown woman with a mind of your own. You don't *need* permission or approval. If you want to get a job, don't let him stand in your way."

"It's not that easy, Megan. Rick says that if I work people will think we have no money. You know, that we are *poor*."

"That's ridiculous! That schmuck you're married to is still living in the Dark Ages. You don't have to be poor to work. You can work just because you want to. "

Joyce shook her head. "Not in our social circle. The only thing that's acceptable is charity work. You know – that's what Annabelle has always done."

"Joyce, please don't compare yourself to Annabelle. That woman has a pea-sized brain and enough loathing to fuel a pipeline."

Joyce took the last sip of her cappuccino and placed the empty cup on the saucer.

"Actually, I think I may have found something...but it's not sure yet."

"Really? What is it?"

"It's at an art gallery in the upper 60s," she said. "You know

I've always loved art. They're looking for someone to help out a few hours a week."

"Joyce, that's wonderful. It sounds perfect for you. Go for it, girl! Maybe you can sell me some Monets, Matisses and Cézannes for rock-bottom prices. Like a 100% discount, what do you say?" I laughed. "Of course, I wouldn't know what to do with all that high-brow art in my shitty apartment, but still..."

"Ha, ha, very funny. Seriously, I think my chances of getting it are really good. They can't pay much and, as long as I'm married to Rick, I don't need the money. So we are the perfect match."

"I'll keep my fingers crossed. And, let's see," I narrowed my eyes, "the Monet goes over the dilapidated sofa, and the Cézanne, shall we say, can be wedged in the corner over the computer desk to hide the peeling wallpaper."

We chuckled but soon Joyce grew quiet. A minute or so passed before she responded.

"Yes, it would be a great job, but it's a pipe dream." She said it in such a low voice, I almost didn't hear her. "Rick would have a fit."

I opened my mouth to answer, to tell Joyce not to give up, but before I uttered any words she abruptly stood up and looked at her watch. It was a gold, diamond–encrusted Rolex. The irony, the bitter irony, was not lost on me.

"Megan, I must run. It's late and I don't want to be stuck in the rush-hour traffic to the Island."

I stood up too, picked up my tote bag, and slang it over my shoulder.

"Let's have lunch soon," I said. "And if you need to talk, or whatever, call me."

We went out into the street. Joyce pecked me on the cheek, started to walk away, and then turned to me again.

"You tell Hayley to go on this trip and have a great time," she said with an odd urgency in her voice. "If she doesn't, she may regret it later. The things you don't do when you are young and carefree, well, you may never get another chance."

Joyce turned and walked toward her parked car. Minutes later her silver Mercedes 500 sped past me. She honked and waved. There she goes, I thought, a bird flying back to her golden cage.

When I got home a piece of paper with Tina's handwriting was scotched to my front door. "Still feeling lousy," it said. "Am going to sleep so don't ring the bell. P.S. Good luck on Friday. Keeping my fingers tightly crossed!"

I opened the door and saw the blinking light on my answering machine. I pushed the button and Mamma's high-pitched voice came on.

"Megan… Megan… you there, eh? Pick up phone! I know you there; I can hear you breathing… Okay, you don't wanna speak to me, so you listen good now, eh? You remember Francesco nephew, Alberto? You know, with glass eye? His wife, Sofia, the big one with lisp, she has cousin, Roberto, and he, Roberto go to South America and to jungle and he attacked by huge monkeys. So you tell Hayley she should stay home, you hear, eh?"

Click.

I laughed. Oh, Mamma, I thought, you really *are* a character.

I opened the fridge and rummaged for something edible. A stale yogurt. Old cold cuts. Some other unidentifiable foodstuff.

I finally settled – by the process of elimination – on a grilled cheese sandwich and an apple. Wait; there was a can of Campbell's tomato soup at the back of the cupboard. A true feast.

I emptied the contents of the can into a pot, added water, and stirred. Even *I* could do that much. As the red mass started to simmer, the phone rang. I rolled my eyes.

"Please, let it not be Mamma with another installment of craziness," I groaned.

I glanced at the caller ID and saw the dreaded number. Annabelle! I briefly considered not answering the phone. That would just postpone the inevitable, I thought. Annabelle would continue calling, haunting me the same way Mamma did. I sighed and picked up the receiver.

"Yes, Annabelle."

"Megan, this not a social call."

"Really? I'm *shocked*."

I hoped that Annabelle could hear the sarcasm in my voice. When did the witch *ever* call me socially? She phoned very rarely; most of the time she sent her directives through her lackey son.

"I am calling about Hayley," she said. Her tone, as always, was icy. "Why you encourage her to quit school just a semester away from graduation is beyond me."

"First of all," I said, as calmly as I could under the circumstances, "I did not *encourage* her to *temporarily* leave school. I merely *supported* her decision."

"You mean to tell me," Annabelle hissed "that you *support* your daughter's decision to quit school?"

"Annabelle, which part of my sentence didn't you understand?" I felt my agitation level rising. "Hayley is not *quitting* school. She is taking a sabbatical. Syracuse University has been around for over 130 years, so we can safely assume that it will still be there when she returns."

I heard a sharp intake of breath. I smiled at the thought that Annabelle was choking on her own venom.

"And how did she get the money for this trip?" she demanded.

"You have been sending it to her, apparently."

There was silence on the line. I could hear Annabelle's breathing.

"I have been sending her money for incidentals," she said, and I heard surprise in her voice.

"Well, consider this trip an 'incidental.' Instead of buying toothpaste, she is going to South America."

"I am not against her traveling per se." Annabelle's voice was cold again. "But she should not leave this country without a proper chaperone."

I snickered.

"A *chaperone*? Annabelle, a twenty–two–year–old doesn't need some spinster governess in a starched uniform following her every move."

Another silence.

"I don't know what kind of mother you are," she finally said in a high-pitched voice. "To allow your daughter, your only child, to go off to third–world countries... well, this is... *shocking*!"

"You have been shocked at my ineptness as a mother for a long time, Annabelle," I said. "I don't see what's different this time."

"Look here. I am not calling to discuss or dissect your past or current shortcomings, of which there are many, I may add. I just wish you'd show, for once, some love and concern for your daughter's safety."

This was like a slap in the face and I had no intention of turning the other cheek.

"I have no idea what you mean and I am not getting into it now," I said, my own voice as icy as hers. "And furthermore, I have no intention of pursuing this subject with you any longer."

I waited for Annabelle's biting retort but none came. Instead she unceremoniously hung up the phone. This was what she always did: when she was finished talking down to me, she just hung up. No goodbye, nothing.

I closed my eyes. One... two... three. Calm down Megan. The bad witch can't hurt you. You are strong, remember? I smiled and took a deep breath.

The soup had become a thick red glob by now, unsuitable for human consumption.

"Shit," I hissed, and poured the contents into the sink.

I ate the cheese sandwich and the apple. Both were stale and tasteless.

That night I dreamt that Martha Stewart came into my kitchen and looked around in disgust. I certainly couldn't blame her.

Next morning I taught two classes. Then I dashed home to have lunch with Hayley, our last one before she returned to Syracuse to pack up her stuff, bring it back here on Saturday, and then fly off to Guatemala on Sunday.

I stopped at a deli and bought cold cuts, some coleslaw and bagels. Then I thought of not seeing Hayley for two or three months and picked up a cheesecake as well.

When I got home the light on my answering machine was blinking. I pushed the button and bingo, Mamma's frantic voice came on.

"Megan, why you never home when I call, eh? All of a sudden you so busy you can't answer the phone? Why you no call me, eh? Anyway, this morning at the store Signora Bonnino come in, you remember, she live near Corona Park, you always say she look like a man and she should shave...so she come into shop and we start talking, and, by the way, she don't have the mustache no more, but anyway, we talk and I tell her Hayley going to South America and she says *Dio mio*, her nephew from Italy go there too and is attacked by mosquitoes the size of pigeons, can you imagine, poor Hayley fighting off pigeons and she no speak Spanish, poor *bambina*, so, tell her..."

Mercifully, the tape ended. I rolled my eyes and started slicing the bagels and spreading the mayo.

Hayley arrived just as I finished making the sandwiches and slicing the cheesecake. She hugged me and sat down at the kitchen table.

"So how was your morning?" I asked.

Hayley had been at the travel agency, making final arrangements.

"Fine," she said, biting into a bagel. "Everything is ready. I have my passport, I have my tickets and itinerary..."

She stopped, put down the bagel and wiped the mayonnaise off her lips.

"Mom, I want you to know that I appreciate your support. You're cool, you know that?"

I put down my sandwich as well.

"Sweetheart, I love you and want you to be happy," I said, my voice choking. "I know you are responsible and trustworthy. And I know you will be cautious."

"Oh, Mom, of course I will be," she said.

She bit into the sandwich again and swallowed another mouthful.

"By the way, that promise I made to go back to school next semester? I intend to keep it."

"I know you will, sweetheart. You don't have to convince *me*."

"Daddy and Grandma?"

"Yes, and Nonna. She has been calling here, leaving weird messages. "

After lunch Hayley spread a map of Central and South America on the table and pointed to all the places she and her friends planned to visit: Guatemala, Venezuela, Argentina, Brazil, Peru.

"You might be fluent in Spanish by the time you get back," I said. "Maybe even some Portuguese too."

"Si," she said, laughing.

At three o'clock Hayley left. I hugged and kissed her goodbye. The feeling in the pit of my stomach was a mix of joy, sadness and apprehension.

Chapter Twelve

The next morning I sat at the kitchen table with the newspaper and a cup of coffee. The phone rang and before I glanced at the caller ID, I knew it was Mamma. It made no sense at all, but the phone rang differently when Mamma called. The rings seemed shriller, more persistent and more urgent.

I could no longer decently dodge Mamma's calls. I sighed and picked up the phone.

"Good morning, Mamma," I said cheerily.

"So, you finally answer, eh? Her tone was accusatory.

"Mamma, it's a wonderful, sunny day," I said, sipping the coffee. "Let's not start it by arguing. Please?"

I took my cup into the living room, sat down, and put my feet up on the coffee table.

"I hear that!" Mamma chided.

"Hear *what?*"

"You put feet on table. How many times I tell you not do that, eh?"

I chuckled.

"Mamma, you used to tell me that when I was fifteen. But I'm a big girl now, you know?

"So, if you so big you should know better. What kind of example you set for Hayley, eh?"

Another chuckle.

"Mamma, Hayley too is a big girl. I'm sure that, by now, she is not going to be influenced in any adverse way by the position of my feet. And anyway, I doubt that anyone can become dysfunctional solely because his or her parents put their feet on the coffee table in the privacy of their living room."

There was a silence as Mamma mulled over this information. I was sure that she tried to recollect the names of Francesco's customers whose children became delinquent after being exposed to the sight of their parents' feet propped up on the coffee table. Mamma's brain was like a huge index cataloguing every possible disease, dysfunction and disaster that could befall those who sidestepped from the socially acceptable straight and narrow road.

Finally Mamma broke the silence.

"You remember Flavia from across hall?" she asked.

Before I could even open my mouth to say that I had no idea who Flavia was, and I didn't want to hear about her maladies, Mamma went on.

"Flavia just had baby. Girl."

I was not sure where this is going.

"Great," I said. "Congratulate her for me."

"So I meet Flavia by elevator and she has baby in one of those slings, you know, where you hang baby on your chest like monkey... but anyway, I tell her make sure you don't let baby travel to South America... And you know what she say?"

"That you should mind your own business?"

"You think you funny, eh? No, she no say that."

Mamma stopped and took a deep breath. I imagined she did it so she could deliver Flavia's message, like some kind of a divine revelation, in one breathless swoop.

"She say that no decent mother do that!"

With that Mamma exhaled and, I presumed, waited for my guilt-ridden reaction.

"I agree with her, Mamma," I slowly said. "I'd think twice about letting a newborn baby go to South America too."

Again, there was silence on Mamma's end of the line. I started to feel sorry for her, for the thinly–veiled, clumsy efforts to stop Hayley from leaving.

"Listen Mamma," I said. "Hayley will leave on Sunday. Please come over for lunch."

Mamma perked up.

"Of course. I bring a dish."

"Great, see you Sunday."

I was about to hang up, but Mamma was still on the phone.

"Oh, before I forget," she said. "Gioia coming over Friday evening. She no see you in *years*. You come, eh?"

"Mamma, you know I like Gioia, but I can't on Friday," I said, hoping that she wouldn't ask for an explanation.

"Why not, eh? It's not as though you have date."

Shit. Did Mamma have a crystal ball?

I took a deep breath.

"Actually, I do."

"WHAT?" Mamma shouted, clearly shocked. "With who?"

"Mamma, why are you so surprised? It's not as though I haven't been on dates before."

"Sure you been," she said, her voice dripping with sarcasm. "I just can't remember *when*."

"Well, it was nice talking to you Mamma," I said. I wanted to get off the phone before she started asking questions.

"Wait," she shouted. "Who is it?"

It was not an illogical question, even coming from Mamma, but I hesitated before answering. Should I tell Mamma the truth – that I would be going out with a younger man I met on the internet – or invent a politically correct date, say, a middle-aged, wealthy Italian I met in church? I decided to tell the truth. I could always do damage control later, I thought.

"His name is Brent," I said cautiously.

"Brent, who?" she asked. "And where you meet him, eh?"

I suddenly felt like a hedging sixteen–year–old.

"Uh, I met him online," I said, and braced myself for the onslaught of *Dio mios*.

"On what line?" Mamma asked, in all seriousness. "You go on date with man you meet in *subway?*"

"Don't worry, Mamma, I didn't meet him on a subway."

"Well, you gonna tell me or no?" she asked impatiently.

A pause. Tell her already, I thought. Otherwise she'll drive you up the wall.

"I met Brent on the internet," I blurted out.

I heard a sharp intake of breath.

"WHAT?" she shouted. "You go out with man you meet on *internet*? You lose your mind?"

"A lot of people meet this way," I continued. I briefly wondered whether I was trying to convince her, or myself. "They chat online, get to know each other and then meet. Sometimes it works out, sometimes it doesn't."

"But what you know about this man?" she asked, her voice

panicked. “How you know he is not criminal, eh?”

“I just *know.* I promise you he won’t be carrying an axe or a hatchet.”

I put the empty cup on the coffee table. Without a coaster. If only Mamma knew!

“So,” Mamma asked, her voice still alarmed. “This, er, Brad, what he do for living and how old he is?”

Did Mamma have some kind of a built–in radar that detected unreleased information?

I closed my eyes.

“He designs websites and,” I lowered my voice, “he is... thirty.”

“Can you speak louder?” Mamma said. “I don’t hear you good.”

“You heard right, Mamma. He is thirty.”

Again, a sharp intake of breath.

“He... thirty?” Mamma asked in a high-pitched voice. “You *mad?”*

I got up from the sofa and went to the kitchen for another cup of coffee. I poured some from the pot into the mug and took it back to the sofa again.

“No, Mamma, I’m not *mad.”* I took a sip of coffee and spilled a few drops on the table. I rubbed them in with my sleeve.

“So what thirty–year–old *boy* want from *you,* eh?” she asked.

“Well, at least I can be sure it’s not the money,” I quipped.

“You crazy, eh,” Mamma declared. “I never hear of no such thing.”

“Well, now you have.”

I looked at my watch. Mamma and I had been on the phone for over half an hour.

“Mamma, I have to go. I teach at ten.”

Actually, I didn’t have any classes that morning but I needed to get away from Mamma.

“You call me after your, er, *date.* I be waiting.”

Mamma hung up. It was still early in the day but I felt as though I had been fighting dragons for hours.

Chapter Thirteen

Thursday night I hardly slept. Thoughts of my impending rendezvous with Brent fluttered around my mind like butterflies. I hatched all kinds of scenarios: sitting in a hansom cab with him, holding hands, even kissing, for heaven's sake. We talked about our lives, our dreams, our hopes for the future. I could feel and hear the flip–flops of my heart, the kind that only a joyful anticipation can bring on.

"STOP IT!"

I abruptly sat up and turned on the bedside lamp.

"This is real life, not some soppy movie, so don't get carried away." I said. "Probably he'll turn out to be a jerk with a vile body odor."

I slid under the covers again and crossed my hands under my head.

"Yes, that's far more likely," I said, staring at the ceiling. "So you'd better prepare yourself to be disappointed. Like, what else is new?"

I lay like this, thinking, until the morning light started to stream in through my curtains.

That morning I taught three classes, but I couldn't keep my mind focused on French conjugation. Every time I thought about meeting Brent that afternoon – and I thought of it every few minutes – I felt a mixture of dread and excitement.

At two I picked up a Greek salad at the corner deli and hurried home. I ate the salad straight from the container while standing in front of the bedroom closet wondering what to wear.

I tossed the empty container and the plastic fork into the trash and then rummaged through my clothes. Was it really possible, I thought, that I had nothing nice to wear?

"Jeans," I mumbled, as I made my way through the shelves and hangers. "Another pair of jeans. Denim jacket. Sweat pants, sweat pants, and more sweat pants. Darn!"

I sat down dejectedly on the edge of the bed. Did I have enough time, I wondered, to dash out, cab it to the GAP and buy some decent clothes? I looked at my watch. Almost three. No way.

All of a sudden I remembered: last month Hayley bought some clothing on sale and left it in the shopping bag in her closet.

I sprang up and ran to Hayley's room. I opened her closet and took out the bag, brought it to my room, and emptied its contents on my bed. There was a short tan denim skirt, and a matching t-shirt and sweater set. I looked at the skirt's size. Eight. Shit!

Last time I bought clothes – when was it, a year ago? – I was size ten. I took off my jeans and pulled on the skirt.

"If I hold my breath and pull in my stomach," I gasped, as I tried to close the zipper all the way up, "I'll be fine. Or," I looked at myself in the mirror, "I'll look like a stuffed sausage."

I glanced at the bedside clock. 3:10 p.m.

"Okay, kiddo, decision time. What will it be; a short skirt that's a size too small or matronly sweats? Ha, it's a no-brainer."

I took the skirt and cut off its tag.

"Vanity wins, and who cares about comfort."

I ran into the bathroom, stripped and took a quick shower. I toweled myself off and opened the cabinet. Let's see. Deodorant? Yes, absolutely. Tylenol? No. Preparation H? I hope not. "That's Mamma's, I must remember to give it back to her," I mumbled. Hayley's perfume samples. YES!

I picked up a couple. One had a musty, woodsy smell; another conjured up images of daffodils and lily–of–the–valley. I hesitated. Did I want to smell like a forest ranger, or a field of flowers?

"What the heck."

I sprayed myself liberally with both.

Now, what about hair and make-up? I usually just let my hair fall, past the nape of my neck, in a messy mass of curls. What should I do? Put it up in some kind of a twist, or tie it up in a pony-tail? I decided to leave it as it was.

I rummaged through Hayley's side of the cabinet again, this

time for make-up. Mascara, taupe eye shadow and a pinkish-beige lipstick. I applied a little bit of each and peered at myself in the mirror.

"Megan, is that *you*? You look surprisingly nice."

I went into the bedroom, dressed in Hayley's clothes and ran my fingers through my hair.

Three-forty.

"It's time," I said, as I checked my appearance in the mirror again. "Go razzle–dazzle him."

I quickly scribbled a note for Tina.

"Wearing Hayley's clothes, make–up and perfume. There ain't no fool like an old fool P.S. Don't uncross those fingers yet. Talk to you soon."

I ran out of the building and hailed a cab. One screeched to a stop in front of me immediately, a rare occurrence at this time of the day. I sat on an uncomfortable vinyl seat with a hole in the middle trying to convince myself that I wasn't nervous.

"Not nervous?" I whispered, "Then why the hell is your heart beating as though it were on amphetamines?"

I told the driver to drop me off at the corner of 49th and 5th, so I could walk the last block. I was afraid that the skirt would rip as I got out of the cab, and what if Brent was there to witness it?

As I approached the Dean and DeLuca, my already fast heartbeat accelerated. I took a deep breath and looked around. Oh, please God, don't let Brent look like Quasimodo. I immediately felt a pang of guilt for having such shallow thoughts.

A very tall, skinny man with a long beard and a ponytail stood in a doorway, staring at me. He wore a T-shirt with a swastika on it and a "Fuck the World" inscription underneath. I raised my eyes skyward. "*Please* don't let this be Brent," I whispered.

Another guy passed me and smiled. His bald head was tattooed with snakes and dragons; his earlobes, eyebrows and nostrils were pierced. I cringed.

I looked around. How I could I possibly find Brent in this crowd, I wondered? Why didn't we exchange cell phone numbers at least?

I turned to look across the street and spotted a young man in sunglasses. He was intently watching the moving hordes. He had dark brown hair and wore tan slacks, a blue shirt and a pair of sneakers. Somehow, I *knew* this was Brent. I looked skyward again.

"Thank you," I silently mouthed.

I crossed the street and, my heart still pounding, stood next to him. He turned toward me and smiled. I noticed his dimples.

"Brent?" I said, trying to keep my erratic heartbeat and breathing under control.

"Yes. And I assume you are Megan?"

"Your assumption is correct," I said.

Brent and I looked at each other in silence.

"You're very pretty, Megan," he finally said.

I was overwhelmed with relief. Of course, Brent had no way of knowing that I was holding my stomach in, which prevented me from smiling. Somehow, I couldn't do both.

"Flattery will get you everywhere," I said, and forced a crooked smile.

"So," Brent said. "What shall we do?"

"You're the tourist here. So it's your call."

"Actually, I have been here quite a few times before. But tell me, where do you go when you want to have a good time?

"I wouldn't know. I haven't had a good time in quite a while."

Brent looked around and then turned to me.

"Are you very hungry?" he asked.

"Not really."

I couldn't tell Brent that a big meal might blow the zipper right off my too–tight skirt.

"My feelings exactly. How about if we get a hot dog, sit over there," he pointed to the skating rink area, "and talk. And maybe later we can go for a walk?"

"Sounds great."

We turned and walked to a hot dog stand and got two, with everything on them.

We took the hot dogs and sodas across the street and sat down on a low wall.

"So," Brent said as he bit into his bun, "do I look like you thought I would?"

I wiped the mustard off my lips.

"Actually, I had no mental image of you. But I can tell you I *am* relieved to see you have no noticeable piercings or tattoos of snakes and dragons."

"You saw him too, huh?"

"How could I miss," I laughed. "And for one heart-pumping moment I thought it was you."

Brent chuckled in response.

"So, is it safe to assume that I'm not a total disappointment"?

"Absolutely safe."

We finished the hot dogs and sodas, threw the trash into a bin, and started to walk toward Central Park.

"Do they still have those hansom cabs there?" Brent asked.

My heart started pounding again.

"I think so."

"Would you like to go for a ride?"

Oh, God, I thought. OH, GOD!

"Yes," I said, trying to catch my breath. "That would be great."

Brent slowed down and turned to me.

"Are you okay?" he asked.

"Yes. Why?

"Well, you look tense. I hope I'm not making you uncomfortable?"

"No, you're not. But I *am* a little nervous. Actually, *very* nervous."

"I'm nervous too," Brent sighed. "I feel like a high school kid out on the first date."

"Well," I smiled, "I wouldn't know how *that* feels since I wasn't allowed to date in high school or in college, for that matter. As I already told you, Mamma was overly protective. Still is, as a matter of fact."

"Are you telling me your mother wouldn't approve of our meeting?"

"I know for a fact that she doesn't," I said.

"And do you have a curfew?"

"I do. I have to be in bed by midnight. But I might be able to stay out longer when I turn fifty."

"Well, that certainly sounds reasonable to me."

We walked through the throngs of tourists. I tried to catch up with Brent but my skirt made it difficult for me to take anything other than tiny geisha–like steps.

Suddenly I felt Brent's hand on mine. He pulled me toward him, pushing a group of Japanese tourists aside. He intertwined his fingers with mine and gripped them tightly.

As we neared the Plaza Hotel we spotted a line of horse–drawn carriages parked to the side. We got into the first one and sat close together on the red leather seat.

The driver turned to us.

"Newlyweds?" he asked, winking.

"Not yet," Brent answered and winked back. I blushed.

The driver turned back toward the white horse.

"Onward, Charley," he told him, nudging gently. "Let's take these nice folks through the park."

The carriage lurched forward and I turned to Brent.

"Well, at least he didn't mistake me for your mother," I smiled. "I mean, there's a considerable age difference between us."

"Oh, c'mon, you don't look like my mother. As a matter of fact, you look like you could be in your thirties."

Really, I thought? I briefly wondered whether Brent would say the same thing if he saw me without any makeup. I remembered how haggard Joyce looked the other day, and she was six months younger than me.

I glanced back at the Plaza, and the memory of my meeting with Annabelle years ago came flooding back. Brent followed my gaze.

"Ever been inside?" he asked.

"Yes," I said. "This is where I first met my former mother–in–law. I've never been back since."

We sat in silence for a few minutes. Was I really riding in a hansom cab with Brent, just as I imagined last night? Quick, Megan, pinch yourself. I furtively pinched my arm. It hurt.

Brent and I turned toward each other and started to talk at the same time.

"You first," he said, laughing.

"I was about to ask about your meeting," I said. I felt less nervous now and my heart rate stabilized. "How did it go?"

"It went very well. I got the contract. A former client is opening a chain of retail stores in Manhattan and he wants me to redesign his website."

Brent stopped talking and turned his head away from me. He looked straight ahead.

"Actually, Megan, I have a confession to make," he said in a low voice.

My heart jumped. Oh, no, I thought, he was about to tell me something terrible!

"What... what is it?" I muttered.

"Well, it wasn't strictly necessary for me to come to New York. Certainly not right away. I could have waited. Truth is," he inhaled and turned to me, "I wanted to meet you. So I kind of finagled this trip."

The dread I had felt just seconds ago was suddenly replaced by euphoria.

"Really?" I asked, my voice high-pitched with excitement.

"Yes, really."

"I'm happy to hear it, Brent, for I wanted to meet you too," I grinned. "As a matter of fact, I have a confession too."

"Oh?"

"I had absolutely nothing to wear. I only own jeans and sweats. So, I raided Hayley's closet and," I pointed to my skirt, "I'm wearing this much too tight and too short size eight skirt on my size ten body."

Brent laughed. His eyes crinkled and the dimples accentuated.

"Well, that size eight skirt looks amazing on your size ten body," he said. "I immediately noticed it but thought it wouldn't be in good form to comment on it the second we met."

"Thank you, but you may not be feeling this way when I start exhaling and the zipper rips."

"On the contrary," he grinned. "I may *love* it when the zipper rips."

Brent reached out for my hand again and we sat in silence, our fingers intertwined.

Rollerbladers and skateboarders passed us by, and the hansom cab had to swerve to avoid a family of bikers.

"Steady, Charley, steady old boy," the driver said, pulling the reins.

He turned toward us.

"Sorry about that folks. But Charley here is used to all kinds of diversions, so no need to worry."

Brent and I nodded.

"I forgot how pretty Central Park is," Brent said as we rode through a path shaded by giant oaks. "I came here with Sean at Christmas two years ago. A long weekend, just us guys. We had a great time skating at the Wollman rink."

"Look." I pointed to the skating rink on our right. "There it is."

"Next winter you and I will have to come here to skate," he said, his gaze following my finger.

Next winter? Again, I was filled with a euphoric feeling, but this time the emotion was more subdued. Take it easy, old girl, I thought. Don't get your hopes up.

I sighed and turned to Brent.

"What is Bradenton like?" I asked. "I've never been to Florida."

"Very nice. Quiet, laid back, lots of sunshine. I love it."

"Don't you miss snow?"

"The white stuff that falls down, immobilizes traffic, and then turns into a grey slush? No way! I don't even own a shovel."

"You guys down south are sissies," I smiled.

"Megan, I'm shocked!" Brent answered. I could see he tried to suppress a smile and to appear poker-faced, but his twitching mouth gave him away. "I haven't heard such braggadocio since...well, since the Civil War!"

We both laughed and Brent edged towards me on the leather seat.

"This may sound like an odd request," he said. "But may I kiss you?"

Kiss? Could this be really happening, or was I merely dreaming?

I turned to Brent and smiled.

"I thought you'd never ask," I said, my heart fluttering.

He released my hand, put his arms around my shoulders and drew me close. His brown eyes were fixed on my mouth. He then lowered his head and put his lips on mine. The slow, lingering kiss sent tingles down my spine.

"That was...nice," I said in a hoarse whisper when our mouths parted. My spine was still tingling and my heart aflutter.

Brent's dimpled face looked down at mine.

"*Nice*?" he grinned. "How about a *wow*!"

"Okay, so I was overly conservative in my assessment. It was *definitely* a "*wow*," I laughed.

"I haven't kissed anyone like that in a long time," he said, looking up ahead. He squeezed my hand and clutched it tightly.

"How many customers of yours did you *ever* kiss?" I asked.

"Bad business practice, huh?"

"To the contrary," I smiled. "It's a *great* practice. If all business owners kissed their clients like that, there would be no dissatisfied customers."

"That's certainly something to consider. And since we're talking business," Brent glanced at his watch and sighed, "we might as well discuss your website."

The website! I hadn't thought about it at all the whole day.

"Gee, what a mood breaker," I sighed. I heard sadness in my own voice.

"Sure is. Seems almost unethical to talk shop while riding through Central Park in a hansom cab. Some folks believe that one can mix business and pleasure but personally I've never been a partisan of this particular theory."

"Tell you what. Let's forget the website for the time being. We can talk about it online. Just send me whatever you have. I'm sure I'll love it."

"Well, okay then, if you absolutely insist," Brent grinned. "You certainly don't have to twist my arm on that point. After all, the customer is always right."

We sat in silence, our bodies close together until we saw the outlines of the Plaza Hotel loom ahead. Brent looked at it and turned to me. There was urgency in his voice.

"Listen, I wish I could stay here longer so we could spend more time together, but I have a plane to catch. I *have to* be back tonight because Sean is with me this weekend."

"Of course," I said, willing my voice not to quiver. "I understand."

The carriage came to a halt. We got off; Brent paid the driver and patted Charley on the back.

"Nice horse you have," he told the driver.

"Well, bye you lovebirds." The driver raised his hat and winked. "You come back, hear?"

"We'll certainly try."

We walked to the curb and Brent turned to face me.

"Believe me, I hate to kiss and run, but I have no other choice."

He raised his arm to hail a cab.

I felt a lump in my throat. The thought of never seeing Brent again filled me with sadness.

"I understand."

A cab stopped in front of us and Brent took my hand into his again.

"I had a great time, Megan," he said in a low voice. "I'm glad we got to meet and spend this time together, short as it was."

"Yes," I said, the lump in my throat growing. "It was short but intense."

Brent brought my hand, still clutched in his, to his lips and kissed it. Then he gently disengaged his hand from mine, opened the cab's door, and turned back toward me.

"See you on the IM"? he asked.

"Yes," I said. "See you on the IM."

Brent got in, closed the door, told the driver where to go, and lowered the window.

"Bye, Megan," he said.

The cab pulled away and, through the back window, I saw Brent waving. I waved back.

As the cab disappeared from my view, I turned away from the curb. I started to slowly walk uptown, wiping the tears from my face with the sleeve of Hayley's sweater.

The moment I stepped out of the elevator, I heard the phone's shrill ring. "That woman *has* to have a built-in radar," I muttered.

I opened the door, went into the kitchen, and peered at the caller ID.

I rolled my eyes and picked up the receiver.

"Hello, Mamma. I'm home, safe and sound, so you can stop worrying," I reported.

"So what happen?" she prodded.

"We had a nice time," I said, feeling a dull ache inside me.

"And...?"

"And *what*?"

"Is this all you gonna tell me, eh?"

"There is nothing more to tell," I sighed.

No, nothing more. The intense moment of joy I had felt this afternoon was short-lived. Now I stood in my kitchen shedding mascara-smeared tears on Hayley's new clothes. I felt very tired, as though whatever physical and emotional stamina I had in me just a short while ago had dissipated.

"Mamma, I'm tired," I said and lay down on the sofa.

"So, what kind of man is he, this, um, Brad?"

"Brent."

"Who?"

"*Brent* is very nice, Mamma," I said. Tears streamed down my face onto the cushion. "Very nice."

Mamma didn't answer for a few moments. I closed my eyes.

"So, you see this Brad again?"

I reached for the box of tissues standing on the coffee table and wiped my eyes.

"I doubt it, Mamma. He lives in Florida."

"*Florida*?" Mamma exclaimed. "Why you don't find nice man right here in New York, eh? Eight million people and you can't find one man?"

"Yes, Mamma," I said, just to make her stop.

"So what time lunch on Sunday?" she asked. I was happy to change the topic, to stop thinking about Brent, even momentarily.

"Noon. I will see you then."

"*Bene*. Goodnight."

I heaved my body – which suddenly felt as though it were made from lead – off the sofa. I stripped off Hayley's clothes and left them in a pile on the floor. There were mascara stains on the sweater.

"I can't deal with the laundry now," I sighed. "First thing tomorrow."

I went into the bathroom, stepped into the shower and stood under a steady stream for ten minutes. I toweled off and put on an old T-shirt. I didn't even have the energy to dry my hair.

I lay in bed hugging my pillow close to my chest. The tears have dried but the emptiness inside me, now that Brent had left, was still a sore, gaping hole.

I drifted off to sleep remembering the touch of Brent's hand, and the feel of his lips on mine.

I woke up at midnight with a parched throat and got up to get a glass of water. As I passed the computer, I noticed a message on the IM.

FloridaBrent: Megan, are you there?

The message was sent half an hour ago. My heartbeat accelerated. Was Brent still in front of his screen? "Please, please be there," I whispered.

MeganM: Yes, I just got up to get some water... So I see you got home okay.

FloridaBrent: Yes, a smooth flight and an on-time arrival.

MeganM: Great.

FloridaBrent: So, what have you been doing since I left?

MeganM: Let's see... reinvented the wheel?

FloridaBrent: Terrific. Just what the world needs.

MeganM: And what about you?

FloridaBrent: I've been missing you.

I smiled.

MeganM: I miss you too. I've been moping ever since you left.

FloridaBrent: So, what are we going to do about it?

MeganM: I don't know. I don't think there are too many options open to us.

FloridaBrent: There are many options open to us.

MeganM: Name one.

FloridaBrent: Let's see. Stay in touch, talk every day, and try to see each other once in a while. That's three.

MeganM: It sounds so far-fetched, unrealistic and, frankly, not very satisfying.

FloridaBrent: Yes, I agree. But that doesn't mean we should give up already.

MeganM: I don't want to give up. I'd like to get to know you better, spend more time with you. But the gap between wanting something and not being able to have it is...

FloridaBrent: Is called frustration.

MeganM: Yes, a terrible feeling. I'm no stranger to it. Anger, you can deal with. But frustration, it kind of eats you up, little by little.

FloridaBrent: Ever heard of a "positive attitude?"

MeganM: Yes. It's over-rated. Stuff fairy tales are made of.

FloridaBrent: Fairy tales are full of hope and a sense of wonder. The world would be a sad place without them.

MeganM: Haven't you noticed? The world is a sad place *with* them.

FloridaBrent: So I take it you don't believe in the idea of Prince Charming coming in on a white horse and sweeping you off your feet?

MeganM: You're right, I don't.

FloridaBrent: I'll have to sprinkle some magic stardust on you the next time I see you. But for now I have to say goodnight. It's late and it has been a very long day. I don't regret one minute of it.

MeganM: Me neither. Goodnight, Brent, and sleep well.

FloridaBrent: Talk to you soon. Take care.

I lay in bed for a long time listening to the thumping of my heart. Then I fell asleep and woke up when I heard the insistent ringing of my doorbell.

Chapter Fourteen

"I'm sorry, sweetheart; I just don't understand how I could have slept so long!"

I stood in Hayley's room wearing my terrycloth bathrobe, a strong cup of coffee in my hand. It was past noon and I felt dazed.

"If I knew you were sleeping, I would have let myself in with the key," she said.

Hayley's little room was now filled with cardboard boxes full of books, clothes and various trinkets she had brought back from her dorm.

"Don't worry, Mom, I'll get it out of your way," she said. "I'll unpack as much as I can and the rest I'll just stow away in the closet."

"I'll help you with it later," I said. "Right now, come and sit with me."

I took Hayley's hand and led her into the living room. She stopped in front of the sofa and looked at her clothes piled up on the floor.

"What..."

"Oh, sweetheart, I'm so sorry, I..."

I put the mug on the coffee table and bent down to gather the clothes.

"You *wore* this?"

"I... Okay, I *did* wear it last night. I'm very sorry I didn't ask your permission, but... well, I was in a hurry and had nothing to wear, and then I remembered you had this stuff stashed in your closet."

Even without looking in the mirror I knew that my face was

red.

"I'll wash it for you this afternoon; it'll be as good as new."

Hayley stared at me wide-eyed.

"Please, sweetheart, don't be upset," I pleaded. "This was the first time I *ever* borrowed any of your stuff. Honest."

"*Any* of my stuff? What *else* did you borrow?"

"Just some make-up. Oh, and the perfume samples..."

"Mom!"

I sighed and bowed my head in embarrassment. I wasn't used to being reprimanded by my own daughter.

"Sorry, darling, I..."

"No, no, Mom, I didn't mean it like that. But, *why?*"

I sat down on the sofa and patted the space next to mine.

"Come sit by me."

Hayley came over, sat down and turned to face me. There was still a look of disbelief on her face.

"Well?" she asked and stared.

I reached for the coffee mug and took a sip.

"I went out yesterday," I said, not looking at her. "With...a man."

I took another sip and cupped the mug in my hands.

"Well, that puts an entirely different spin on things," Hayley exclaimed. She had a big grin on her face. "Now I *understand* why you had to wear the mini skirt. You had a hot date!"

"Not exactly a *hot* date," I smiled. "At this point in my life I don't want to be burned."

"What are you telling me, Mom?"

I hesitated. Should I tell Hayley about my meeting with Brent? Would she think I was crazy to go out with a man I met online only days ago? A much younger man, at that.

Hayley stared at me.

"Mom, you're confusing me. What's going on?"

I put the empty mug on the table.

"Well," I said haltingly, "I did have a date last night, but it certainly wasn't what you'd call a *hot* one."

"Really, who with?"

I hesitated again. My gaze was fixed on the mug. What should I tell her first, I wondered? That I met him online, or that he was only eight years older than she was?

Hayley nudged my arm.

"C'mon Mom, out with it," she said with a smirk. "Don't tell me you were out robbing cradles."

I was so startled, I started to cough and couldn't stop. I jumped up, ran to the kitchen and filled a glass with tap water. I drank it in one go.

Hayley watched me from the living room, an amused expression on her face. I walked back to the sofa and sat down.

"So," she asked. "How old *is* he?"

I averted my eyes.

"Thirty," I mumbled.

Hayley burst out laughing.

"*Thirty?* Way to go, Mom! Who is he?"

"Well," I cleared my throat. "His name is Brent. He lives in Florida. He is designing a website for me. We started chatting online, and for some reason I still can't quite fathom, I got drawn to him. Then yesterday he came to New York on business, for one day, and we met."

"And?"

"And that's it."

"Well, what do you think of him?"

"He is very nice," I sighed.

"Oh, Mom, that's fantastic," Hayley said and pecked me on the cheek. "I'm *so* happy you met someone."

"Hold your horses, Hayley. We only met once. And don't forget that he lives in Florida. I'm not sure I can handle a long–distance relationship."

"Mom, a long–distance relationship is better than no relationship. If you like this guy, things will work out."

I turned to Hayley and smiled.

"I appreciate your optimism, sweetheart. But what about the age difference? You know, fourteen years?"

Hayley pursed her lips.

"Big deal. Age has nothing to do with it. Besides, lots of men are attracted to older women."

"Really?"

"Yes, really."

"And why would that be?"

Hayley narrowed her eyes.

"I read an article once," she said slowly, as though trying to remember every detail. "It said men find older women more interesting, challenging, willing to try new things and experiment sexually."

"Really?" I laughed out loud. "Isn't it amazing what you learn from your kids."

"So you see, you have a *good* thing going."

I moved closer to Hayley and gave her a big hug.

"Sometimes I wonder who's the mother and who's the daughter here. Thank you for your invaluable insight, and for your support, of course. "

"I hope you remember those words when *I* show up at home with a younger man." she said with a mischievous grin on her face.

Hayley and I spent the day doing laundry and rummaging through the boxes she brought from Syracuse, deciding what to keep and what to discard.

"I just can't help worrying about you, sweetheart," I sighed, as I folded two pairs of jeans and placed them in Hayley's backpack. "I don't think I've worried about you as much since your sophomore year."

"What happened in my sophomore year?"

"You came home one weekend and I saw the Pill in the bathroom cabinet. I knew you dated before, of course, but this was the first indication I had that you... well, you *know*."

"Had sex?" she laughed. "Well, at least I was being responsible about it. And I really did care about Danny. Who knows, if he hadn't gone off to grad school, we might still be together."

"I was relieved that you were being responsible, yes," I smiled. I never told Hayley about how *she* was conceived. "But I still worried. That's what mothers *do*, sweetheart."

"Nonna worries. Grandma Annabelle worries. But *you?* You've always been cool."

"Thank you, sweetheart. I'm flattered. But," I sighed, "even the coolest of Moms worry. *Especially* when their kids go off into the big blue yonder."

Hayley put down the clothes she was folding and came to me. She placed her arms around my neck and we stood in the middle of the room hugging.

"I love you, Mom," she said into my shoulder. "And," she raised her head and looked me in the eyes, "I'll be *very* careful out there. Promise."

"And you'll keep in touch, right?"

"Absolutely."

In the evening we ordered a pepperoni–and–mushroom pizza and took it next door to Tina's. She still looked frail and her skin had a greyish tinge to it.

"I can't shake this bug, so no pizza for me," she said. Her voice had a whispery hoarseness to it. "You guys enjoy it though. I'll sit with you and sip my ever so delicious green tea."

"Tina, you *must* go see a doctor," I said, biting into a slice. "I'll go with you if you want."

"Yes, Tina," Hayley seconded. She had cheese and tomato sauce smeared all over her mouth and chin. "You don't want me to worry about *you* while I'm trekking through the jungle, do you?"

Tina smiled.

"*I* should be the least of your worries while you're in the jungle."

"Stop it you two." I swallowed the last bite and reached for another slice. "Don't make me feel more frazzled than I already am."

Now that I had managed, at least to some extent, to alleviate my worries about Hayley's trip, I didn't want any more disturbing information to enter my psyche.

"If you get a chance, you absolutely must go to the Galapagos islands. They are magnificent," Tina said in a low, almost inaudible voice. "Freddie and I went there a couple of times."

"Yes, he told me about it. You went snorkeling and a fish or some other sea creature bit him on the toe, right?" Hayley asked.

"Actually, I think he just stubbed his toe on a rock or a shell, or something." Tina smiled. "But by the trail of blood you'd think he was attacked by a giant shark."

Tina finished her tea and slowly stood up, holding on to the edge of the table for balance.

"Sorry guys, for being such an ungracious hostess. But," she whispered, "I'm so fucking tired. If I don't drag myself to bed right now, I'll just fall asleep right here at the table."

Hayley and I stood up.

"Come, give me a hug," Tina whispered and stretched out her arms. Hayley went to her and the two of them embraced.

"Have a great time out there, and don't forget to tell me *every-*

thing."

"Of course. And you must promise me that you'll go see a doctor," Hayley demanded.

"I promise. First thing Monday."

Tina waved at us and left the kitchen. We heard the shuffling of her feet down the hallway and the sound of the bedroom door closing softly behind her.

"Jesus, Mom, she looks really sick," Hayley whispered. "What do you think she has?"

"I don't know. Stomach flu can really wipe you out."

We cleared the table, picked up the leftover pizza and left Tina's apartment.

Mamma arrived at eleven, carrying veal Marsala and scalloped potatoes in two baking pans. While the food was warming in the oven Hayley and I set the table, laughing at Freddie's underwater encounter with fish or rock. Although we talked in muted tones Mamma overheard us.

"What?" she said, her voice panic-stricken. "You gonna swim with *sharks*?"

"Oh no, Nonna, of course not," Hayley laughed. "Mom and I were just remembering the conversation we had with Tina last night. She and Freddie were snorkeling off the coast of Ecuador and he stubbed his toe and bled as if sharks attacked him."

"You not gonna snorkel, eh?" Mamma demanded in a high-pitched voice.

We all sat down and Mamma dished out the food.

"Well, we will, probably. Snorkeling is not dangerous. It's fun, and you get to see coral reefs and..." Hayley's voice trailed off when she saw Mamma's panicked expression.

Mamma sat wide-eyed and motionless, the serving spoon held mid-air, staring at Hayley. Her breathing was labored.

"You...you do no such thing!"

Hayley took a sip of water and turned to Mamma.

"Nonna," she said in a calm, steady voice. "I cannot go on a trip like this and not do all these fun things. I mean, what's the point?"

"Exactly!" Mamma exclaimed. "What for you need to schlep over there where everything is dangerous, eh?"

Mamma picked up her fork.

"Eat," she commanded.

Hayley stared at her plate as though thinking of a rational response to counter Mamma's convoluted argument. I knew exactly how *that* felt.

"Nonna, New York is a dangerous place too. Muggings, robberies, all kinds of gratuitous violence."

"*Si*," Mamma nodded. "When your mother was young I never let her go nowhere, eh."

"Nonna, what kind of life is *that*?"

"*Safe* life. You stay here, finish school, find nice boy. What you need to swim with sharks for, eh?"

"I'm *not* going to swim..."

"Hey, you two," I said cheerily. "Let's not talk about catastrophes and disasters, okay?"

"Okay," Mamma said. "But we must talk about diseases."

Hayley and I exchanged furtive glances.

"Francesco niece, she has husband. He has brother who go to South America, or maybe Africa, I don't know no more. Anyway, he touch some kind of animal or maybe tree, I don't remember. He get very, very sick, *poverino*. So, don't touch no trees or animals and don't forget to wash your hands with soap over there." Mamma turned to me. "You give her enough soap, eh?"

"Yes, Mamma."

Hayley glanced at me and rolled her eyes; I smiled at her and winked.

"And," Mamma continued, "don't forget to call. They have phones there, *vero*?"

"Oh, Nonna, *of course* they have phones there."

I chuckled. Mamma's twenty–year-old black rotary phone was not exactly the epitome of modern technology. And she was asking whether there were phones in South America? Incredible.

"And what you gonna eat there, eh?" Mamma asked. "Promise me you don't eat no monkeys."

Hayley pushed her half–empty plate away. I too had lost my appetite.

"Okay," she said. "I can promise you *that*."

She got up and put her plate, glass and cutlery in the dishwasher.

"Excuse me. I have to finish packing," she said, and went to her room.

"But you don't finish eating," Mamma called after her.

"I'm not hungry anymore."

While Hayley packed I cleared the table and Mamma washed the dishes.

"I hope nothing bad happen to her over there," Mamma sighed and shook her head. "I still don't understand why you let her go. What kind of mother..."

"Mamma, *stop* it!"

I threw the dish towel onto the table and sat down. Mamma's comments managed to re–ignite my own doubts about Hayley's trip. *Was* I wrong in letting her go, in not trying to stop her? No, I was not going to fall into Mamma's trap.

"Why everybody in this house upset with me, eh?" Mamma whined.

"Forget it, Mamma," I said dryly. "Let's not fight, for Hayley's sake. She'll be leaving very soon. I don't want her to go on a sour note."

Mamma folded her apron and put it, along with rubber gloves and two baking dishes, into a shopping bag.

"And how is it *my* fault, eh?" she asked.

I took a deep breath.

"You always manage to create a conflict," I said, not looking at her. "You can never be happy for anyone, or let *them* be happy. Hayley is looking forward to this trip. Let her enjoy it."

"You *crazy*!" Mamma's voice was agitated. "You don't know what you talking about."

My heart started to pound.

"*You* don't know what you're talking about." My own voice was agitated too; I tried to slow down and not sound frantic. "You haven't been out of New York in fifty years, and yet you're such an expert on foreign disasters. If *you* want to believe that nonsense about getting sick from touching trees, go ahead. But don't spread this shit like some kind of a revelation and spoil it for Hayley."

I exhaled. From the corner of my eye I saw Mamma standing by the kitchen sink, her mouth open. She stared at me.

I turned my head to face her.

"Please, Mamma, don't say anything," I sighed. "I don't want to fight. We can talk about it another time, but not now."

Mamma turned away and muttered something in Italian.

At two o'clock we hailed a cab. We were dropping Mamma off in Queens on our way to the airport. The tension was almost palpable and we rode in silence. Hayley looked through her airline tickets and printed itinerary; Mamma sat between us, hugging the shopping bag containing the baking dishes close to her chest. She stared straight ahead.

The cab stopped in front of Mamma's building. She turned to Hayley and planted two wet kisses on her cheeks.

"You...be careful out there, eh?" Mamma said in a low voice. "And you call me!"

"Yes, of course, Nonna." Hayley put her arms around Mamma's neck and pecked her on the cheek.

Mamma got out. As the cab pulled away from the curb, Hayley and I turned and waved. Mamma stood still, hugging the shopping bag. She looked so sad and lonely, I felt sorry for her.

I turned to Hayley and took her hand.

"Listen, sweetheart, as difficult as Nonna can be sometimes, she loves you very much and she worries to death. So please, call her as often as you can."

"Yes, Mom, I will try."

At the airport Hayley introduced me to her traveling companions: her old roommate, Carrie, and three boys, Jeff, Matt and Alex.

"Stay together and take good care of each other," I said, my voice breaking,

"Yes, ma'am," Jeff replied. "We'll be careful."

The five of them checked in. Hayley came to me and put her arms around my neck.

"Mom, stay cool," she whispered into my ear. "And don't worry about me, I'll be fine."

"I know sweetie," I said, my eyes stinging. "Please, e-mail regularly if you can, or call collect. Just stay in touch."

I wanted desperately not to sound like Mamma.

"Of course I will, Mom. And," she smiled and winked, "good luck with that thirty-year-old hunk!"

I laughed and smoothed Hayley's unruly curls.

"I love you, sweetheart," I whispered through the tears that were now gaining momentum.

"I love you too, Mom."

One more hug, a last wave, and Hayley left. I watched her walk through the security and a feeling of sadness overwhelmed me.

"Oh, Hayley," I whispered. "Godspeed."

Back home I sat in front of the screen and waited for Brent to log on. Had I become so dependant on him that I couldn't even spend an evening away from the computer, I wondered? I remembered reading about people who became so addicted to the internet that they didn't lead "normal" lives anymore. Damn, was I becoming an internet junkie too? How pathetic.

But the moment I saw Brent's name on the screen, my mood lifted.

MeganM: My daughter tells me that you and I deserve a fighting chance.

FloridaBrent. She is right. What do *you* think?"

MeganM: I'm willing to give it a try. But how do we go about it, living so far apart?

FloridaBrent: Ye of little faith! Haven't you ever heard of airplanes?

MeganM: That's quite a long commute for a date, isn't it?

FloridaBrent: I don't know about you, but I'm willing to fly the extra mile.

MeganM: More like a thousand miles.

FloridaBrent: My take on it is that we can't give up before giving it a fair chance. I don't know about you, but I'd probably spend the rest of my life wondering what could have, might have been.

MeganM: Yes, I agree. I don't want to live with regrets.

FloridaBrent: Good, let's think of how we can make it happen. After all, Rome wasn't conquered in a day.

MeganM: No, but the world was created in seven.

FloridaBrent. Actually, in six, I think. On the seventh day He rested."

MeganM: By the way, how long *did* it take to build Rome?

FloridaBrent: I don't know. You're the Italian here. Nor do I know how many Romans it took to change a light bulb... ha, ha!

MeganM: Probably far too many. Hence the fall of the Roman Empire.

FloridaBrent: I'm sure that's one version you'll never see in history books.

MeganM: Thanks, Brent.

FloridaBrent: For what?

MeganM: For cheering me up. This banter, though silly and bordering on idiotic, is doing me a lot of good.

FloridaBrent. Megan, I really think we'll make it.

MeganM: Beautiful music together?

FloridaBrent: The very best.

MeganM: I 'm looking forward to hearing it.

FloridaBrent: You'll...stay tuned?

MeganM: Is there no end to your jokes?

FloridaBrent: No.

MeganM: That's good; I like men with a sense of humor. I actually haven't known any, but I like them.

FloridaBrent: Then I 'm your guy.

MeganM: You may very well be...We'll see.

FloridaBrent: We'll talk tomorrow?

MeganM: Yes.

FloridaBrent: Are you home around lunchtime?

MeganM: I should be. I only have two morning classes.

FloridaBrent. We'll talk tomorrow then. Oh, by the way, check your e-mail, will ya?"

MeganM: Why?

FloridaBrent: You'll see.

I logged off the IM and checked my e–mail. There was a message from Brent directing me to "Click on the link below." I did.

I sat for a long time staring at the bright blue screen. A French flag waved in the right hand-corner; pictures of the Eiffel Tower, Notre Dame Cathedral, the Sacred Heart Church, and boats on the Seine were lined up on the left. Below there were several links entitled "Facts about France," "Facts about Paris," "Recipes for French dishes," and "French verbs and their conjugation." I smiled.

In the middle of the page, in red block letters, there was a message: HERE YOU CAN PUT ANYTHING YOU'D LIKE. JUST REMEMBER: THE LAST CHAPTER HASN'T BEEN WRITTEN YET.

I laughed, turned off the computer, and, on a happy note, went to bed.

Chapter Fifteen

Monday morning my phone rang at 8:30. Could it be Hayley, calling to report a safe arrival? I jumped out of bed and grabbed the phone. It wasn't Hayley. It was Mrs. Schuler, a secretary at the "Y," informing me that there was a power outage in the building and my classes were cancelled.

I showered, put on jeans and a sweater, and knocked on Tina's door.

"Hey, Tina, it's me!"

I heard the familiar clicks of locks and bolts, and the door opened.

"Come in. Want a cup of something?"

I followed Tina to the kitchen. I noticed that her gait was slow and unsteady.

"No, thanks," I said, and sat down at the table. "How are you feeling?"

Tina sat across from me. I cringed at the sight of her thin and emaciated face.

"I'm going to see the doctor today," she said.

"That's good. Hopefully he'll give you something to make you feel better. Maybe you need antibiotics."

"Who knows," she sighed. "I'm just so weak; I can hardly stand up anymore. I mean, I haven't been able to hold any food in over a week."

"Maybe there's something in the water," I quipped.

Tina laughed.

"Well, whatever it is, I hope the doc has an antidote for it. I'm becoming such a coach potato, it's indecent."

"Do you want me to go with you?" I asked. "My classes were

cancelled, so I'm footloose today."

"Thanks, but Lizzie is coming over this morning. She'll drive me."

Tina's niece, Lizzie, was a graduate student at Columbia. The previous year she announced that she was a lesbian and introduced her roommate, Sherry, as her "partner." Since that day Tina had been the only family member that did not shun Lizzie.

"So," Tina looked at me and smiled. "How did it go with Brent?"

"It was great. He turned out to be a really terrific guy."

"And?"

"I can't answer that. It's too early to know how this will turn out."

"Listen, we never know how *anything* will turn out." Tina said.

She slowly stood up, went to the sink and poured herself a glass of water. She downed a couple pills.

"Imodium," she said. "It's been my best friend for the past week."

She brought the glass back to the table and sat down.

"So, if you want my advice, and I'm sure you do," she said, "go for it. Explore it. Give it a chance to grow. If it doesn't go anywhere, at least you've tried. And if it does, well...invite me to your wedding."

"Oh, Tina, *stop* it." I laughed. "Marriage is the farthest thing from my mind."

"That's because you haven't met the right guy yet," she said. "And I know I'm partially responsible for that."

She started to cough and took a sip from her glass.

"Well, I'd better start getting ready for the doc's appointment."

I stood up.

"Let me know what the doctor says and if Lizzie doesn't show up, just ring the bell. I'll go with you."

"And you promise me you won't let Brent get away, hear?"

"Yes, Mother," I shouted back from the hallway.

Inside my apartment the answering machine blinked. Oh no, Hayley must have called and I wasn't here to talk to her.

I pushed the "play" button.

"Hi, Mom," she said, breathlessly. "I just have thirty seconds to leave this message. So anyway, we got to Guatemala fine, no problem. Don't worry and tell Nonna not to worry, and I will call again in a few days. Okay? Bye, love ya!"

Click. End of message.

Relieved, I went to the kitchen and poured myself a cup of coffee. As I brought it to my lips, the doorbell rang. Probably Tina, I thought. She wanted me to go to the doctor with her after all.

I put the mug down on the counter and headed for the door.

"Coming!" I yelled.

One lock, one chain, one bolt. Finally I opened the door.

Was I hallucinating? Could it be...?

"BRENT!" I screamed. "WHAT ARE YOU DOING HERE?"

Brent stood in the doorway, grinning.

"Is this how you greet a weary traveler?" he asked.

I looked at Brent, at his smile, his dimples, his ruffled hair and I couldn't move. I just stood there, staring like a star struck teenager.

"Does this mean that you're *not* happy to see me?" he asked.

"Uh, er, I... Oh, Brent, I'm sorry. I must sound like a monosyllabic idiot. It's just that you being here is such a surprise."

"A good one, I hope?"

"A great one, of course," I said and moved out of the way. "Come in."

Brent walked into in the hallway and opened his arms.

"How about a hug? You know, to make me feel welcome."

I edged closer to him and we stood in the middle of the hallway, hugging, for a good minute. Finally I took his hand into mine and led him to the sofa.

"Sit down," I said. "And tell me... what are you doing here?"

"Well, when we talked online last night I got this brilliant idea, a real brainstorm: I decided to catch the first New York–bound flight out of Tampa and drop by for a visit. And – ta da! – here I am."

"Brent, this is absolutely incredible," I laughed. "You never told me you were so impetuous."

"You never asked," he said with a grin.

"But how... how did you find me? You don't have my address."

"Elementary, my dear Megan. I looked it up online in the White Pages. Fortunately, there is only one listing for Megan Moseley."

"And what would you do if I were not listed?" I asked.

"Then I would have to go to Plan B."

"And that is...?"

"I'd have to run through the streets of Manhattan and do my impression of Marlon Brando," he said. "You know, cup my mouth and shout *Megaaaan, Megaaaan!*"

"I guess it's a good thing my name is not Stella, huh?" I laughed.

"Well, it does sound more Italian than Megan."

I inched closer to Brent and took his hand.

"How long can you stay?" I asked.

"I take the last flight out tomorrow evening. So that leaves us," he looked at his watch, "thirty hours. That's 1,800 minutes or 108,000 seconds."

"Well, then, I suppose we shouldn't waste any more. What would you like to do?"

"I came here to be with you. Whatever you'd like to do is fine with me."

"Let's see, have you eaten? Or should we have an early lunch?"

"It depends. Are you cooking or are we going out?"

I took a pillow and threw it at him.

"Very funny, ha ha ha. You think I'll poison you?"

"If you cook? Well, there is always that possibility. So I cast my vote for eating out. My treat."

Brent and I went out. He put his arm around my shoulders and I put mine around his waist. As we walked toward the corner diner I suddenly knew, beyond any doubt, that I wanted this relationship to work out. I wanted it so badly, it hurt.

"What do you want to do next?" Brent asked as we exited the diner.

"I know!" I exclaimed. "Let's go back to Central Park and take a hansom cab again. Maybe we'll find the same one."

We took a cab to the Plaza, got out and looked around.

"There he is," Brent said excitedly and pointed to a white horse.

We approached the carriage and Brent patted the horse's back.

"How are you, Charley?" he whispered.

The driver looked at us and raised his hat.

"Nice to see you again, folks," he smiled. "Shall we go for a ride?"

"Yes, please."

We snuggled together on the red leather seat.

"Who would have thought we'd be back here so soon again?" I said. "This is truly incredible."

"Yes, and this time I don't have to run out on you."

"Not immediately, anyway," I smiled. "Not for another 1,200 minutes."

Brent put his arm around my shoulders and kissed me on the top of my head.

"You know, apart from my former wife, I never cared enough for anyone to ever *want* another date. I got bored very quickly."

"And what makes you think that you won't get bored with me?" I asked.

"Well, I flew in for the second date, didn't I? That should be an indication of my interest."

"And you're sure that you're not bothered by the age difference?" I asked, hesitantly.

"If I were, I wouldn't be here," Brent said. "What about you? Are *you* bothered by the age difference?"

"If I were, I wouldn't be here either," I smiled.

"Well, that's settled then," Brent grinned and shook my hand. "I officially pronounce us compatible."

We rode in silence for a while. After we passed the Wollman rink Brent nudged me.

"This is where we kissed on Friday," he whispered. "Shall we give it another go?"

"Absolutely."

Brent's right arm encircled me and with his left hand he raised my chin. Our mouths touched and our lips locked. We kissed until the carriage lurched to a stop.

"Will I see you folks again?" the cabbie asked after Brent paid him and patted Charley again.

"I certainly wouldn't rule it out," Brent said.

We walked around Manhattan holding hands, looking at store windows, and, every once in a while we stopped to kiss. At five Brent looked at his watch.

"I'd better find a hotel room for the night," he said.

"Don't be silly. You can stay with me."

Brent grinned.

"But what will the milkman think?"

"I said *stay* with me, not *sleep* with me. You can use Hayley's room."

I couldn't deny my growing feelings for Brent, but I wanted to go slowly, savoring every moment. I stopped and turned toward him.

"I'd like to take this one step at a time," I said. "I want to make sure that I won't end up getting hurt."

"You can never be sure of that, Megan. That's the nature of life."

"Yes, I know," I sighed and thought of what had happened with Joe. "Been there."

We got a Chinese takeout and took a cab back to the apartment.

"I want you to meet a good friend of mine," I told Brent when we got off the elevator on my floor. "Tina's been ill so she looks really bad, but I'm sure she'll never forgive me if I don't introduce you to her."

I rang Tina's bell.

"Hey, it's me, Megan," I hollered. "There is someone here who wants to meet you."

"Coming!" Tina shouted back.

She unlocked and unbolted the door and opened it a crack. Maybe it was only my imagination but I could have sworn she looked even more haggard than she did that morning. Her skin was pasty and her eyes sunken, but her face lit up at the sight of Brent.

"Well, well, who is *this* handsome guy?" she asked and opened the door wider.

"Tina, this is Brent. He... he just showed up on my doorstep this morning."

"Really? How come good-looking guys don't show up on *my* doorstep? Oh, never mind, just look at me."

She wrapped the bathrobe tighter around her.

"Come on, Tina, you've been ill," I said. "And speaking of which, what did the doctor say?"

"He scheduled me for some tests on Thursday. In the meantime he gave me a miracle drug that is supposed to help me keep the food down."

"That's good," I replied. "If you want me to go with you, let me know. "

Tina turned to Brent.

"So how long are you staying here?" she asked.

"Unfortunately, I have to go back tomorrow. But," he squeezed my hand, "I intend to be in this neighborhood very often."

"Well, then, our paths will surely cross again," Tina smiled. "And hopefully next time I will look better. I assure you I don't usually look like an old hag."

"I will look forward to seeing you again, Tina," Brent said. "And I hope you'll feel better soon."

Tina came closer to me, as if to kiss my cheek, but instead she whispered in my ear.

"Great guy. He's a keeper."

She winked at me and shut the door.

That evening, after we devoured the spare ribs, spicy beef with onion and egg rolls, Brent and I sat on the couch and talked.

"So what do you want to be when you grow up?" he asked, his arm around my shoulders.

"Let's see. How about a great chef?"

Brent laughed.

"I guess it's never too late to learn, but please, *please* don't practice on me."

"Why, have I scared you off already?"

"Not yet. But I *am* curious. How did you manage to feed your child if you don't know how to cook?"

"Easy," I said. "Frozen food, canned food, fast food, ready–to–cook food. I always served home–cooked meals; it's just that they weren't cooked in *my* home."

"I like your style," Brent grinned and kissed my forehead.

We talked late into the night and by two a.m. we turned off the lights and snuggled on the sofa.

"You know," I said into the darkness, "I can't believe how comfortable I feel with you. We've only been together for such a short time, but it's as though I've known you forever."

"I know," he whispered into my ear. "I was just thinking the same thing."

We drifted off to sleep holding each other. The last thing I was aware of was how well our bodies fit together on the narrow sofa, and how melodic Brent's soft breathing sounded to my ear.

The next morning I awoke disoriented. Where was I? I was lying on my side, but I wasn't in bed. I tried to prop myself up on my elbow but something heavy pinned me down.

It took me a few moments to realize that I was lying on my living room sofa and the heavy "object" was Brent's arm across my shoulders.

I wanted to move into a more comfortable position, but I didn't know how to do it without waking Brent. I was trying to flex my legs without nudging him when the shrill ring of the phone startled me. Shit! I gently moved Brent's arm and got up. As I tiptoed to the kitchen to pick up the phone I peered at the clock. Eleven. How could we have slept for nine hours without moving our bodies?

"Hello," I croaked into the receiver.

"What's the matter with you?" Mamma demanded. "You sick or something?"

"Er, no, Mamma, I'm fine," I whispered.

"So, you hear from Hayley?"

Goodness, in all the excitement of being with Brent I had forgotten to tell Mamma that Hayley was safe and sound. I felt a pang of guilt.

"Yes, Mamma, she just called this morning," I lied. "She is fine and sends her love."

"So why you whispering, eh? Is somebody with you?"

Was there *nothing* I could hide from Mamma? I was about to whisper that there was no one here, but in a moment of lucidity intermingled with a touch of defiance I decided what the hell, Mamma had the right to know. And *I* had the right to live my own life.

"Brent is here," I said.

"Brad? You tell me he live in Texas."

"No Mamma, he lives in Florida. But he came to New York yesterday to see me. So he's here now."

There was a long pause as Mamma digested this worrisome information.

"So why you whispering, eh"?

I shut my eyes.

"I'm whispering," I said slowly and deliberately, "because *Brent* is still sleeping and I don't want to wake him up."

So there, the cat was out of the bag. The floodgates were open.

I leaned against the kitchen counter waiting for Mamma's reaction. I felt like a rebellious teenager cockily informing her mother that she was seeing an unsuitable boyfriend.

"Brad sleeping there? In *your* house?"

"Mamma, it's *Brent*, B-r-e-n-t. And yes, he is sleeping here. In *my* house."

I heard a sharp intake of breath.

"You lose your mind, eh?" Mamma's high-pitched voice was not exactly soothing and I moved the receiver away from my ear. "You let stranger sleep in your house?"

"Actually, Mamma, he's not a stranger. We got to know each other pretty well last night."

Another intake of breath. As soon as the words were out of my mouth, I realized how they sounded to Mamma. I wanted to explain, to tell her that Brent and I didn't have sex, but when I opened my mouth to tell her, I thought better of it. I'm an adult and I don't *have to* justify my actions to Mamma, I thought. A smile crossed my lips.

"Listen," I simply told her. "I have to go now. But I will talk to you tomorrow. Bye, Mamma."

As I hung up the phone I felt as though a big burden was finally, at long last, lifted from my shoulders. I didn't *have* to placate Mamma anymore. I didn't *have* to walk around her on eggshells. I could, and would, live my life openly, defiantly if necessary, without the slightest trace of remorse.

"YES!" I mouthed and smiled. "I'm a big girl now."

I turned on the coffee pot and went back to the living room.

Brent was awake, sitting on the sofa.

"Hi," he grinned. "Was I dreaming, or did we really fall asleep on the couch?"

"You weren't dreaming. We did sleep together."

Brent's hair was mussed up and he had five o'clock shadow. He saw me looking at him and brought his hand to his face.

"Don't tell me. I need a shower, a shave, and these clothes look like I slept in them."

"Don't worry about it, you look adorable."

Brent got up and stretched.

"Can't say that this was the most comfortable bed I ever slept in," he said. "But you're by far the best bed mate."

We spent the afternoon walking in Greenwich Village.

Afterwards we drank cappuccino and split a cheesecake at the Village Delight Café.

“Megan, I would like you to come to Florida very soon,” Brent said over coffee. “Please?”

My lips broke out into a smile, and my heartbeat accelerated.

“I would like that,” I said. “I will see what I can do about my classes. Maybe I can re-schedule them.”

“Please try. And plan to stay at least a week.”

The thought of spending a full week alone with Brent filled me with a sudden, unbounded elation.

At five p.m. we stood at the curb in front of the coffee shop. Brent hailed a cab.

As one screeched to a stop in front of us, he turned to me and gave me a bear hug.

“See you soon?” he asked.

“Very soon,” I said, and meant it.

Brent got into the cab, but before closing the door he leaned out and looked up at me.

“I’ll miss you,” he said.

I felt tears well up in my eyes.

“Me too,” I sniffled. “Me too.”

Brent waved and shut the door.

“Damn, this is the second time in four days that I’ve stood at a curb and watched Brent’s cab drive away,” I said, and wiped away a tear from my cheek. “And this is the second time in four days that I’ve cried over a man.”

The joy I had felt only moments ago at the thought of spending a week in Florida, was now replaced by a feeling of emptiness in my heart.

Chapter Sixteen

On the way home from the Village, I made a decision: as soon as I possibly could I'd go to Bradenton to visit Brent.

The next morning I told the students in my French course that I had an unexpected opportunity to visit a friend in Florida, and that I'd be going there the following week.

"This will be the first time in over twenty years I'd be missing classes and my first vacation *ever*," I said. I felt a bit guilty about running out on my students on such short notice, but I also knew that no amount of guilt would stop me from going.

"Don't worry about us, dear. We can survive a week without French," Mrs. Kupfer, a perky octogenarian, told me. "It's not as though we're planning to traipse through Paris with our canes and walkers any time soon. So you go, enjoy yourself, and don't worry about us old fogies."

I knew that from a financial standpoint this was not the wisest of decisions, for not only would I be foregoing my meager wages, but also dipping into my sacrosanct "for emergencies only" savings account. So what, I thought defiantly as I walked back home at lunchtime. This was an *emotional* emergency. By the time I reached my street, my mind relegated this trip from pure luxury to pure necessity.

As I neared my building I noticed a small, thin woman pacing by the outer door. She wore a pair of wrinkled slacks and an over-sized sweater. She turned toward me and I cringed. Joyce. I had never seen her looking so unkempt. I started to walk faster.

"Hi," I said breathlessly. "What's up?"

"I just got here." Her eyes were red; her face puffy and

blotched. "Wasn't sure whether you'd be home."

"Well, let's go in and talk," I said, and took Joyce by the arm. "All I can offer, at such short notice, is a sandwich and a can of Campbell's soup – mmmmm, good!"

Joyce chuckled.

"You mean, if you *knew* I'd be coming you'd *cook*?"

"Negative, but I might have gotten a fresh loaf of bread instead of serving you bagels with a freezer burn."

We stepped into the elevator and I pushed the button.

"Don't worry about it," Joyce sighed. She opened her bag, retrieved a few tissues and dabbed at her eyes. "I'm not at all hungry."

I opened the door. Joyce followed me to the kitchen and sat at the table. I rummaged through the cabinets and took out two cans.

"Tomato or chicken noodle?" I asked. "I'm not sure which one is better."

"Just a cup of coffee for me, Megan. Instant is fine."

I put the kettle on and scooped a spoonful of coffee into two mugs. Joyce continued to sit, silently staring at the table.

"Joyce, it's obvious something's up," I said. "Is it Rick?"

"How did you figure *that* out? Because I show up at your doorstep looking like something even an alley cat wouldn't drag in?"

I turned toward her and smiled.

"Your self-deprecating and sarcastic comment would be funny under different circumstances," I said.

I poured boiling water into the mugs, brought them to the table and sat down across from Joyce.

"I'm not concerned about your looks," I said, as I took a sip of the hot liquid. "I'm concerned about the cause."

Joyce put two sugar cubes into her mug and stirred the coffee.

"I... I... left Rick."

"No shit? Congratulations!"

I saw tears streaking down Joyce's cheeks and immediately felt guilty.

"I'm so sorry, Joyce. I had no right to sound so jubilant."

I had always felt that Rick was a lowlife and that Joyce would be better off without him, but perhaps this wasn't a good time to drive home that point.

I reached back toward the counter, grabbed a roll of paper

towels and put it in front of Joyce.

"Forgive me?"

"Of course." Joyce reached for the roll, tore off a wad of paper, and dabbed at her face.

"So what happened?" I asked.

"Last night we had a huge fight about this art gallery job," she said in a croaky voice. "Rick said that if I decided to work I should pack my stuff and get out."

I brought my chair closer to Joyce's and leaned toward her.

"Joyce, that jackass has no right, no right whatsoever, to give you an ultimatum like that. What century is he living in? You're not his slave or his doormat. You don't have to put up with his crap!"

"He has been berating me for wanting to work," Joyce sobbed. "He said that if I ever embarrassed him like that he'd throw me out without a penny. That, on top of all the other fights we've been having, and his verbal abuse, did it. I have been so miserable for so long. Something just snapped in me. I packed my bag and left. Please tell me I'm not making a terrible mistake," she implored, wiping her eyes with a paper towel. "I need to hear that."

I took Joyce's hand.

"You are *not* making a mistake. Not in the long run. It will probably be hard in the beginning, but as time goes by it'll get easier and better. And getting your self-esteem and respect back is priceless."

"I hope I won't regret it. I mean, what do I know about being alone? And how will I manage by myself? I've never had to worry about money, about anything."

"Joyce, lots of women have been where you are, and managed. My own situation was somewhat easier perhaps because I had only been married a short time, so I looked on it as a bad but brief episode. If I had spent two decades with Joe, as you have with Rick, it would have been more difficult for me to walk away."

"It's just that it's such a huge change," she muttered, staring into her mug. "My life, as I know it, is over. And I'm so scared that I won't manage on my own."

"Believe me, being alone is not a bad thing. As a matter of fact, it can be comforting to know that you are your own person and not a slave to a schmuck."

Joyce dabbed at her eyes and blew her nose. I felt very sorry for her.

"Listen," I said, "this ain't exactly the Ritz, but you're welcome to stay here, in Hayley's room, for as long as you need. Especially, since I won't be here the whole of next week."

"Thanks," Joyce said. There was a faint glimmer of a smile on her face. "But I talked to my sister this morning. She and her husband are going to their house in Aspen for a month, so I'm going to stay at their place on east 82nd."

Joyce took a sip of her coffee, paused, and looked at me.

"What do you mean, you won't be here the whole of next week? Where are you going?"

I hesitated. Was this a good time to tell Joyce, whose marriage was on the rocks, about Brent? I didn't want to be insensitive, but how could I *not* share this news with my best friend.

"Well," I took a deep breath, "I got to know a guy online recently. He came to New York twice, we hit it off really well, and now I'm going to visit him in Florida. How's that for an incredible and weird story?"

Joyce stared at me wide-eyed. Her mouth was open but nothing came out.

"Don't tell me this news made you speechless," I smiled. "Say something. *Please.*"

"I'm trying to think. You met a man online and now you're flying to Florida to be with him?"

"That's it, in a nutshell. Ain't life stranger than fiction?"

"*This* is stranger than fiction. I mean, did you think this through?"

"Oh yes," I grinned. "And I'm sure that I'm doing the right thing."

"What do you know about him?"

"Let's see. His name is Brent. He has an eight–year–old son, owns a website design business, he's bright, funny, loves to read, and has the cutest dimples. And, oh yeah, he's thirty."

"What...did you say?" Joyce looked at me incredulously. "*Thirty?* As in three-oh?"

"Yes, as in three-oh."

Joyce pushed her empty mug toward the center of the table and leaned back in her chair. She sat in silence, staring at the wall in front.

"That is all you're going to say?" I smiled. "Hellllloooo?"

Slowly Joyce diverted her gaze from the wall back to me.

"Believe me, I would be very happy if you met someone special. God knows you've been alone for far too long. But this Brent, I just don't know," she sighed. "It just doesn't sound promising on the surface."

I hesitated. If this were anyone else I'd tell her to mind her own business and stay out of mine. But Joyce was my oldest friend. I wanted to hear her out.

"Why do you think it doesn't sound promising?" I asked.

"Well, the way I see it, and I'm willing to admit that at the moment I'm very bitter, which may prejudice the way I look at men, is that sustaining a relationship is a hard gig. So if you complicate it further by – in this case – a considerable age difference and the long distance factor, what realistic chances are there for this to work out?"

"Yes, distance might be a problem, but I don't think this relationship is automatically doomed because of the age difference," I said. "Besides, the age difference per se isn't an issue. It's only an issue because *I* am older than Brent and not the other way around. If Brent were fourteen years older nobody would bat an eyelid. Older men with younger women are considered normal. But the opposite looks suspicious and demands an explanation, doesn't it?"

"Yes," Joyce nodded. "That has a ring of truth to it."

"What possible rational explanation is there, except that it offends traditional, mainstream socio-cultural values?"

"I'm not sure I know how to answer that," Joyce said, "except that men, no matter how old, are more immature than women of the same age. And probably because of that they seem to prefer younger women... sexy bimbos who feed their egos."

I knew Joyce was referring to an affair Rick had a few years ago – no doubt one of many – with a young department store sales clerk.

"That's the commonly–held view," I agreed. "But it's not necessarily true."

"If I tell you that going to Florida is a bad idea," Joyce said quietly, "would you listen?"

I laughed.

"Joyce, I don't even listen to my own mother."

"Of course not, but you *should* listen to your best friend."

I closed my eyes. An old memory was emerging from the back

of my mind and pushing its way out. I smiled.

"Did I ever tell you the story of my mother's teeth in a pickle jar?" I asked.

"No. But I'm dying to know what this has to do with your trip to Florida."

"Once, when I was fourteen or so, I woke up in the middle of the night hungry and went to the kitchen to look for a snack. I opened the fridge and saw a pickle jar in the back. It was clearly labeled "Dill pickles." So I grabbed it, brought it out and set it on the counter. But even in the dim light I saw, to my utter horror and disgust, that the jar contained not a single dill pickle, but rather Mamma's dentures."

Joyce chuckled.

"You're kidding."

"Would I kid about a serious matter like that?" I laughed. "So I quickly put the jar back in the fridge. The next morning I asked Mamma why on earth she kept her dentures in a pickle jar in the refrigerator instead of in a glass on her nightstand, which I thought most denture wearers did. And you know what she answered?"

"No," Joyce said. "But I really want to hear it."

"First she said that I shouldn't scavenge for food in the middle of the night because it would spoil my appetite for breakfast. You know, Mamma and her weird theories."

"Yes," Joyce responded impatiently, "but what about the teeth?"

"I asked her why she kept them there and she said, 'Why not? Is there a law against it, eh?' I said 'No, Mamma, there's no law against it, but that's not what most people do.' And she answered that just because most people placed their dentures in a glass on a nightstand didn't mean that *she* couldn't do it differently."

"It's a funny story, Megan, but what do your mother's teeth in a pickle jar have to do with Brent and your trip to Florida?" Joyce asked. "I assume there's a connection?"

"Indeed there is. It made me realize that there isn't just one way of doing things, but many. Just because most people put their dentures in a glass doesn't mean that a pickle jar isn't a viable alternative. And just because most people do not have the kind of relationship Brent and I might have, doesn't mean that he and I can't make it work. So, that's my 'teeth in a pickle jar' theory." I stopped to catch my breath. "You know, at the time I thought that maybe I had misjudged Mamma, that maybe she wasn't as square as she appeared to be. For a while after this incident I had these fantasies that Mamma would drop her guard and her hip and unconventional side would emerge. Of course," I sighed, "that never happened."

"Perhaps that hip, unconventional side of Mamma is still there," Joyce suggested slowly, "but buried so deep inside her, somewhere in the hollows of her subconscious, that she isn't even aware of it."

"Yeah, right," I laughed. "And that side of her awakens just once in a century, like Brigadoon!"

Joyce laughed out loud. She again dabbed at her cheeks with the paper towel but her eyes were dry.

"Seriously though, you know what's really strange?" I asked.

"*Everything* you just told me is really, really strange."

"What I mean is that this particular incident with Mamma's teeth made a big impression on me at the time. But then I forgot all about it. I hadn't thought about it or even remembered it until now. So," I took a deep breath, "I think it was *meant* to come back to me here and now."

"And why would that be?"

"Because. I had always, more by compulsion than choice, walked a beaten path – Mamma's path. With very few exceptions I never dared to stray from that path. Until now. Meeting Brent has created a pivotal point in my life. It makes me want to take chances, to do crazy things, to reshuffle the stifling status–quo."

"Sounds to me like you're going through a midlife crisis," Joyce offered.

"Who knows; maybe I am. It's certainly long overdue and I'm going to enjoy every minute of it. So there." I retorted with a smile.

A quick glance at Joyce's puffy face immediately filled me with remorse. I felt as though I was gloating in the face of her misfortune.

"Joyce, I'm sorry," I said, and patted her hand. "Here I'm rhapsodizing about my new–found freedom of thought and action, while your marriage is crumbling. How very insensitive of me."

"Oh, no, don't say that. Just because this... thing is happening to me doesn't mean the world will stop in its tracks. As for you and Brent, it's true that I have my reservations. But," she smiled, "I'll keep an open mind and root for you."

Joyce stood up, put her mug in the dishwasher and threw the dirty, crumpled paper towels into the trash.

"There's one thing I have to do right away," she said and picked up her handbag. "I want to go to the gallery and see whether they still want me. I hope they haven't hired anyone yet. God knows I'll need the money."

I walked Joyce to the door and kissed her on the cheek.

"Remember, all major life changes are difficult," I said, hugging her. "But sometimes *not* changing is the hardest thing of all. You *will* manage. You *will* survive. And you *will* be okay."

"Amen," Joyce sighed and walked out the door.

"You outta your mind!" Mamma shouted into the receiver when I finally told her, the day before my departure, that I would be going to see Brent. I had purposefully delayed breaking this news for as long as I decently could.

"Mamma," I said, "believe me, I'm *not* out of my mind. I know what I'm doing. "

"Remember Franco, our old neighbor?"

"Mamma, I just love your lack of transition. It makes me think of a butterfly, flying from one flower to another in no discernible order."

"I don't know what you talking about, eh. But Franco, remember you always say he creepy old guy. Anyway, he now live in Bayside, but still come to store, although now he *stumble* not walk because he had his bad leg amputated, that's the word, *vero*? And nobody to take care of him because his wife, may she rest in peace, die a couple years ago. Remember, she..."

"Mamma!"

"Okay, okay, so Franco he walk in, er, *stumble* in on crutches into store, *poverino*, and say his nephew, Angelo, he live in Florida and invite him to visit but he, Franco, afraid to go because there sharks all over Florida and what happen if one attack him and he can't run, only stumble, eh?

"Mamma," I said slowly, as though talking to a child. "I solemnly swear that if I spot a shark I will not stumble. I will *run*. Fast. So you can rest easy. Okay?"

An audible sigh and a long silence followed. I imagined that Mamma was desperately searching for another impediment to my trip.

"What about your classes, eh?" she finally asked.

"I was able to reschedule."

"How you can just leave your job like that, eh?"

"Mamma," I said wearily, "I'm not exactly teaching at Harvard."

Another silence.

"So this, er, Brad, is serious?"

"I don't know, Mamma, it's too early to be sure. But it's the most serious I've ever been about a man. "

A long sigh.

"Why you no find somebody right here, eh? You forty-four-years-old and I still worry about you."

"You're right, Mamma, I *am* forty-four-years-old, but you don't *have* to worry about me," I said. "You *choose* to worry."

"I worry because you lose your mind, eh," she huffed into the phone.

I closed my eyes and willed myself to stay calm. One, two, three, four. I slowly counted to ten, took a deep breath, and opened my eyes again.

"Teeth in a pickle jar," I said out loud.

I threw in the bait and waited to see whether Mamma would bite. Would the mere mention of the old incident refresh Mamma's memory? More importantly, would it – miraculously – bring back the unconventional Mamma I had briefly encountered all those years ago?

"What? What you talking about, eh?"

"Oh, never mind," I sighed. "I'll call you in a week, when I get back. In the meantime, try not to worry. Please?"

"Wait..." Mamma said, with the usual urgency in her voice, but I was already hanging up. I wanted nothing to spoil my trip to Florida.

I went into the bedroom and opened my closet. I had to pack because I'd be leaving early the next morning.

"Here you are, standing in front of your closet again, with places to go but nothing to wear," I said.

And this time I couldn't even borrow Hayley's clothes because she took all her hot weather garb with her. It was only the beginning of March but I imagined that it would be warm in Florida.

I pursed my lips and rummaged through stacks of old T-shirts.

Ah, a pair of shorts. I forgot I even owned one. I finally settled on five tees, the shorts, two pairs of jeans and a windbreaker.

"Not exactly glamour wear, but what the heck," I mumbled as I looked at the pile on my bed. I picked up the lot and placed it in a large travel bag Hayley had left behind.

Next I went to the bathroom to pack my toiletries. Toothbrush and toothpaste. Shower soap, shampoo and sunscreen.

I smiled and opened the medicine cabinet. There, nestled between Tylenol and the cough syrup, was a small box. I had gotten it earlier in the week. I took it out, opened it and counted. Four little pills were missing. I must remember to take the fifth one tomorrow morning, I thought.

I had taken the plunge and gotten the Pill. The day after I decided to fly to Florida I had gone to see my doctor. I sat in the waiting room nervously fidgeting with the strap of my tote, blushing like a pimply teenager about to embark on her first sexual experience.

Dr. Pierce was matter–of–fact and straightforward. She examined me and gave me the prescription. If she wondered why a forty–four–year–old woman suddenly needed the Pill, she didn't let on.

I had the prescription filled on the way home and immediately took the first pill. Then I shared this bit of news with Brent during our new ritual: the nightly phone call.

"That's great, Megan," he exclaimed. "I will finally be able to start taking *hot* showers!"

Of course, I decided not to let Mamma in on this potentially traumatic bit of information. How many mothers were there who'd throw a fit after learning that their forty–four–year–old daughters took the Pill? Probably just one. *Mine*.

Actually, as excited – and impatient – as I was at the thought of having sex with Brent, the prospect also filled me with some trepidation. I hadn't been with a man in a very long time and I felt totally rusty.

"I've lived like a vestal virgin for *years* and now, at forty–four, I'm about to have sex with a thirty–year–old? How's that for luck?" I laughed so hard, my eyes were tearing up. Then I said, somewhat defiantly, "And if they want to bury me alive, so *what*?"

I zipped up the bag and placed it in the hallway. Then I went out the door and knocked on Tina's. She hadn't responded to my knocks the whole week and I had started to seriously worry about her.

“Open up!” I said in a stern voice. “FBI!”

I heard a faint sound, like a heavy shuffling of feet. The locks and bolts clicked, and the door opened to reveal Tina’s ravaged face. I hoped she didn’t see me wince.

“Okay, so I fibbed,” I said in an effort to bring a smile to her face. “It’s not the FBI. *C’est moi.*”

“Yeah, you *really* had me fooled,” Tina said.

She turned and walked back slowly and painstakingly. I came in, shut the door, and followed her into the living room.

Tina lay down on the sofa, closed her eyes, and covered herself with a blanket. She looked frail and skeletal; her black hair had streaks of grey in it.

My heart started to pound and I silently, inwardly, willed it to calm down. I sat down in an armchair and leaned toward Tina.

“I’ve been knocking on your door the whole week,” I said softly. “Where have you been?”

Tina breathed in and opened her eyes.

“I was in and out of the hospital for a series of tests,” she murmured. “They were inconclusive, so the doctor sent me to the hospital for more. Blood tests, sonograms, X-rays. And still no results.”

“Why didn’t you tell me? I could have gone with you.”

“Oh, don’t worry. Lizzie has been around much of the week, and her partner, Sherry too.”

“So, how are you feeling now?”

“Well,” Tina took a deep breath, “I’m not sure how to answer it. The medication the doc gave me is helping me keep the food down, but I really wish they’d tell me what the hell is wrong with me. I mean, I’ve been like this for almost three weeks now. Enough already.”

She shivered and pulled the blanket all the way up to her chin.

“And what’s up with you?” she asked. “I’ve been meaning to ask about Brent.”

“Well, as a matter of fact, I’m going to Florida tomorrow morning. For a week.”

“That’s terrific.” I saw a faint smile come to Tina’s face. “I really hope this works out for you. And how is Hayley?”

“Great. She e-mailed the other day about trekking through

Guatemala, visiting the Mayan ruins of Tikal, and being very impressed by the Pacaya volcano. "

"Ah, yes. It conjures up wonderful memories for me. Please give Hayley my love."

"Sure will."

Tina shut her eyes again. Her slow, rhythmic breathing told me that she was falling asleep.

I stood up.

"I'll go, Tina," I whispered. "You take care of yourself, hear? I'll call you from Florida."

"Don't even *think* of me while you're over there, frolicking," she whispered back. "Have a great time."

I tiptoed to the sofa, gave Tina a peck on the forehead, and quietly left. A feeling of unease started to creep in but I pushed it away.

"Everything will be fine," I said, as I let myself into my apartment. "It *has* to be."

The phone started to ring as I bolted the door.

"If it's you, Mamma, I'm not home," I said out loud. "Do you hear me, Mamma? I'M NOT HOME!"

I looked at the caller ID but didn't recognize the number. When I picked up the receiver I heard crackling noise on the line.

"Mom, are you there?"

"Hayley! What a surprise. How are you, honey?

"I'm great, Mom."

"And where in the world are you?"

"I'm still in Guatemala City, and I decided to call you, instead of e-mailing, to tell you that I met the most wonderful, amazing guy, and... I'm in love."

What? Hayley has been gone for how long? It couldn't have been long enough to meet a man *and* fall in love.

"Mom, I know what you must be thinking," Hayley piped up, "but believe me, this is *it*. The real, true love. Head over heels."

"Wow, honey," I said, and hoped that Hayley would not discern my utter astonishment. "And who is this wonderful, amazing man?"

"His name is Pedro. He is a local doctor who works with the poor. He is the most generous, giving, loving person *ever*."

"He sure sounds terrific," I said, trying to keep concern out of my voice. "How did you meet him, so quickly?"

"Must be fate. Our local guide here introduced him to our little group. The guide and Pedro have been friends for twenty–five years. Since kindergarten, I think."

Kindergarten? Twenty-five years? Was Pedro *that* much older than Hayley?

"Honey," I asked, willing my palpitating heart to slow down. "How old is Pedro?"

"That's the best part, Mom!" she exclaimed. "He is thirty."

My throat suddenly felt very dry. I thought that I would choke.

"Thirty?" I managed to croak out. "Brent is thirty too."

"I know," she laughed. "Isn't it great? Pedro and Brent can be buddies."

Oh, *great*. My boyfriend and my daughter's boyfriend were the same age. What could be more normal, more conventional than that?

I swallowed some saliva to moisten my throat.

"Life sometimes works in strange and unexpected ways," I finally said. I felt that the statement was general enough to cover all kinds of contingencies: mine, Hayley's and Joyce's.

"I'm so excited," Hayley went on. "This trip is definitely the best thing that has ever happened to me. Please be happy for me, Mom."

I suddenly remembered how encouraging and non-judgmental Hayley was about Brent. Pull yourself together, Megan, I mentally chided myself.

"Of course I'm happy for you darling," I said, willing my voice to be cheerful. I was, at that point, too astonished by the news to be naturally cheery. "Will I get to meet this wonderful, amazing Pedro?"

"I sure hope so, Mom. We'll try to get a visa for him to come back with me."

"I'll be looking forward to that," I said, relieved that Hayley was not considering staying in Guatemala for good. "And by the way, I'm off to Florida tomorrow. To see Brent."

"Really? That's terrific," Hayley said in the same breathless voice she had just used to announce her love for Pedro. "I'm so glad this is working out."

"Well, I don't know for sure yet whether this is working out. But I'm hoping."

"Mom, I'm keeping my fingers crossed. One hand for you, one

hand for me."

"Oh Hayley, I do love you. I'd like to hug you right now, but I guess we'll have to take a rain check on that."

"I love you too, Mom, but I have to run. These calls are expensive."

"Sure, honey, I understand," I said. "Thank you for calling. Please keep in touch. And say hello to Pedro for me."

"Will do. And have a great time in Florida."

Hayley hung up. I leaned against the kitchen counter, crossed my arms and thought about Hayley and Pedro, Brent and myself.

"How much weirder can this get?" I said, and started to laugh.

Chapter Seventeen

In the plane I tried to read, but the mounting excitement over my imminent meeting with Brent prevented me from focusing on the text. Ever since I had made the decision to go to Florida I had tried to prepare myself for a possibility that this relationship, still very much in its nascent phase, may bite the dust once Brent and I got to know each other, warts and all. What would I do then, I had asked myself more than once. Would I be able to get over the disappointment? Would I just gracefully slip back into my so–called life, or would I have to drag myself back, kicking, screaming and crying?

Stop it! Given the choice between the cold logic of *what ifs* and flip-flop flutters of my heart, I opted, perhaps naively, to listen to the latter.

Any qualms I still had when I arrived in Tampa were quelled the minute I saw Brent and threw myself into his arms.

An hour later I stood in the driveway of Brent's home, a small white stucco ranch surrounded by palm trees and a white picket fence.

"Welcome to my humble dwelling," he said, opening the front door. "As they say, *mi casa es su casa.*"

"I never figured you for a white picket fence kind of guy," I laughed.

"What can I tell you, I really *am* June Cleaver at heart."

Brent grabbed my hand and led me inside. A small entryway opened to a white-tiled living room, a kitchen with a breakfast nook, the master bedroom, and Sean's room. Outside there was a small patio shaded by palms. For a man's house the place was tidy, with only a few scattered books lying on the kitchen table. It certainly put my own messy apartment to shame.

"Brent, this is lovely," I said. "It looks cool and crisp, and very inviting."

He cocked his head and chuckled.

"Are you telling me that this house *doesn't* need a woman's touch?"

"Certainly not *this* woman's. I couldn't care less about frilly curtains and matching throw pillows. This place is perfect as it is."

"Well, you haven't seen everything yet."

Brent led me to the kitchen and opened a side door.

"Voilà, the master's lair," he said.

Brent had converted the spacious garage into his office. A large table piled with papers stood against one white-washed wall and filing cabinets against another. A computer and a copying machine sat on a desk in the corner.

"So this is where you work."

"Yes, not exactly a long commute."

I walked over to Brent's computer and touched the keyboard.

"And this is where you were sitting when we first met?" I asked.

Brent came over and put his arm around my waist.

"Yes, I like to think of this computer as the cornerstone of our relationship," he said. "Maybe we should enshrine it."

"Maybe we should. We could name it 'Exhibit A' on the walk down the memory lane."

That afternoon Brent took me for a drive around Bradenton. We passed quiet residential streets lined with palm trees and then drove along a drawbridge. Boats and catamarans sailed through the shimmering waters of the bay.

"Brent, this is beautiful," I said.

"Most people have heard of St. Petersburg to the north and of Sarasota to the south. We're sandwiched in between but not as well–known."

"You're right," I said. "I, for one, have never heard of it."

"Then let me be your guide. We're south of Tampa Bay and north of the Manatee River. The population here is roughly 50,000 including yours truly. The first settlers were Timucan Indians; they came here over 1,000 years ago. In 1539 the Spanish explorer Hernando DeSoto arrived and led his army of 600 conquistadors ashore near the mouth of the Manatee River in search of gold, which they never found. Three centuries later a certain Josiah Gates came upon the manatees, which the Spanish settlers called the 'sea cow, and when he laid out his settlement here he called it after the manatees. Hence 'Manatee County,' in which Bradenton is located. The city itself was named after another settler, Joseph Braden, who arrived here in the 1850s and grew sugar cane. Our claim to fame, aside from miles of sandy Gulf beaches, is Tropicana orange juice. How many people drink it in the morning and know it comes from Bradenton?"

"Not many, I guess, unless they read the fine print on the label. Brent, I can't believe how all this information just rolls off your tongue!"

"What can I say, I'm a walking encyclopedia," he chuckled.

"I can honestly say that you're the first walking encyclopedia I have ever known. Please take this as a compliment."

Later we went to a beach restaurant and ordered broiled grouper. From our seats we watched the sun disappear behind the horizon, trailing vibrant streaks of red and orange in its wake. As dusk turned to darkness, we zipped up our windbreakers, took off our sneakers, and walked on the cool sand.

"I can't believe how quiet it is here," I said, looking down at the imprints of our bare feet in the wet sand. "After living in New York my whole life, this is culture shock!"

"I like the energy of New York, but, as far as I'm concerned, nothing beats a moonlit walk on the beach under a dark, starry sky," Brent said.

"Yes, there's something ethereal about walking in the dark in a vast, open space, our path lit only by the stars. I guess I'm being sappy, huh?"

Brent stopped and pulled me closer to him. We stood huddled together in the breeze, which had become cooler since the nightfall.

"There's nothing even remotely sappy about being moved by a moonlit walk on the beach under a dark, starry sky," he said. "That's how poets get inspired.

Walking with you under a sliver moon
Millions of stars lighting up the sky
My heart is beating with the rhythm of waves,

And murmurs of the breeze."

"Who wrote that?" I asked.

"A local poet. His talents are unknown to anyone beside himself."

"So I suppose I never heard of him?"

"Yes, you have, you lucky, chosen one. It's me."

"You're kidding, right?" I asked, surprised. Brent was clearly no Robert Frost, but the mere thought that he wrote such sentimental verses touched me.

"I never kid about my poems."

"How many have you written?"

"Including this? One. I composed it, or rather ad-libbed it, as we walked. Like it?"

"Well, it shows how agile your mind is," I laughed. "That's certainly admirable."

"I'm not sure whether I'm discerning admiration or sarcasm in your voice?"

"How about a little of both?"

"Fair enough. Shall we head home?

We turned around and walked back. Suddenly Brent stopped and pointed skyward.

"Look, Megan, there's Polaris, the North Star," he whispered into my ear, his voice muffled by the wind. "See it?"

I looked up and immediately spotted the bright star.

"Yes," I whispered back. "There's something magical about the North Star. Like the human heart, it is the only true compass for one's life journey."

"I never thought about it that way," he replied. "But what a great analogy."

We started to walk again.

"I'm sorry to say I haven't been listening to my heart often enough," I sighed and snuggled closer to Brent. He put his arm around my waist and held me close. "I've made decisions based purely on what other people, namely Mamma, were telling me."

"And now?"

"That star up there," I looked up again, "is going to be my only guiding light."

"That's the way it should be. If you listen to your heart, you can't go wrong."

"Well, you *may* get hurt."

"Are you referring to us?" Brent asked. "You think that I will hurt you?"

"Maybe not intentionally. But there's always that possibility."

Brent stopped and brought his lips to my ear. His breath warmed up my earlobe.

"I'm willing to take a chance, to follow the North Star," he whispered. "Are you tagging along?"

I breathed in the cold, salty air and looked up at the sky again. There it was, shining and twinkling.

"Yes, Brent," I whispered.

I showered and slipped under the blanket on Brent's bed. As I pulled it all the way up to my neck to cover my nakedness, my heart rate accelerated to an aerobic workout level.

Brent came into the room a few minutes later, his hair still wet. He unceremoniously discarded the towel that was wrapped around his waist. I diverted my gaze.

If Brent noticed my discomfort he didn't say anything. He slipped under the covers next to me. He smelled of soap and shampoo; his still–damp skin sent shivers through my body.

He turned to me and grinned.

"We have to stop meeting like this."

"Ha, very funny," I said. His flippancy did nothing to alleviate my nervousness. I continued to shiver under the sheets.

Brent reached down and cupped my left knee in his hand.

"Megan, you are trembling. I didn't know you were *that* excited to be with me."

I forced a smile.

"Nah, I'm just suffering from jerky knee syndrome."

"Really? Just be careful where you're aiming it. Certain parts of my anatomy are dangerously close by."

Brent inched closer to me and wrapped his arm around my chest.

"I may as well tell you," I whispered. "I haven't had sex in ages, and even before then it was a rare occurrence."

Brent didn't say anything for a while and I started to feel very awkward, as though I were some kind of oddity. I turned my back to him and buried my face in the pillow. The acute discomfort I felt was exacerbated by the thought of my naked body next to Brent's, exposed, vulnerable, with no place to hide.

"I think it's safe to assume that sex is like riding a bike," he finally said and nibbled on my neck. "Once you learn how, you never forget. "

"Well, I haven't ridden a bike in a long time either," I grumbled into the pillow. "Not since the fourth grade, I think, when Mamma decided it was too dangerous."

"Okay, forget the bike analogy. I'm sure that once we... uh... get into it, your memory will be refreshed very quickly."

I turned around and faced Brent.

"You can't possibly imagine what it's like to be a forty–four–year–old woman with hardly any sexual experience," I mumbled into his chest.

"You're right," Brent said, his chest heaving with laughter. "I can't possibly imagine what it's like to be a forty–year–old woman with hardly any sexual experience. You're not going to hold *that* against me, are you?"

I smiled. Brent's laughter was contagious and his wit the most effective relaxant. I felt the tension and nervousness leave my body.

I reached for the blanket, pulled it over my head and held it up with my arm to form a tent–like cocoon.

"Care to join me?"

"Ooh, you brazen woman." Brent grinned and slid down next to me.

The feel of his skin against mine sent tingles all over my body. I snuggled to him and intertwined my legs with his. Even our heartbeats blended. I shut my eyes and let my senses roam free.

When I awoke the following morning I was on my side facing the patio door. Brent was behind, spooning me, his arm across my waist.

"Fancy finding *you* here," he murmured. "And I thought it was only a dream."

"It wasn't a dream," I said groggily, my voice hoarse from little sleep. "And it looks like I learned to ride that bike again."

"Well, you know what they say about practice," he whispered into my shoulder.

"Oh, Brent," I laughed. "Don't tell me you want us to do *that* in Carnegie Hall."

We spent the next three days sightseeing, taking long walks along the beach, watching sunsets and starry skies, and cocooning under the blanket.

On the fourth day I woke up and my first conscious thought was that I loved Brent. I had no way of knowing whether Brent had reached the same emotional level as me, and I was afraid that a premature confession of my love might scare him away. An inner voice whispered softly that it was too soon, too early to share these feelings with him. I decided to wait.

That night, as we lay in bed, Brent was very quiet. He stared intently at the ceiling and I sensed, by the furrow between his brows, that he was deep in thought.

"Is anything wrong?" I asked and immediately felt my body go into a tensing, tightening spasm of despair.

Was Brent having second thoughts about us? I shut my eyes tightly to keep the tears from welling.

A full minute passed – I could hear the ticking of the bedside clock – before Brent stirred. He turned to me and kissed my forehead.

"Nothing is wrong," he said. "*Au contraire,* I have been very happy these past few days. The happiest I have ever been."

A sense of relief filled every crevice of my body. I could feel the tension evaporate and warmth flow through my muscles, relaxing them into a mushy softness.

"Actually," Brent continued, "I was thinking of the way our bodies mesh. Did you notice how, when we walk, our hands reach out and clasp, and our arms entwine at the same precise moment, as though we had carefully rehearsed and choreographed each movement?"

"Yes," I said. "I did notice. And also how each curve, bend, fold, nook and cranny of our bodies fit perfectly together. It's as though they were custom–made for each other."

"Yes. I know exactly what you mean."

We lay in silence for a long moment. I wiggled into Brent's arm, put my head on his chest and listened to the faint, rhythmic beating of his heart.

"Penny for your thoughts," he said.

"Nothing, really."

"Okay, you drive a hard bargain. I'm upping the bid. A buck?"

I laughed.

"Haven't you heard? Curiosity killed the cat."

"That's okay," he said. "I'll still have eight lives left."

Suddenly his tone grew serious.

"Megan," he whispered, "*please* share your thoughts with me. Tell me, were you thinking about us?"

I opened my mouth to tell Brent that I was in love with him but no words came out. The thought of rejection, and of the ensuing pain, hovered in the forefront of my mind.

"I'm *always* thinking about us," I finally said. "Aren't you?"

"Yes, of course I am."

There was an eerie sadness to his voice. I sensed that we were playing a silly cat–and–mouse game, and that we both knew it.

"By the way, I'd like you to meet Sean tomorrow," Brent said after a long silence.

The mood, the intimacy and the closeness we had shared just moments ago were gone. It was as though our souls had reached out for each other, touched, fondled and caressed briefly and then, sad and dejected, scattered into different directions.

"It's not my day to have him, but he's off from school early and Cindy said it would be okay for me to pick him up."

"I'd love to meet Sean," I said, and briefly wondered whether this meant that Brent was serious about our relationship. "Tell me about him."

"He's a good kid, even if he *is* my son," Brent chuckled. "And he has the strangest hobby for a third–grader. He collects shells."

"There is nothing strange about that," I defended. "It seems very appropriate for Florida."

"Well, most boys his age are into action figures, or sports. But Sean loves going to the beach and collecting shells. His room is full of them."

"I think it's a lovely hobby."

"Well, this may sound chauvinistic and I apologize if it does," Brent said. "But a man doesn't want his son to have a *lovely* hobby. However," he sighed, "if shell collecting makes Sean happy *and* keeps him out of trouble, I' m all for it."

The next afternoon we drove to Sean's school. Brent parked and stood by the wire fence; I sat in the car with butterflies in my stomach.

What if he doesn't like me, I thought. What if he thinks I'm too old for his father? So many "what ifs" rushed through my mind, I had to remind myself that he was an eight–year–old boy and probably too young to form such rash judgments.

I turned my head and saw a small boy running toward Brent. With his dark hair and dimples he was a smaller version of his father. I smiled.

Brent hugged the boy, took his backpack and pointed toward the car, saying something. Sean turned and looked at me. I waved. As the two of them approached the car I opened the door and got out.

"Sean, I want you to meet someone very special," Brent said. "This is Megan."

The boy looked up at me timidly.

"Hi, Sean," I said and stretched out my hand. "It's a pleasure to meet you."

We shook hands and he turned to his father.

"Is this your girlfriend?" he asked.

"Yes," Brent said, and smiled.

Sean didn't respond. He looked up at me again, cocked his head, and, after a moment's silence, he asked:

"Do you have kids?"

"Yes, a twenty-two-year-old daughter," I replied. "Her name is Hayley."

The intent look on Sean's little face told me that he was mulling over the information. Suddenly, he turned to Brent.

"Dad, I'm hungry," he said. "Can we get pizza?"

"Of course, son. Let's go."

We drove to the food court at the DeSoto Square mall. While Brent got the pizza and sodas Sean and I sat at a table and talked.

"Are you and Dad getting married?" he asked.

"We haven't known each other very long," I smiled.

"How long do you have to know each other before you get married?"

"It's a very good question, Sean, but I'm not sure how to answer it," I said, and wondered why this little boy was asking about marriage in the first place. "I suppose it's not a matter of how long you know somebody, but how well."

Brent brought the pizza and gave each of us a slice.

"Ta-da! Three slices of pepperoni pizza delivered right to your table. How's that for service?"

He sat down between Sean and me and we all took the first bite.

"I hope this pizza is not going to spoil your appetite for dinner," Brent told Sean. "I'd hate to upset your mom."

Sean reached for a napkin and wiped tomato sauce off his lips.

"We're having macaroni and cheese tonight. I'll eat it," he promised.

I turned toward the boy.

"Sean, your dad tells me that you are an expert on shells. I bet you have quite a collection."

"Yeah," Sean answered with his mouth full. I remembered Mamma's admonishments about talking with food in the mouth, and smiled.

He swallowed the pizza and turned to me.

"I have about two hundred right now. I had more before my little sister got into my room."

He took another bite.

"Do you collect shells too?" he asked.

"Oh, no. I live in New York. Not too many shells there."

"There are over three hundred species along the coast of southwest Florida," Sean said earnestly, and for a moment I forgot that the boy was only eight. "Mollusks that create shells flourish in the Gulf waters."

"Really? I had no idea."

"Yeah, there are no reefs in the Gulf that break the incoming water and the flat bottom lets the seashells reach the shore unbroken."

"I'm impressed." I laughed. "I can't believe you're only eight and you know stuff that most adults have no clue about."

We ate in silence for a few minutes and then Sean turned to Brent.

"Dad, if you and Megan get married, will you have a child?"

I almost choked on a pepperoni, but Brent kept a straight face.

"We haven't figured it out yet, son."

"Well," Sean said, swallowing the last piece of his pizza, "if you do, I hope it's a boy. Girls suck."

Brent grinned, but, wisely, didn't say anything.

Afterwards we drove Sean home.

"It was nice to meet you," I said. "And thanks for the tutorial on seashells. It was very interesting."

"The collection and study of mollusk shells is called conchology," Sean said as he vigorously shook my hand.

"Wow. You really are smart, Sean," I laughed. "Now I know from whom your dad got his brains."

Brent chuckled, gave Sean a bear hug and ruffled his hair.

"See you soon, son," he said. "Stay out of trouble. And be nice to your sister."

"Girls suck!" Sean shouted back before disappearing through the side door.

"He is fantastic." I told Brent on the way home. "What a kid."

I tried to remember Hayley at the same age. Was she as knowledgeable about any particular subject as Sean was about seashells? No, I could not recollect one single interest – aside from maybe building up her Barbie and Ken collection – which she had been as passionate about. That Sean was one precocious kid.

"You are the first woman I have ever introduced to Sean," Brent said. "I never cared enough about any others."

This was the first time Brent had alluded to his previous girlfriends. I wondered about them, but I didn't want to pry.

"And how many were there, exactly?" I smiled.

"Hmm... fifty or sixty. But who counts?"

"*Sixty?* Brent! Are you, by any chance, pulling my leg?"

"Why? Don't you think I'm capable of having so many girlfriends?" he smiled.

"Yes, if you had started when you were six."

"You're right; in my zeal to impress you, I've grossly exaggerated. There were maybe ten of them, total. But," he turned to me and grinned, "*you* are my best girl."

"Well, I'm honored. And I meant what I said about Sean. He is a great kid. And *you* are a great father to be so involved in his life."

Brent stopped at a red light and squeezed my hand.

"I try," he said. "That's all any of us can do. Try."

"Yes, but not all of us make that effort," I said as the car lurched forward. "Take Joe, for example. He hasn't been much of a father to Hayley. He used to have his secretary call to tell me Mr. Moseley wished to see his daughter, and would I kindly have her delivered in the afternoon. *Delivered*! Can you believe that? So I said. 'And how would Mr. Moseley like his daughter delivered? By UPS or FedEx?'"

"Even way back then you were a funny girl, huh?" Brent laughed.

"You find this funny? I didn't, though now, twenty years later, I can see a certain humor in it. Anyway, since Joe's office wasn't that far from the apartment, I put Hayley in the stroller and walked. My mother–in–law, the witch of all witches, was always there. She literally snatched the baby from my arms and cooed at her like an injured pigeon. Sometimes Stanford – that's Joe's father and the only human in the family – would come in and play with Hayley. As for Joe, he would just stand by his desk like a tree in the Petrified Forest, not moving, not smiling, and not saying a word. Can you *imagine*?"

"No," Brent shook his head. His expression was that of disbelief. "I can honestly say that I can't."

"And later, as Hayley became older, Joe had his company chauffeur pick her up on Fridays after kindergarten and drive her to Long Island for the weekend. In the beginning she was eager to go, because it's a huge house with a beautiful garden, and so it was a novelty. But after a while she cried and threw temper tantrums every time she was to go. When I asked her why, she said she wasn't allowed to do anything in the house; she was told by Annabelle not to touch anything. She couldn't even play in the garden because Annabelle told her not to walk on the grass. Then," I had to pause to catch my breath, "Annabelle bought her a pony to ride on, but the pony was kept in a stable miles away so she hardly ever saw him."

"And how is Joe with her now?"

"Hayley kind of gave up on the idea of having a father–daughter relationship with Joe. She never told me, but I think it broke her heart. As time went by their contact petered out to occasional visits, birthdays, holidays, that kind of thing. A few years ago Joe married some stuffy blue–blood with a British accent – so Hayley tells me – who basically just ignores Hayley. At least he's been generous with money. He has always paid for everything: clothes, braces, college. I could never have given her that on what little I earn."

"That's incredible, Megan," Brent said as he turned into his street. "I really feel for Hayley. I mean, financial help is a good and necessary thing, but it can't replace *emotional* support."

"Yes, I know, " I sighed. "I made my peace with this a long time ago. I see Joe as a sick person. Not physically, but something must have happened to him in childhood to stunt his emotional growth. That 'something' was probably Annabelle. From what little I heard, she coddled and overprotected him, and made him believe that she was, and would always be, the most important person in his life. He probably doesn't even go to the bathroom without first informing Mommy and getting her permission. The amazing thing is that Hayley harbors no resentment toward Joe. She just accepted the situation and got on with it."

Brent pulled into the driveway but didn't get out of the car. He sat staring at the steering wheel. Then he turned to me.

"Listen," he said. "Do you want to go home now, or are you up for a little more driving? I'd like to take you to one of my favorite places."

"*Now* he tells me about it!" I exclaimed. It was a relief to stop thinking about Joe's failures as a father and focus on something pleasant for a change.

"Well, I planned on taking you there eventually. So, shall we go?"

"Definitely. I'm holding my breath."

"Nah, don't do that," he smiled. "It sounds very uncomfortable."

We laughed and Brent started to drive again.

"Where are we going?" I asked.

"Anna Maria Pier. It's a beautiful, small island off the northern part of Bradenton."

Twenty minutes later we parked at the foot of the pier, a narrow boardwalk jutting into the water, flanked on both sides by fishermen.

"Let's go," Brent said and reached for my hand.

We walked toward the bungalow at the end of the pier, my sneakers making a soft thumping sound on the uneven wooden planks. A pelican swooshed by me, flying dangerously close to my head. I ducked in a hurry and Brent laughed.

"C'mon, don't tell me a tough New Yorker like you is scared of a little birdie."

"A *little* birdie? That pelican was humongous. Is he on steroids, or what?"

"Nope. Just lots of sunshine, fresh air and Gulf fish."

Brent took my hand again and we resumed walking. Suddenly he stopped and looked intently at the water, as though trying to spot something in the distance. I followed his gaze.

"What are you looking at?" I asked, and narrowed my eyes. "I see nothing but the horizon, and the brilliantly blue, clear sky."

"I'm not looking at anything specifically," he said quietly. "I'm thinking."

"About?"

Slowly he turned to face me.

"I brought you here for a reason. This is the perfect place to tell you... what I've wanted to tell you for days."

My heart started to beat so fast, I thought it might jump out of my chest and land, splashing, in the water.

Brent took both my hands into his and pulled me closer. His forehead touched mine.

"I love you, Megan," he whispered. "I love you so much."

Within seconds I felt tears well in my eyes and run down my cheeks.

"I think I knew that I loved you after my second trip to New York. But I didn't know how to tell you. I didn't want to jump the gun only to find out that my feelings were not reciprocated."

"Oh, Brent."

I put my arms around his waist and my head against his chest.

"I love you too," I mumbled, "and I too was afraid to tell you. For the same reason."

"Silly us," Brent said. He sounded relieved.

"Yes, silly us."

We stood in the middle of the boardwalk hugging, our arms entwined, our hearts beating in unison.

"What are we going to do, Brent?" I asked. "I'm going back to New York in two days."

I felt Brent's chest heave as he breathed in and then slowly exhaled.

"I don't know, Megan," he sighed. "I haven't quite figured it out yet."

We walked back to the car in silence. Suddenly Brent turned to me.

"Stay with me Megan," he said with urgency in his voice. "Just stay here and don't go back."

"I'd *love* to stay here, Brent. But... how?"

"We'll think of something."

That night I lay in Brent's arms listening to his soft, rhythmic breathing. Fancy that, I thought and smiled. I'm forty–four–years–old and I'm loved, at last.

Chapter Eighteen

"Andie is coming by tonight," Brent announced the next morning as he put a glass of orange juice in front of me.

"Your sister?"

"Yes, the one and only." He put two mugs of steaming coffee and a plateful of buttered rye toast on the table. Then he opened the fridge and took out two jars.

"Strawberry jam or grape jelly?"

"Grape jelly," I said. "Let's live dangerously."

Brent placed the jelly in front of me, sat down and took a sip of his coffee.

"What's the matter? You're not eating?" I asked, as I spread the jelly on the bread.

"Nah," he smiled. "I want to keep my girlish figure."

I bit into the toast.

"Terrific. *You* are watching your girlish figure and fattening *me* up with buttered toast."

"Nothing's too good for my baby," he laughed. "Next time I'll even serve you breakfast in bed."

"Terrific, I'll be a bed–ridden fatso!" I chuckled. "So, what time is Andie coming?"

"After she picks her boys up from little league practice. You'll see, they are quite a handful."

"Well, if you continue to force–feed me like this, I'll be quite a handful too," I laughed. "A handful of fat."

As I nibbled on the crust I tried to remember what Brent had told me about his sister. She was older and overprotective, but what else?

"Tell me about Andrea," I said. "You haven't talked much

about her."

"Well, she always looked out for me, her 'baby brother.' When I got older she used to set me up on dates. Fortunately, she had some gorgeous girlfriends."

"Terrific. Just what I need to hear."

"Don't worry, that was way back when. These days I'm capable of finding my own women, and," he inched closer and kissed my jelly–smeared lips, "I happen to be *very* happy with the one I have."

I smiled and cleaned my sticky hands with a napkin.

"Anyway," Brent continued. "I had an e-mail from a customer this morning. He wants me to drop by, so I think I'll go see him when Andie gets here. That way the two of you can get acquainted."

"Okay," I said. I thought of how easily I had connected with Sean. Getting acquainted with Brent's sister should be a piece of cake. "I'd love to meet Andie. And," I smiled, "I might as well tell you: I love you. I know there's no transition between the two subjects, but I just *had to* tell you."

Amazing, I thought. I had never uttered these words to any man before, and yet they slid off my tongue so naturally.

"Wanna go back to bed?" Brent took the last sip of his coffee and winked.

"*Now*?"

"Yes, *now*."

"But we just got up."

"What kind of an excuse is that?"

"You're right," I chuckled. "It's a lousy excuse."

We put the plates and mugs into the dishwasher and went to the bedroom.

"It's only ten in the morning, for heaven's sake," I laughed.

"So? It's evening in Japan. "Besides, what we are about to do is not at all time–sensitive."

Later that day, as I sat on the patio with a glass of ice tea, a station wagon pulled into the driveway. Two boys dressed in little league uniforms ran out, followed by a slim woman with shoulder–length brown hair. She wore tight jeans and a halter top that left very little to the imagination.

Brent came out of his office and playfully jostled with the boys.

He pecked the woman on the cheek, said something, and pointed to me. The boys ran onto the patio and started to climb up a palm tree.

"Megan, this is my sister, Andrea, and my hellion nephews, Matthew and Brian," he said.

Andrea turned and looked at me. Her face was more angular than Brent's, and her features harsher. She stared at me for what seemed like the longest time.

"Hi," she finally said, her thin lips curved, more like a grimace than a smile.

I had a distinct, very uncomfortable feeling that Andrea didn't care for me at all. I briefly wondered how she could have formed an opinion so quickly.

I took a deep breath.

"Hi," I answered, in as cheery a voice as I could muster.

"Okay, guys. I have some business to attend to. You two get acquainted. And," Brent looked at the boys hanging from the raffia, "make sure the kids don't wreck the house. Or the grounds it stands on."

He came to me and kissed me on the lips. From the corner of my eye I saw Andrea watching us with a stern look.

"Love you. I'll be back in a couple of hours. Meanwhile, you two enjoy yourselves."

He waved and left. I watched his car back out of the driveway.

Andrea sat down at the table and looked at me.

"So, Megan, Brent tells me you live in New York."

"Yes. Manhattan."

"And how did you two meet? With you living in New York and all?"

"On the internet," I smiled. "We hooked up online."

My smile disappeared the moment I saw Andrea's facial muscles twitch and tighten. Where did I see this stern look before? Annabelle! Oh, shit.

"On the *internet*?" she said, slowly. "But *why?*"

"Because it's *there*?" I quipped, but immediately saw that my answer didn't amuse Andrea one bit. She sat staring at me, as though trying to figure out whether I was pulling her leg.

Finally she stirred.

"I'll have you know," she said haughtily, "that Brent doesn't *have to* hook up with women on the internet. He has never had any problem meeting girls."

"I'm sure that's true. But nevertheless that *is* how we met."

"And are you single? Divorced? Never married?"

I felt like telling this nosy person to mind her own business, but, as Brent's sister – was it possible that she was adopted? – Andrea deserved answers that other officious busybodies did not.

"I have been divorced for many years," I said, trying to keep my voice friendly.

"Any children?"

Jesus. I felt like I was in a courtroom, being interrogated by a hostile attorney.

"Yes. My daughter, Hayley, is a senior at Syracuse University, though she is currently traveling in..."

I heard a sharp intake of breath. Andrea jumped in before I could finish the sentence.

"A *senior?* How old are you, Megan?"

Terrific. I felt like Andrea was wielding an axe over my head, which she would lower as soon as I revealed my age.

"I'm forty-four," I said.

I quickly decided, as I sat looking at Andrea's harsh face, that I would not be intimidated by this unfriendly woman, whose blood ties to Brent were incomprehensible to me.

For a few moments Andrea didn't say anything. She just sat across from me under a palm, looking into the distance. Finally she cleared her throat. I got a frightening *déjà-vu* feeling of Annabelle clearing her throat before coming in for a kill.

"I can certainly see why a woman your age would want to be with someone like Brent," she said in a slow, deliberate voice. "But for the life of me I can't imagine why my brother, who could have any woman he wanted, would be interested in someone so much *older*."

I felt a sudden sharp pain in my chest, as though I were being stabbed in the ribcage. I winced.

"Ask *him*," I responded through teeth clenched in pain and anger. "He is the only one qualified to answer."

I slowly inhaled and exhaled, and felt the sharp pain turn into a dull ache. I desperately wanted to appear cool, poised and unruffled by Andrea's outrageous attacks. But the combination of nerves and self–consciousness prevented me from taking the high road.

Instead of getting her two brats out of the palm tree and just leaving, Andrea continued to stare at me, as though trying to see how many wrinkles lined my face and how many grey hairs sprouted from my scalp. Suddenly I felt old. Old and weary.

"Megan," she said after a long pause. "I know my brother better than anyone, certainly better than you can know him after only a few weeks. I can tell you that women have always found him attractive, gravitating toward him like bees toward honey. Just think, in five years you'll be almost fifty, while Brent will only be thirty-five, a prime age for a man. Do you honestly think that he will want to be with you *then,* when *young* women will be flirting with him? Given the choice, and temptation, who do you think he will choose?"

"Our age difference is of no importance to either of us," I said, hoping that Andrea couldn't hear my pounding heart. "Why does it matter to *you*?"

"Megan, listen to me." She inched her chair closer to mine. Her voice was friendlier and softer now, but I could see through the phoney chumminess. "The age difference may not *seem* like a big deal now, but think five, ten years down the road. You'll be in your mid-fifties. Is this fair to Brent?"

She leaned over and patted my hand, a condescending gesture that wasn't lost on me. I withdrew my hand abruptly and stood up.

"Well, I guess I'd better heave my old bones out of here." I tried to speak calmly, although I was seething inside. "It's almost the early–bird dinner hour for us old–timers."

From the corner of my eye I saw Andrea grin. I couldn't see, nor did I care at that point, whether this was a grin of amusement or triumph.

I opened the sliding door, stepped into the bedroom and closed the blinds. I curled up on the bed, and a few minutes later heard Andrea's car back out of the driveway.

Only then did I allow my tears to flow. Sobbing, I thought about Andrea's words. What if she were right? Brent and I had never really delved into the age difference; we talked about it briefly and jokingly, and quickly dismissed it.

Oh, God.

Suddenly, I saw with the clarity and lucidity that eluded me before, that I was a naïve fool to believe Brent and I had a future. I had allowed myself to live a delusional life and to have hopes that could not be fulfilled, willingly exposing myself to heartbreak and pain. Was I suffering from temporary insanity?

I hugged a pillow and cried so loud that I didn't even hear Brent's footsteps on the carpet. I simply felt the soft tapping of his hand on my shoulder and his mouth close to my ear.

"Megan, what happened?"

With Brent's arrival, my sobs slowly abated. I reached for a box of tissues on the nightstand, dried my face and blew my nose. I turned and saw concern on Brent's face.

"It's... not going to work out," I said in a low, hoarse voice. "You and I... it won't work."

Brent's face flinched.

"What? What the hell are you saying?"

I tried to steady my erratic breathing.

"I... don't think... don't believe that we can overcome the age difference. I mean, fourteen years is... a lot."

"I see." Brent moved away from me and sat on the edge of the bed. "And you just realized it *now*?"

"Yes. I've been thinking while you were gone."

"And you came to this idiotic conclusion all by yourself?"

"Well..." I sniffled

"It was Andie, wasn't it?" He fixed his gaze on me. "WASN'T IT?"

His voice was rising, on the verge of yelling.

"She and I... talked. She brought certain things to my attention, things I haven't thought about before."

"What *things*?"

I took a deep breath.

"She said that five, ten years from now you'll be interested in women your age. I mean, I'll be in my fifties, and you..."

"What kind of bullshit is this?" he shouted. "And you *believed* this?"

"Well..."

Even in the dim light I saw that his eyes were moist, and I wondered whether it was from the anger or the pain.

"This hurts me a lot," he said. His voice was calm now, almost inaudible. "I always knew that Andie was a control freak, but I never thought she'd stoop this low." He paused and I could see that he was searching for words. "That's Andie. But you... how can *you* possibly believe this... this absolute hogwash? You really believe that I'll just toy with you, string you along, and then drop you when a newer, younger model comes along? You really think so little of me?"

"Brent, I don't doubt your love. Or your integrity."

"Then how can you not trust me?"

"I *do* trust you. But we are talking about things that may happen *years* from now. You might feel differently *then.*"

"This comment proves that you have no faith in me after all," he answered. "You *don't* trust me."

Brent put his head in his hands and sat, hunched, on the edge of the bed. After a long silence he straightened and turned toward me.

"What are we going to do, Megan? About us?"

"I don't know." I sniffled and reached for another tissue. "I *should* go home tomorrow, as planned. I'm just so confused right now. What Andrea said wreaked total havoc in my head."

Slowly Brent got up and stood, staring at me, at the foot of the bed.

"I can't sleep with you tonight," he said. There was sadness and weariness in his voice. "I can't be next to you and hold you in my arms knowing you are so confused. I will sleep in Sean's room."

He turned to leave.

"No, Brent, this is *your* house." I started to get up. "*I* will sleep in Sean's room."

"Never mind."

He left the room and shut the door behind him.

I fell back on the bed and again felt the tears' wetness on my cheeks. Immediately, conflicting thoughts and emotions started to swirl in my head like a tornado. Should I run after Brent, beg him to come back? Should I forget, discard, laugh off everything Andie said?

I wanted so much to do that, but something, a nagging doubt that was gnawing at me, kept me from leaping up and running after Brent. Andie's words took hold of me, gripped me, and I couldn't just dismiss them and pretend that they didn't affect me.

I sighed and shut my eyes. I slipped into the twilight zone, the purgatory between restlessness and sleep, and I stayed there until the sun started to stream in through the blinds.

I got up, showered, dressed, and threw my clothes into the bag. I moved around the bedroom like a robot, trying to suppress the ache that was making its way from somewhere deep inside me to the surface.

I came out of the bedroom and went into the kitchen. Brent sat at the table, a mug of coffee in front of him. He was unshaven, his hair was mussed up, and he still wore the same clothes as last night.

"Hi," I said.

He raised his head and looked at me.

"I made coffee," he said in a flat voice. "You'd better hurry if you don't want to miss your flight."

I poured some from the pot into a mug and sat down across from Brent. He didn't look at me; his eyes were fixed on his mug.

"Did you get any sleep at all?" I asked. "It looks like you didn't even get out of your clothes."

"I didn't," he said in a gruff voice.

He stood up, rinsed his mug and put it, upside down, on the counter. He then went to the bathroom and I heard water running in the shower.

God, what have I done, I thought as I sat alone, my hands circling the mug. I wanted so much to snuggle up to Brent, to put my head against his chest. I wanted to feel his closeness one last time, but I knew that I couldn't ask Brent to hold me until I silenced, one way or another, the turmoil that Andrea's words had unleashed in me.

Brent came into the kitchen. He was showered and shaved, and wore a clean pair of jeans and a T-shirt. His face was inscrutable, as though he had put on a mask to disguise his pain.

He picked up the car keys from the counter and turned to me.

"Time to go," he said in an emotionless, flat voice.

He walked toward the front door. I got up, rinsed my mug, dried it, and put it back in the cabinet. I didn't want Brent to return from the airport and find my mug on the table, a still-fresh reminder of my presence.

I picked up my bag and followed Brent outside. He was already sitting in the car, with the motor running. As soon as I got in he sped off, driving so quickly I didn't even have time to turn around and look back at the house where I had spent the happiest week of my life.

We sat in silence. Brent was rigid and motionless, and looked straight ahead. He didn't glance at me at all. I suddenly felt like a useless piece of trash that was being disposed of in the quickest way possible.

Stop it, Megan. I closed my eyes and took a series of short, shallow breaths. I *deserve* this for doubting Brent's love, for questioning his motives. I shut my eyes tighter and tighter to stop the tears from running.

"Brent," I finally said and turned to look at his profile. "I don't want to leave without telling you that... I love you."

His facial muscles twitched and his Adam's apple moved, but he didn't say a word. He didn't turn to look at me or acknowledged in any way that he had heard me.

"I don't want you to think that I'm going because I don't love you," I continued. "I'm going because..."

"You are *confused*. Yes, you told me."

"Yes, I am. I need some time to think, to work it all out in my mind. But I will call you every day, promise."

"No."

I felt a sudden wave of pain wash through me and overwhelm me like a powerful gust.

"No?" I quivered. "You don't want to talk to me anymore?"

"I was up the whole night, thinking," he said, still not looking at me. "I tried to find some kind of logic in all this. And I realized that you are just not ready for the suddenness and intensity of this relationship. One day we were chatting idly on the internet, and the next we were madly in love. I'm totally comfortable and secure in my feelings. But maybe this has been too overwhelming for you, and you need the time and distance to figure it all out."

"Brent..."

He raised his hand to signal that he hadn't finished speaking.

"Please hear me out. As much as I hate the thought of being away from you, I want you to be absolutely sure of this relationship. I want you to be sure that this is what you want, and that there are no impediments, real or imaginary, in our way. Take your time, as much time as you need. But please, don't call me until and unless you are *absolutely sure*. Don't play yo–yo with my emotions."

I covered my face with my hands and sat like this, trying not to cry, until the car came to a stop.

"Do you want me to go in with you?" Brent asked. We were outside the terminal.

I wanted him desperately to go with me, but I sensed that it would only prolong the pain. I couldn't do this to Brent, and I couldn't do it to myself either.

"No, it's okay," I said.

I turned around and took my bag from the back seat.

"Well, I guess I'd better go now," I said and opened the door. "Goodbye, Brent."

I quickly got out of the car and entered the terminal without a backward glance. I didn't want Brent to see the tears streaming down my face.

Chapter Nineteen

I came home, dropped the bag in the hallway and went straight to my bedroom. It was the middle of the afternoon, but I curled up on the bed and cried until I fell asleep.

I woke up hours later. Thirsty, I went into the kitchen and poured a glass of water. As I carried the glass back to the bedroom in a robotic daze, I glanced down and noticed that I had slept in my clothes. My brain nudged me take them off but my hands were too weak, too listless, to execute the task. I lay down again and hugged the pillow. I closed my eyes wishing for a deep, restful sleep to take me out of my misery.

As the sun's first rays shone through the window, I finally fell asleep. When I awoke and looked at the bedside alarm clock I was startled to see that I had slept for seven hours.

As I tried to heave myself out of bed I felt queasy. When did I have my last meal? Could it have been dinner at Brent's house the day before yesterday? I slowly trudged into the kitchen, made some coffee and opened the cabinets looking for something edible. I found a box of saltine crackers and ripped it open.

I suddenly remembered Brent standing in his kitchen, making blueberry pancakes for breakfast. The memory was like a stake driven through my heart and I immediately started to sob.

"Pull yourself together Megan," I said sternly, and wiped the tears away with a kitchen towel.

After two cups of strong coffee I got up from the table, took off my wrinkled, sweaty clothes and went into the shower. I stood there for half an hour, letting the hot water rinse off shampoo and soap, and soothe my tense, sore muscles.

"Oh, how I wish I could wash away the ache from my heart," I sighed.

I stepped out of the shower feeling refreshed and re-energized. I put on a tracksuit, toweled off my damp hair and made a mental list of all the chores I should be doing: E-mailing Hayley. Seeing Tina. Calling Mamma and Joyce. I desperately wanted to keep as busy as I possibly could to keep my mind off Brent.

I went back to the bathroom to hang up the towel and caught a glimpse of myself in the mirror. I gasped at the image. My hair, though freshly washed, was drab and lifeless. My eyes were puffy from crying, and my face blotchy.

I sighed and picked up the phone to call Mamma. I dreaded speaking to her, but I felt duty–bound to check in.

"Hello!"

"Hello, Mamma. I'm back."

"So, how was it?"

I didn't want to tell her, not while there was no resolution, about what had happened in Florida.

"Fine."

"Eh, you stay with strange man for whole week and all you tell me is *fine*?"

I shut my eyes and took a deep breath.

"Yes, Mamma. That's all I can tell you right now."

"Right now? You mean you tell me more *later*?"

"Possibly."

I heard Mamma's breathing on the phone, a series of rapid, short breaths. I desperately wanted to change the subject, to divert Mamma's attention, to bring some semblance of normality into the conversation. Of course, the word *normality* could not really be used in conjunction with Mamma, but I had to steer the conversation away from Florida and Brent.

"By the way," I said, trying to sound upbeat, "I spoke to Hayley. She's in Guatemala, and she says she is in love."

I braced myself for a panic-stricken, hysteria-driven retort. I didn't have to wait long.

"*Dio mio*!" Mamma shouted. "I hope is not some South American punk. A couple years ago Francesco's niece come back from Uruguay, or Paraguay, or one of them countries, with salsa dancer. God forbid. "

"No, Mamma. He's a doctor."

"What kinda doctor, eh? In grass skirt with paint on his face?"

Despite an ache that permeated my soul, I laughed.

"Mamma, you watch too much Discovery Channel. No, Pedro is a *regular* doctor."

"Eh, millions of respectable doctors in this country and she go to Guatemala to find one?"

I was slowly reaching the end of my tether. Emotional upheaval aside, I could take Mamma's digs in small doses only.

"Mamma, I have to go. Lots of things to do today," I lied. "But I'll call you again soon. Bye."

I hung up. Now what?

Let's see. I talked to Mamma, so I could cross that off my "to–do" list.

Tina.

I went next door and knocked. I heard footsteps and the door opened slightly to reveal Lizzie's face.

"Hi," I said. "Tina around?"

"She's napping, Megan," Lizzie whispered.

"How is she feeling?" I whispered back. "And what did the tests show?"

Lizzie turned around as though to make sure that Tina was asleep. She then stepped into the hallway and softly closed the door behind her.

"I'm afraid it's bad news," she said, her voice quivering. "She has ovarian cancer."

I felt a tingling feeling from my head to my toes.

"My God. How bad is it?"

"It's bad." Lizzie took a crumpled hankie from under her sleeve, and dabbed at her eyes. "Pretty advanced by now."

"And... there is no hope?" I asked and grabbed a stair railing for support. My head started to spin and I was afraid I'd fall down.

"No," she shook her head. "It would take a miracle."

I gripped the railing tighter. There was one question I needed to ask, one answer I wanted to hear. I formed a sentence in my mind and opened my mouth, but no sounds came out.

I shut my eyes and took a deep breath.

"How long does she have?" I finally blurted out.

"The doctors can't say for sure. They think probably a couple of weeks."

Weeks? The tingling in my body morphed into tremors, but I was too distraught to make a concerted effort to stop the shaking.

"How is she taking it?" I asked.

"Surprisingly enough, not too bad." Lizzie said, tucking the handkerchief under her sleeve again. "She is philosophical and introspective about it."

"When can I see her?"

"I'll ring your doorbell when she wakes up. Maybe later today."

Faint and dizzy, I went back to my apartment and closed the door. Tina is dying, I thought, as I sat down on the floor of my hallway, my back against the wall. I was nauseated, my head turned, my heart palpitated, and I was short of breath. Within minutes I was in the throes of a panic attack, gasping for air like a fish out of water.

"Slowly, breathe slowly."

I lowered my head between my knees and tried to pace my breathing.

After what seemed like hours but couldn't have been more than fifteen minutes, my heartbeat and breathing were steady. I slowly stood up and, still holding the wall for balance, made my way to the bathroom. I wet a washcloth and wiped droplets of perspiration from my forehead.

Ovarian cancer. The thought of this insidious, devastating disease ravaging Tina's body brought tears to my eyes. I remembered how she used to bounce Hayley on her lap while Freddie danced the rumba in the living room. Or how she brought little trinkets for Hayley from various trips she and Freddie used to take. A wooden, hand-carved elephant from Mozambique. A tiny silk kimono from Japan. A stuffed kangaroo toy from Australia. All these keepsakes were still boxed up in Hayley's closet.

I felt so thoroughly exhausted, emotionally rather than physically, that I knew I couldn't bring myself to execute any more tasks. I lay down on the bedroom carpet and curled up into a foetal position. As I closed my eyes and hoped for oblivion, an image of Brent's smiling, dimpled face jumped out at me. I started to sob uncontrollably, my sadness over Brent and Tina merging and inflating a huge ball of pain around my heart.

I woke up, disoriented, when I heard the doorbell. It took me a while to realize that I was lying on my bedroom floor and that it was dark outside. How long had I been sleeping? It must have been hours.

I slowly got up and went to the front door.

"Yes?" I said in a hoarse voice. "Who is it?"

"Megan? Is that you? It's Liz. Tina is awake now, if you want to see her."

"Oh," I said. "I'll be there in a few minutes."

I went to the kitchen and drank a glass of water, then on to the bathroom to brush my teeth and comb my hair. I recoiled at the sight of the haggard face in the mirror.

I went next door and knocked. Lizzie opened and stared. Was she taken aback by my appearance too?

"Tina's in the bedroom," she said.

I walked into Tina's room and saw her sitting up in the bed, propped up by pillows. She wore a colorful silk caftan Freddie bought for her in India. Out of her terrycloth bathrobe she looked, ironically enough, better and healthier than before.

But as I got closer I noticed that her face was gaunter and thinner. She turned her head toward me, smiled, and stretched out her hand. I took it and sat down on the edge of the bed.

"What happened to you?" she asked, taking in my own haggard appearance.

"Oh, it's a long story," I said. "But I don't want to talk about *me*."

I squeezed her hand.

"How are *you* feeling?"

"Well," she said, still smiling, "I think it's safe to assume that I won't be running the New York marathon this year."

"Tina, you *never* ran any marathons."

"I know. So I guess now I'll have to cross that feat definitely off my list, huh?

"Oh, Tina. How can you be cracking jokes, when..."

I couldn't finish the sentence because I felt tears welling in my eyes. Again. I briefly wondered whether a human being could run out of tears. Were we given a certain lifetime quota, or was there an unlimited supply?

"Please, don't cry," Tina said softly. "I only have two wishes. One, that there are no tears. Two, that I'm allowed to stay here until the end. I don't want to go to the hospital."

"Are you in pain?" I asked.

"Actually, it's not too bad. See this? A morphine pump. The

best thing since sliced bread."

She repositioned herself on the pillows and continued speaking.

"For quite a while now I have had this feeling, like a premonition of sorts, that I would soon be reunited with Freddie," she spoke softly, with no sadness or sorrow in her voice. "A few times I saw him in my dreams and, although he didn't say anything, I sensed that he was waiting for me. I can't logically explain how I knew it, but I did. So, you see, I'm looking at this illness as the beginning, not the end. I'm at peace with it. Not, of course, that I have any other choice."

"But Tina, maybe you're giving up too soon. Perhaps it's not terminal. What about chemotherapy?"

"Are you kidding? Do you want me to go meet Freddie without a full head of hair?"

I smiled. This was probably the worst time to smile, but I couldn't help it.

"If you really want to know," Tina continued, her voice growing weaker, "there's nothing, at this stage, that modern medicine can do."

"Is there anything *I* can do? To make you more comfortable?"

"Lizzie is staying with me and she has been great. But please, come and visit."

She closed her eyes and a shiver run down my spine. I clasped her hand tighter.

"Don't worry, it's not the final curtain time yet," she said, her eyes still closed. "It's just that medicine the doctor gave me. It puts me to sleep. Sorry."

I gently released Tina's hand, got up and tiptoed out of the room.

Lizzie sat in the kitchen, reading the newspaper. When she saw me, she folded it and put it down.

"So what do you think?" she asked.

"She seems to have made her peace."

"Yes," Lizzie said. "She has."

I turned toward the door.

"I'd like to come back again tomorrow. Please let me know when she is up to it."

"Yes, of course, I will."

"Goodnight, then," I said, although my body clock was so

screwed up, I didn't know what time it was.

"Goodnight."

Back in my apartment I finished up the box of crackers I had opened that morning and washed them down with a cup of green tea. There was one more thing I had to do and I was dreading it. I had to e-mail Hayley.

I turned on the computer, went into my mailbox and typed in Hayley's address. I hated to be the bearer of bad news and spoil her trip, but given the close bond between Tina and Hayley, she had to know.

I ate the last cracker, dusted the salt off my tracksuit, and started to type.

"Sweetheart," I wrote.

"I'm afraid I have some terrible news. I just found out that Tina was diagnosed with ovarian cancer. It is in the terminal phase and at this point there is nothing that can be done. Apparently she only has a couple of weeks left. I saw her a while ago and, despite the gravity of her condition, she seems to be in good spirits.

I know how much you love Tina, and I suppose that you will want to see her, but I imagine it may not be easy to re-arrange your trip and come back. I will leave it up to you to decide.

Please call collect as soon as you read this message.

Love, hugs and kisses,

Mom."

I clicked the "send" button and turned off the computer. I yawned and stretched. Was it possible to be tired again after so much sleep? Or was it just a symptom of my emotional distress?

I lay down in bed and shut my eyes. Before long I fell into a deep sleep.

When I woke up the next morning – and my bedside clock confirmed that it *was* morning – my first thought was that shit happens.

My second thought, once my muddled mind was a bit clearer, was that I had to make an effort to come out of my zombie-like state. That meant staying awake during daylight hours, putting on a little make–up so the scary face staring back at me from the mirror didn't look like a blotchy mess, eating my usual diet of canned and frozen foodstuff, and teaching again.

What about Brent? All I knew was that I could not possibly

focus on the relationship while poor Tina was dying next door.

I went through the day like a robot. Whenever a thought or a memory of Brent resurfaced in my psyche, I immediately suppressed it.

"Not now," I whispered, "Tina first."

In the evening I saw Tina again. How could a person become frailer and more emaciated overnight, I wondered, as I looked at Tina's stick–like arms and bony hands. She sat in an armchair under a blanket, her feet propped up on a chair. She turned toward me when I walked into the room and put the tea cup she was holding on a side table. Her hand shook, rattling the fine bone china saucer.

"Come sit by me," she said and pointed to the sofa.

"Would you like another cup of tea?" I asked.

"No, don't bother," she said in a low voice. "But please make yourself one if you'd like. I know I'm remiss in my hostess duties but scurrying around the kitchen isn't as easy as it used to be."

"I was never one for scurrying around the kitchen," I quipped. I desperately wanted to make Tina smile.

"Yes, I know." she said with a faint smile on her face. "Betty Crocker you ain't."

She looked at me for a long time.

"So how is Brent?" she finally asked. "And how was Florida?"

I told her. By the time I finished, I couldn't suppress my tears any longer.

"Let me understand." Tina shifted slightly in the chair and I saw her wince in pain. "You choose to listen to his sister as though she were some kind of a prophet, rather than listening to your own heart?"

"Andrea has a point," I sighed.

"A *point?* All she has are warped, twisted, convoluted arguments."

"And what if she is right? Should I, *can* I, dismiss what she said just because she's a bitch? Or should I give this some thought, mull it over?"

Tina closed her eyes. I took it as a sign that she was falling asleep, but she stirred and opened them again.

"Listen," she whispered. Her voice grew weaker and I strained to hear her. "No relationship comes with a lifetime warranty. That's why whatever good things come our way are a blessing.

Love, *real* love, is so hard to find. Some people wait for it their entire lives. Some never find it. *You* were lucky to find it, and yet you are throwing it away."

"But what if Andrea *is* right? What if in five, ten, or whatever years, when I'm showing my age, Brent gets tired of me?"

"Okay, for the sake of the argument let's assume that it *may* happen. Then you will have five, or ten, or whatever years of love, happiness and companionship. At the end of the day that is far, far better than five, ten, or whatever years *without* love, happiness, and companionship." Tina paused, took a series of quick, shallow breaths, and continued. "Take Freddie and me, for example. He left me first, but how I loved the time we spent together. He is gone, but the wonderful memories are still in there," she pointed to her heart.

"Tina, I wish I knew what to do."

"Just *don't* do anything you'll regret later," she said, her voice a whisper now.

Tina's eyes closed again and this time her slow, rhythmic breathing told me that she had fallen asleep.

On the way out I passed Lizzie folding laundry on the kitchen table.

"She fell asleep in the armchair," I whispered.

"Don't worry about it. I'll help her into the bed later."

I came inside the kitchen and started to fold a blue pillowcase. We folded in silence because I couldn't bring myself to ask the next question.

"Do you think that, as the end nears, she will suffer?" I finally asked.

"Her dosage of morphine was increased this morning. Hopefully, that will keep her pain–free."

I turned to leave, then turned back.

"And how are *you* holding up, Lizzie? It can't be easy on you."

"Oh, don't worry about me," she sighed. "I'm managing. Sherry comes in from time to time to help out."

"Well, if you need any help, running errands, sitting with her so that you and Sherry can have some time off, just let me know."

"Thanks, Megan."

I opened the door.

"Goodnight, then."

"Goodnight."

"**My** God, this is *terrible*!" Joyce exclaimed when I told her about Tina.

We sat in a coffee shop on Eighth Avenue, my first "social" outing since I got back home four days ago.

"I go to see her ever day, but it's getting more and more difficult to talk to her. She just falls asleep in the middle of the conversation, poor thing." I stopped and took a sip of my cappuccino. "And I still haven't heard from Hayley. I don't even know whether she saw my message."

I put my cup down and looked at Joyce. I noticed that her hair was styled and highlighted, her clothes trendy. She looked healthy and relaxed.

"Leaving Rick did wonders for your looks," I smiled. I was glad to steer the conversation away from Tina's condition. I wanted to talk about something *positive* for a change.

Joyce put two teaspoons of sugar in her latte and stirred.

"Well, I figured that I needed a makeover. I realized that I couldn't work at a Manhattan art gallery looking like a frumpy Long Island housewife."

"How is the job going?"

Joyce took a sip and put the cup down. I noticed that she no longer wore her wedding band.

"Fine. I really like it, and I like Tom, the man who runs the gallery. It's not much money, but I'm managing for now since I'm living rent–free at my sister's. Of course, I won't be able to freeload forever."

"Did you see a lawyer? Hopefully Rick will pay through the nose."

Joyce shook her head.

"I don't want Rick's money. Otherwise, I will never be free of him."

"I must say, I'm pleasantly surprised at how well you are handling all this," I said. "If I recall, the last time we talked, which was not that long ago, you were a mess. And look at you now."

Joyce smiled.

"I still have my moments of doubt. Have I done the right thing? Should I go back to him? But you know what? I'm happy the way I am and I've discovered that I *don*'t want to go back to him."

"What is Rick saying now that you are gone?"

"I thought that he would be raving and raging when I left. But no. I heard through the grapevine that he immediately started to see other women and bring them to the house. So that place is now jinxed for me."

"Well," I said, "it just proves that he wasn't worth much to begin with. You're much better off without him."

Joyce nodded.

"That's what I'm thinking too. What took me so long, I'll never know. But, enough! I want to know about your trip to Florida. And about Brent."

I felt a lump in my throat and tears making their way to the surface.

"Oh, no," Joyce said, watching me. "What happened?"

I told her.

"So, you see, you were right when you warned me about the age difference," I said.

"Megan, the last time we talked I wasn't exactly of sound mind. I take back everything I said about the age difference. And I apologize for speaking out of turn."

"C'mon. You have the right to express your views just as I have the right to disagree with them. Though I'm sorry to say that in this case you were right."

"Megan, I was *not* right. Those were the views of someone whose capacity for clear thinking was greatly diminished."

"So you're saying that the age difference *doesn't* matter?"

"I don't know that I have an opinion one way or the other," she said. "But if you love each other, get along and have tons of things in common, then yes, age shouldn't be an obstacle. *I* should be that lucky."

I closed my eyes and breathed deeply. I thought of what Joyce had just said, and Tina's words jumped back at me too. They were both right: I *had* acted rashly and stupidly.

I opened my eyes and immediately felt the tears.

"I'm afraid I made such a mess of it," I whimpered. "I ran out on the man I love because his bratty sister scared me off. And now I'm suffering."

Joyce stretched out her arm across the table and patted my hand.

“I’m sure the situation is not hopeless. Besides, you know my motto: ‘you fuck up, you clean up.’ So maybe you have some mending of fences to do.”

“Thanks for these words of wisdom. There’s nothing like a dose of philosophical perspective when you screw up your life,” I smiled sadly.

“Well, you did inject some sanity into mine when I was reluctant to leave Rick. So I’m returning the favor in kind.”

That evening I sat, as usual, by Tina’s bedside. Keeping up a conversation was a big effort for her; her voice was very low and sometimes I had to strain to hear her. Her breathing was rapid and her words punctuated by grimaces of discomfort. I went back to my apartment feeling lonelier than I ever had in all the years of living alone.

I heard the ringing of the phone even before I opened the door. I ran in and grabbed the receiver.

“Hello?”

“Mom, this is *so* horrible.”

Even the bad connection couldn’t disguise Hayley’s sobs.

“I only got to read the e-mail now, tonight. How is she?”

“I wish I could tell you that she is better. But it doesn’t look like she will go on for much longer.”

“Mom, Pedro called the airlines for me. The earliest I could fly out would be on Sunday.”

Sunday. Four days from now.

“Okay, honey. I’ll be waiting.”

“Do you think Tina will still be... I mean, will I get there in time to see her?”

“I hope so, sweetheart.”

“Oh Mom, this is *so* unfair. I mean, *why?*”

“Honey, I wish I had an answer to give you,” I said. “But I just don’t know.”

I heard Hayley sniffle.

“I will e-mail you my flight details as soon as I know for sure.”

“Yes, honey, okay. I’ll get you at the airport.”

“Mom?”

“Yes?”

“I love you. And I am sorry if I haven’t told you that often enough.”

My eyes filled up with tears.

"Thank you, sweetheart," I whispered. "I love you too."

"Hayley is coming to see you on Sunday," I told Tina the following day.

Her eyes were shut and I wasn't sure whether she could hear me. But she stirred and smiled.

"Hayley! How is she?"

"She is very disturbed by what is happening to you," I said. "As we all are."

"Well, I'm not too crazy about it either," she whispered.

She groaned and grimaced as though the mere fact of breathing was painful. I took her hand into mine. It felt small and slim, almost like a child's.

"Listen," she said, slowly turning her head toward me. "I want to tell you this while I can still talk."

I placed my face closer to Tina's.

"What is it?"

"After I go, this apartment will be Lizzie's. She and Sherry are living in a studio and I want them to be comfortable. As for all the stuff here, tell Hayley that she can take whatever she wants. She used to love those Indian beads..."

Tina's voice drifted off. She closed her eyes and I stood up to tiptoe out of the room. But as I turned away from the bed, I felt her hand grip mine. I turned back toward her.

"You won't forget to tell Hayley, right?" she whispered, her eyes still shut.

"No, of course not."

Tina's hand slipped away from mine, and she fell asleep.

The next three days passed slowly. In the morning I taught my classes. In the afternoon I sat with Tina, drank countless cups of coffee and thought, with longing, of Brent. Several times I picked up the phone, and a couple of times I even went as far as dialling his number.

"What if he can't forgive me?" I muttered, as I clutched the phone close to my ear. "How will I deal with the pain, in addition to everything else that's going on?"

I always ended up hanging up before Brent answered.

Saturday evening Tina clasped my hand.

"I think...it's time for us to say goodbye," she whispered in a hoarse, croaky voice.

"Tina, no!"

My chest started to heave even before my eyes teared up.

"Yes. I don't want to go without saying goodbye to you."

She tightened her grip on my hand.

I moved as close to her face as I could and kissed her on the cheek. It was soft and cool.

"All right, then," I sobbed. "Goodbye, Tina. Thank you for being such a great friend to Hayley and me. Our lives will never be the same without you. I have only wonderful memories of our years together and I will cherish them forever." I stopped and wiped the tears from my eyes and cheeks.

There was a faint smile on Tina's face.

"You take care of yourself. Have a happy life."

"I will try, Tina," I croaked out. "And you, you say 'hi' to Freddie for me."

"I shall," she smiled and shut her eyes.

I ran home and threw myself on the bed. I wept the whole night.

"Hello, sweetheart." I hugged Hayley and held her, tightly, close to me. "How was your flight?"

"Okay," she said, yawning. "I haven't slept much in the past forty-eight hours and I'm exhausted."

"You'll get some rest at home."

"No, Mom. The first thing I'll do is see Tina. How is she?"

"She is slipping away," I sighed. "Yesterday she wanted us to say goodbye; it was so heart–wrenching. I'm happy you got here in time."

At home, we put Hayley's luggage in the hallway and immediately went next door. Lizzie opened the door, smiled and hugged Hayley.

She led us into the kitchen.

"A very odd thing happened," she said in a hushed voice. "Tina has been almost comatose for the past twenty–four hours. But just a couple of hours ago she opened her eyes and asked, her voice as clear as a bell, 'Is Hayley coming today?' When I said yes, she smiled, sat up – *by herself*, which she hasn't done in a week – and hardly slept since then."

"Can I see her now?" Hayley asked.

"Yes, of course."

We went into the room and I saw Hayley cringe at the sight of Tina's gaunt, weary face. But then she ran to the bed and gave Tina a bear hug. I was afraid she would crack Tina's brittle bones.

"Okay, you two," I said, "I'll leave you alone."

I kissed Tina's bony cheek and walked out.

"I'll be back tomorrow," I told Lizzie. "I want to give the two of them some time together."

Time to say hello and goodbye.

I made Hayley a tuna sandwich and set it, with a glass of peach ice tea, on the kitchen table.

Half an hour later Hayley walked in, her face streaked with tears. She came over and hugged me.

"Oh, Mom," she sobbed.

I patted her back.

"I know, sweetheart, I know."

We stood like this for a full minute, reluctant to let go of each other. Finally Hayley wiped her tears, sat down and bit into the sandwich.

"I didn't realize I was so hungry," she said, and drank almost the whole glass in one go. "Or thirsty."

"How was Tina just now?" I asked.

"She seemed surprisingly animated for someone who is so ill," Hayley said, and took another bite of her sandwich. "But in the end she just closed her eyes and fell asleep, in mid–sentence."

"Yes," I said, "she has been doing it a lot."

"She told me how happy she was to see me. That made me feel good."

Suddenly Hayley paused, put down the sandwich and stared at her plate.

"Sweetheart, what's wrong? I asked. "Besides the obvious."

Hayley didn't answer and she looked as though she were searching for the right words to break some ominous news. I had an uneasy feeling that what she was about to tell me was not good.

Finally she raised her head, looked at me and took a deep breath.

"Mom, just now, when I saw Tina, I told her something. I meant to tell you first, but when I saw her lying there, looking so ill, I thought I should tell her right away in case, you know, in case

I won't be able to talk to her anymore."

"What is it, honey?"

I asked the question, but with the foresight which could only be called "mother's intuition," I already knew. I knew, but I needed to hear it from Hayley.

"I'm pregnant, Mom."

I gasped and staggered to the nearest chair. I felt like a character in a play where a calamity happened in each act. Was there no end to it, I wondered? We sat in silence, my daughter and I, avoiding each other's eyes. Memories of the day I told Mamma *I* was pregnant flooded back; now history was repeating itself. I have come full circle, I thought.

"Pedro?" I finally asked.

"Yes. We found out the day before I left."

"I see."

I desperately searched for the right words, the words I longed to hear from my own mother.

"Well," I said. "This is a surprise."

I immediately regretted blurting out such a shallow remark, but I felt as if my brain had slowed down and I was suffering from cerebral burnout. *Was* there such a condition? Oh, never mind, Megan. You can't think clearly and you can't formulate your thoughts. Worse, you don't even know what your thoughts *are*.

Hayley's gaze was fixed on mine. I saw a flicker of fear in her eyes.

"Mom, are you angry at me?"

Those words gave me the jolt I needed.

"Angry? Of course not, sweetheart, just stunned. I've been under a lot of stress lately, and this news is so unexpected."

Hayley laughed nervously.

"Does this mean that you are happy with this news?"

Happy? I didn't even know anymore what happiness was.

"Yes, sweetheart," I said and patted her hand. I needed time to figure out my true feelings, but until then I wanted to be supportive of Hayley. "I *am* happy for you, for us."

Of course, I couldn't include Mamma in this statement.

"I'm *so* relieved. I wasn't sure how you would react, although of course I *should* have known," Hayley said. "And Tina, by the way, was ecstatic."

"I'm glad you were able to tell her."

I stood up and refilled Hayley's glass.

"So, when is the baby due?" I asked.

"I'm not sure, exactly. I need to go see a doctor while I'm here. Can you believe it, I must have gotten pregnant the first time Pedro and I... were together."

I suppressed a chuckle. Yes, Hayley, I can believe it. I couldn't help thinking that my own life was being eerily replayed.

"And what does Pedro think of it all?"

"He is very happy too," Hayley said. "Even though this wasn't planned. He said it was probably fate, and that it would all work out."

We sat at the kitchen table for the next two hours, drinking ice tea, talking about the baby and Hayley's plans to go back to Guatemala to marry Pedro.

At about 10 p.m. there was a knock on the door. I saw Lizzie through the peephole, her face clearly distraught.

I opened the door and looked into her red-rimmed eyes.

"Tina died fifteen minutes ago," she whispered.

Hayley and I pulled Lizzie inside and the three of us stood in the hallway, hugging.

"How did she go?" I asked, when my sobs finally subsided.

"You know I told you how she was alert this morning, waiting for Hayley? Well, as soon as Hayley left, she closed her eyes and slept. Then, fifteen minutes ago, she woke up, opened her mouth as though to say something, and then shut her eyes again and stopped breathing. It's like she was holding on for Hayley's sake and then she just let herself go."

Long after Lizzie left and I put my crying daughter to bed, I sat on the sofa in the darkened living room. I looked though the window at the dark sky speckled with thousands of blazing stars. And then I spotted it: shining brightly, brighter than the other stars, was Polaris.

I closed my eyes and started to sob. At first, they were soft, inaudible sobs, which quickly became more vocal and gained momentum. They became so powerful that they almost sent my body into convulsions.

I stood up, staggered to the phone and dialed a number. Although it was well past midnight, the phone was picked up on the second ring.

"Brent," I wailed. "Tina just died and Hayley is pregnant, and

I miss you *so* much."

"I'll be there as soon as I can," he said. "I'll try to catch the first flight out."

"Thank you, Brent," I sobbed in relief.

"Megan?"

"Yes?"

"I sensed that you'd be calling tonight."

"How?"

"I'm sitting on the patio, looking at the North Star, re-membering our walk on the beach."

I gasped.

"I saw it too just now," I whispered. "And something nudged me to pick up the phone and call."

"I'll see you soon, babe," Brent said softly.

I hung up, clutched the phone to my heart and lay down. The last thing I saw, before I shut my eyes, was a shooting star.

"Goodbye, Tina," I whispered, and then fell into a deep sleep.

Chapter Twenty

I slept surprisingly long and well, and was awakened by the doorbell. At first I was disoriented; then I remembered the events of last night: Tina's death, Hayley's announcement.

I got up, went to the door and peered through the peephole.

Brent!

I was suddenly aware of my haggard appearance, tear-streaked face, puffy eyes, wrinkled sweats and T-shirt.

I considered dashing to the bathroom for a quick shower and a dab of make–up. Oh, what's the point? Only a major overhaul would change my appearance now.

My heart beat faster as I unlocked and unbolted the door.

Brent stood on my doorstep with a grin, much the same way as he did the first time he flew in for an impromptu visit. If he was disturbed by my appearance, he didn't let on.

"I see that your welcome mat is out again," he quipped.

I pulled him in and threw myself in his arms. We stood in the hallway, in the same spot that Lizzie, Hayley and I had stood last night, hugging and kissing.

After a long holding–tight session, he pulled away and looked at me. I suddenly become self–conscious and ran my fingers through my hair.

"What's the matter, you don't like my 'just–out–of–bed' look?" I asked.

"Well, to be perfectly honest, I prefer your '*in*–the–bed look,'" he grinned. "I missed that look."

"Yes," I said softly, "I missed it too. That, and so much more."

I led Brent into the kitchen.

"Coffee?" I asked. "You must have been up very early."

"Yes, but fortunately, I was able to get on the first flight. But listen, let me make the coffee. I got some bagels and cream cheese at the corner deli. You just relax and tell me everything."

I sat down and watched as Brent brewed the coffee, sliced the bagels and spread the cream cheese.

"I could get used to this life," I sighed.

"That's what I'm hoping for," he winked.

He put two mugs on the table, poured the coffee and set the plate with bagels in front of me.

"Eat," he said and sat down near me.

I laughed. "You sound just like Mamma."

"You're right, that *is* worrisome."

Brent put a teaspoon of sugar into his cup and stirred it.

"So tell me," he said.

I took a deep breath and related all the events of the past two weeks. Tina's illness, her heart-wrenching death, Hayley's announcement of her pregnancy.

"Incredible," Brent said, shaking his head. "So much happened in such a short time."

"And throughout it all," I whimpered, "I missed you so much."

Brent reached out for my hand, brought it to his lips and kissed it.

"I missed you too," he said. "Not an hour went by that I didn't think of you. You were my last thought at night and the first one in the morning."

"I picked up the phone so many times. I even dialed your number, but I always chickened out and hung up. How's that for a really immature, irrational behavior?" I smiled.

"Well, you've been under a lot of stress." Brent stood up and refilled our mugs. "Tell me, how do you feel about your daughter's pregnancy?"

How *did* I feel? Aside from the initial astonishment, I didn't yet have the time to assimilate this news.

"Well, I'm concerned, naturally. Who is this Pedro? I know nothing about him except what little Hayley told me on the phone. Also, what does this mean in terms of her future? So, you see," I sighed, "there are a lot of unanswered questions."

I took a sip of my coffee and continued.

"Remember the story of my own unplanned pregnancy? I did tell you, right?"

Brent nodded.

"So, it goes without saying that I will stand by Hayley and be as supportive as I possibly can. How could I not be, when she seems to be following in my footsteps so precisely."

Brent laughed and opened his mouth to retort. But before he could say anything, I raised my hand.

"If you are going to tell me that an apple doesn't fall far from the tree, please don't." I smiled. "I mean, it's obvious. It's staring me in the face."

"I'm glad you can see the humor in this."

Suddenly Brent's expression grew serious. He stared into his coffee mug for a long moment, and then raised his eyes and looked at me.

"So what about us, Megan?" he asked softly.

"I'm sorry I ran out on you like that," I said. "Please forgive me."

"Listen," Brent sighed, "my sister, though I love her dearly, can be an ass sometimes. She and I had a talk about what she said to you. Believe me, she feels very bad. You must know by now that her opinions and mine do not converge."

"I know. It's just that I'm afraid of being hurt. I put my heart and soul into this relationship."

"Megan, I promise, I swear, that I will never intentionally hurt you. That would hold true whether you were twenty-five or fifty-five."

I couldn't help smiling.

"And will you still need me when I am sixty-four?"

"You silly woman," Brent laughed. "When you're sixty-four, *you* will need *me*, not the other way around."

Brent edged closer to me and took both my hands into his.

"Listen," he said, a solemn expression on his face. "I want us to get married."

I felt a shiver go down my spine.

"Oh, Brent," I said. "But *why?"*

"Why *not*?"

"I mean, what *for*? We can be together. We don't *have* to get married."

"True," Brent said. "We don't *have* to get married, in the same way that you and Joe, or Cindy and I, had to. Isn't it far better to get married not because we *have* to, but because we *want* to? For all the *right* reasons?"

"Brent, you're such an idealist."

"Is that a yes?"

I remembered Tina's words: I could either choose to be happy with Brent, or miserable without him.

I felt a tear forming in the corner of my eye and then slide, slowly, down my cheek. For the first time in many days I was not crying out of despair.

"Brent," I said, and wiped the tear away. "Let's get married."

Brent got up from his chair, came to me and kissed me on the lips.

"I accept your proposal," he said, his face buried in my hair.

"I feel like we should be drinking champagne," I chuckled. "But all we have is this here coffee."

Brent brought the coffee pot and refilled our cups.

"There's just enough left for half a mug each," he said. "But I suggest we look at it as mugs half full, not half empty."

"Cheers," I raised my mug.

"Here's to us."

We emptied our mugs in one go, as though they contained shots of vodka.

"So," Brent said, as he set down his mug. "We are now officially engaged."

I laughed.

"Super. I haven't been officially engaged in twenty–one years."

We still sat at the table, holding hands, when Hayley came in.

"Hi," she said sheepishly.

She stood in the doorway in her pyjama, surveying the scene.

"Hayley, this is Brent," I said excitedly. "He just got here this morning. And guess what – we're getting married!"

Hayley's face broke into a smile.

"Really? Boy, Brent, you sure are a fast worker."

She ran to me and threw her arms around my neck.

"Oh, Mom, I'm *so* happy for you," she whispered into my ear. "And he is *soooo* cute."

She turned to Brent and planted a kiss on his cheek.

"I've always wanted to have a cool stepfather," she said. "You'll do just fine."

"Thanks. I shall certainly strive to live up to that honor."

Hayley sat down and reached for the plate.

"Bagels and cream cheese," she said. "Yum."

"Brent brought them."

"Any guy who brings food into my mother's kitchen has got my vote," she said and took a bite.

We sat in the kitchen talking, eating and laughing. I felt an occasional pang of guilt thinking of Tina. But didn't I promise her that I'd try to be happy?

"Where are you going to live?" Hayley asked.

Brent and I looked at each other with puzzled expressions.

"It seems like we have to work out a lot of details," I said with a grin. "When and where to get married, where to live."

"And," Hayley said with a twinkle in her eye, "how to break this news to Nonna."

Mamma! How will I ever tell her about my marriage *and* Hayley's pregnancy?

Hayley must have read my thoughts.

"Maybe we shouldn't tell her until *after* you get married," she said. "As for me, how about if I just send her a birth announcement?"

The three of us laughed in unison. Tina would approve, I thought. She was probably looking down on us right now, beaming.

We talked a little longer, discussing marriage, pregnancy, Mamma. Finally Hayley glanced at her watch and got up.

"I'd better shower and get dressed. I'm supposed to go see Dad. And Grandma Annabelle." She rolled her eyes dramatically. "And you think *you*'ve got problems."

Hayley went to her room and Brent turned to me.

"She is lovely, Megan," he said.

"Yes. How do you think Sean will feel about her? He already said in no uncertain terms he didn't want another sister."

"A *baby* sister. He didn't disqualify older ones."

We cleared the table and put the plates and mugs in the dishwasher.

"How long can you stay?" I asked.

"I have to take the last flight out tomorrow," he said. "My departure was kind of unplanned and hasty, and I have some outstanding projects to finish this week. But let's talk plans, and see how we can make everything happen."

"Brent," I said and cupped his face in my hands. "There is one thing I haven't told you in a long time."

"What is it?"

"I haven't told you how much I love you."

"Funny, you took the words right out of my mouth."

We spent the rest of the day talking logistics.

"Personally, I don't believe in long engagements," Brent said. "What's the point? Either you're ready to take the plunge, or not."

"Brent," I said, "what if we are being too hasty?"

"What if we're not?"

"But how can we be sure?"

"Megan, I *am* sure. I can't prove it scientifically, but right here," he pointed to his heart, "I'm certain."

"And you have no doubts?"

"That I love you? That I want to be with you?" He shook his head. "No."

We sat on the sofa, holding each other.

"So," he said. "Any ideas as to date and place?"

"Oh, Brent, this is so sudden. On first thought, the two logical places are either here or Bradenton. I think we can eliminate eloping to Las Vegas."

"Oh well," he rolled his eyes dramatically. "My lifelong dream of getting married by an Elvis impersonator is biting the dust."

"You know what would be cool?" I asked.

"Getting married in Alaska?"

"Actually, quite the opposite. Marrying on the beach in Bradenton at sunset. Just the two of us and a justice of the peace. And, of course, Sean. Low key, yet romantic. What do you say?"

"It's certainly a possibility. But what about Hayley and your mom?

"Hayley will likely be back in Guatemala. As for Mamma, I really don't know. There's just no telling how she'll react."

"Listen," I told Hayley that evening. "I figured out how to tell Nonna about my marriage and your pregnancy."

"Send her smoke signals?" Hayley laughed.

"Not exactly. I'll call her tonight and tell her about Brent and me. God help me. Then tomorrow, on the way to the airport, we'll drop by her house so she can meet Brent. While we're there, I'll invite her to dinner here and we'll tell her about the baby then. How does this sound to you?"

"Well, it's certainly worth trying," Hayley said. "Who knows, her reaction may exceed our expectations. Like Dad's."

Hayley told me about her meeting with Joe.

"He took me out for a snack and I told him about Pedro. I could see that he wasn't thrilled with the idea of a Guatemalan son–in–law, but he didn't really say anything. And then I told him about the baby."

"And?"

"And he just sat there, staring into space like he was searching for the right words. You know what I mean?"

I knew, of course, what Hayley meant. I was sure Joe was staring into space because he was remembering my own announcement of our impending, unplanned parenthood.

"Uh...yes. So what *did* he say?"

"He just asked what my plans were and whether I was sure that Pedro would stand by me. I assured him that he would."

"Good," I said. "But I'm sure this was just the calm before the storm."

"Grandma Annabelle?" she asked.

"Yup. I'm sure it won't be long before we see her broom hovering overhead."

That evening, as Brent and I lay in bed, I reached for the phone and dialed Mamma's number.

"I really don't know what's the big deal," Brent remarked. "She's your mother. If you're happy, she'll be happy."

"Ha! You're talking about *normal* mothers. I'm talking about *mine.*"

Mamma picked up on the third ring.

"Hello, Mamma," I said, willing my artificially cheerful voice not to betray my nervousness. "I have some sad news, but happy news too."

"What happen?" she asked, her voice alarmed.

I told her about Tina's passing last night. Mamma seemed genuinely touched.

"I say a prayer for her tonight," she said. "May she rest in peace."

"That's sweet, Mamma," I said. "And, by the way, Hayley is here. She flew in yesterday, got to see Tina for a bit. Let's get together for dinner later this week."

"Yes, of course. She okay?"

"Terrific. She'll... tell you about it herself."

There was a lull in the conversation as I tried to figure out how to gently break the news of my marriage.

I took a slow, deep breath.

"There is one more thing, Mamma," I said, and immediately felt my heart doing flip–flops in my chest. "Brent and I are getting married."

There. I shut my eyes tight and waited. On the other end of the line I heard a sharp intake of breath, the sharpest I had ever heard from Mamma.

"But you tell me you had *happy* news for me!" she shrieked.

"This *is* happy news, Mamma."

"You mean, you serious?" Her voice was so shrill, it hurt my ear. "You marry this Brad, who is thirty and live in Texas?"

"His name is Brent and he lives in Florida," I said, trying to stay calm. "But yes, that's the guy I'll be marrying."

"*Santa Maria, madre di Gesu!* What wrong with you, eh?"

"I'm sorry you feel this way, Mamma," I quietly said. "I wish you could be happy for me."

"I wish I be happy for you too," she screamed. "But you don't give me no reason."

"Mamma, you always said you wanted me to get married again."

"*Si*, but not like this. Remember Antonio, Gioia's neighbor? He ask long time to marry you."

"Mamma, you can't be serious. *Antonio?* The one with no teeth?"

"No *front* teeth," she specified. "So, he not the best looking man in the world, *e alora*? At night all cats are grey."

"True, but I'd have to look at him in the daylight too," I laughed.

I closed my eyes and silently counted to ten.

"Listen" I said, "how about Brent and I stop by tomorrow around three o'clock. He has a plane to catch in the evening, so we could drop by on the way to the airport."

I waited for Mamma's response, but none came.

"Mamma?"

"Fine," she said curtly, as though she were doing me a huge

favor. "Come at three. Don't be late. You think I don't have nothing to do the whole day, eh?"

She hung up.

"Sweetheart," I said to Brent as I got under the covers next to him. "Tomorrow you're in for a treat."

"That takes care of tomorrow," he said, a devilish, dimpled grin on his face. "What about tonight?"

"Sorry," I said, with a mock look of shock, "but I'm engaged."

I stirred the next morning when the phone started to ring.

Sleepily I picked up the receiver and recognized Annabelle's number. Shit.

"Yes?" I said in a croaky voice.

"Megan, I am calling about Hayley."

I propped myself up on one elbow.

"Let me guess. You're *shocked*."

"As a matter of fact," she said icily, "I am."

"Great. Thanks for calling me at eight in the morning to tell me that."

"The hour is irrelevant," she hissed. "We have a major problem on our hands."

I shut my eyes and tried to sound calm.

"Annabelle, it's true that Hayley's pregnancy is unexpected. It's also true that it is ill timed. But there is nothing we can do about it now other than accept it and deal with it the best way possible."

"Why couldn't she have been more careful?"

"That's a very good question, but I'm afraid *I* can't answer it. And, it's a little too late to be asking it now. "

"Ha," she declared dramatically, "I should have known! This is all you have to say about it?"

"Yes, Annabelle, this is all I have to say about it," I sighed.

"Haven't you learned anything from your own experience?" she hissed.

"Yes," I said, and yawned. "I learned to stay away from people who send out bad vibes."

I could almost see Annabelle's thin lips pouting in disapproval.

"I'll be happy to discuss Hayley's plans with you as soon as they are finalized, and, hopefully, at a more decent hour of the day," I said. "Right now, if you'll excuse me, I'd like to get back into bed with my fiancé."

I hung up and looked at Brent's bemused face.

"Who was *that?*" he asked.

"Annabelle, Joe's witch of a mother. She was the original fodder for the evil mother–in–law jokes."

"Speaking of mothers–in–law," Brent said, stretching, "today is the day I get to meet *my* infamous one. I'm shuddering as we speak."

I looked at Brent's mischievous grin.

"Yes, I can see that."

We got up, showered and sat at the kitchen table sipping coffee. Hayley showed up in the doorway, her face ashen.

"Hail to the lovers," she said.

"Hi, honey. How are you this morning?"

"Well, *now* I'm officially pregnant," she sighed. "I have morning sickness."

"Oh, why don't you come and sit down," I said. "How about a cup of tea and some saltine crackers? They used to settle *my* stomach when I was pregnant with you."

I stood up to make the tea.

A sudden vivid, bittersweet memory of my own pregnancy sent quivers through my body. Has it been twenty–two years already? And now my daughter, the product of an awkward romp on a sofa, was expecting her own unplanned baby. For an odd coincidence this really *was* an odd coincidence.

"Mom, are you okay?"

I turned around and saw both Hayley and Brent staring at me with concern.

"Yes, of course," I said. "Why?"

"You made this weird noise. A sharp intake of breath, like something was hurting you."

"I'm fine," I smiled. "As a matter of fact, I was remembering being pregnant with you. Seems like yesterday."

"Did you have morning sickness too?"

"Oh yes," I said and put some crackers on the table in front of Hayley. I poured boiling water into a mug and dipped a tea bag in it.

"As a matter of fact, one of the more enjoyable memories I

have is puking all over Annabelle's marble bathroom. You know, the downstairs one with gold fixtures. It was a very Freudian experience."

Hayley and Brent laughed in unison. I placed the tea in front of Hayley, refilled Brent's mug, and sat down.

"So," I said, "what are your plans for today?"

Hayley picked up a cracker and bit into it.

"I'm going to see Dr. Felder this afternoon. Tina's memorial service is tomorrow. Then I'd like to book my return flight to Guatemala City."

"Sweetheart," I sighed. "I understand that you want to be with Pedro. But frankly, I can't help worrying about the state of health care there. I imagine that it's not the best place for a pregnant woman."

Hayley stared into her tea cup. She blew on the hot liquid and took a slow sip.

"Yes, medical care is pitiful there. I should know because Pedro is a doctor. But I don't intend to stay very long. Our plan is to get married and get Pedro a visa. I certainly hope to come back in plenty of time before giving birth."

Hayley put the cup down and bit on the cracker again.

"But what about the two of you?" she asked. "What are *your* plans?"

Brent and I were awake until three a.m., talking.

"Well, if everything works out, I'll go down to Florida after you leave. We'll get the ball rolling then. One of Brent's neighbors is a Presbyterian minister and Brent is sure he'd marry us. On the beach, at sunset."

"That is *so* romantic. Of course, I would love to be there too, but I hope you understand that I can't, under the circumstances," she said apologetically. "I mean, all this is kind of unexpected."

"I'd love to have you there, sweetheart, but I totally understand. Besides, it will be a very simple, no–frills ceremony."

"Yes," Brent jumped in. "I won't be wearing any frills."

Hayley laughed and I looked at Brent sternly.

"*Excuse* me," I said and tried to keep a straight face, "but we're having a private conversation here. Do you mind?"

I turned to Hayley.

"After the wedding," I continued, "I'll come back, pack up and try to rent this place out. Certainly the extra income will come in handy. Hopefully by then you and Pedro will be here so we can have a belated post–wedding reception. How does that sound to you?"

"It sounds perfect and totally doable. And if everything works out we will make it a *double* post–wedding reception."

Suddenly Hayley started to laugh.

"What?" I asked.

"I was just thinking. What if we have not just a double reception but a double baby christening?"

"Surely you must be joking. Imagine becoming a mother at *my* age."

"Hey," Brent grinned, "it *could* be done."

"Stop you two. There will be no baby sibling. But, "I turned toward Hayley, "you'll have a step–brother. Sean is eight and really cute."

"Cool," Hayley smiled. "I'm looking forward to meeting him. I promise to take my 'older step–sister' duties very seriously."

With that she stood up and stretched.

"Well, I feel better, so I'd better take myself out of here," she said. "I have a few errands to run, buy something presentable to wear for Tina's service and then the doc's appointment."

She turned to Brent.

"Listen, good luck with Nonna today. She is really pretty harmless, once you ingratiate yourself with her."

"Thanks for the heads–up," Brent sighed.

That afternoon, as Brent and I sat on the subway on the way to Queens, I tried to prep him for Mamma.

"Once you win her over, she'll love you forever," I said. "That's the good side."

"I dread to ask what the bad side is. I'll be thrown to the lions?"

I laughed.

"Who knows. Mamma thinks I should be marrying the toothless Antonio."

We got out at Continental Avenue and 71st Street, just two blocks from Mamma's apartment.

"You know," I said as we crossed the street, "it would be so much easier if you were Italian. Are you absolutely sure you don't have even one drop of Italian blood in you?"

"Absolutely sure," Brent sighed. "Just the luck of the Irish."

As we neared Mamma's building I glanced up and saw her looking furtively from behind a curtain.

"This is where I grew up," I said, pointing to the five-story brick building. "Lots of memories."

Mamma must have been hovering behind the door because she opened it even before I pressed the doorbell. She wore a swirling floral skirt and a crisp white blouse. Her hair was freshly washed and set.

"Hello, Mamma," I said and pecked her on the cheek. "This is Brent."

Mamma looked up – she was only five feet tall – and extended her hand. Brent took it and smiled the dimpled smile, which, I hoped, would melt Mamma's heart.

"Mrs. Gigliardi, I am very pleased to meet you."

Mamma nodded stiffly and led us into the living room. The small table was covered with the heirloom hand–embroidered tablecloth that used to be her grandmother's, and set out with her best china, which she hadn't used since Papa's funeral.

"I made chocolate cake," she said, not looking at either of us. "You like some?"

"That would be great, thank you," Brent said.

He sat next to me on the sofa and I thought about how strange it was to see Brent in my childhood home. And stranger still – he was the *only* man I had ever brought here to meet Mamma. Not even Joe had set his foot in this place.

"You like some coffee too?" Mamma asked.

"Yes, please," he said. "No cream, just one sugar."

Mamma scurried into the kitchen and Brent turned to me with a worried look.

"Megan," he whispered, "look at this china. It's paper-thin. I'm afraid I'll break it."

"It's Mamma's 'good' china," I whispered back. "It's quite an honor. Just keep your hand steady, that's all."

"But, I'm not used to drinking from such fancy stuff," he said, still in a hushed tone. "I mean, how does one hold it? What if it slips and I spill the coffee all over this tablecloth, which looks very old."

I put my hand on Brent's.

"Relax, sweetheart. Just try to make the best of it."

"Easy for you to say." Brent eyed the table with growing concern. "This is an accident waiting to happen. Your mother will think that you are marrying a clumsy buffoon."

I started to chuckle just as Mamma came in, wearing an apron and carrying a chocolate cake and a pot of coffee. She set the cake stand and the pot on the table, poured coffee into a filigree cup and handed it to Brent.

"The sugar here," she said, opening a bowl.

Brent looked at the delicate, tiny silver spoon in the hand-painted sugar bowl. His hand hovered over it and then he withdrew it.

"Um, it's okay," he said. " I'll drink it black."

Mamma sliced a piece of cake and placed it in front of Brent.

From the corner of my eye I saw his worried face. He picked up the plate gently, held it in his hand, but his fingers couldn't quite grasp the tiny spoon. He put the plate ever so gingerly back on the table and turned to Mamma.

"Mrs. Gigliardi, this is a wonderful cake."

"How you know, eh?" she asked gruffly. "You not taste it."

"Well, the cake *looks* delicious." I saw that Brent was struggling for words. "And the coffee *smells* out of this world."

Mamma settled down on the settee across from us.

"You better no get used to *these* smells," she grumbled. "You don't get nothing home–baked from Megan, eh."

"Actually, I have made brownies in the past," Brent said. "I have a young son, and he and I are quite a team in the kitchen. Of course, only simple recipes, nothing like this."

I finished my cake and put the plate back on the table. Brent cleared his throat.

"May I use your restroom?" he asked.

"What?" Mamma croaked.

"It's there," I pointed to the door in the hall.

Brent got up and walked to the bathroom. As soon as the door closed behind him Mamma turned to me and hissed.

"Brad don't like my cake."

"Mamma, the cake is delicious. It's just that Brent," I lowered my voice, "is afraid he will break your china."

"He probably not used to eat from nice china," Mamma sniffed. "They eat from paper plates in Texas."

"Mamma," I laughed, "how on earth do you know *that*?"

"You always think that I don't know nothing," she huffed. "You think I stupid, eh?"

Before I could answer, Brent came back into the living room and sat down near me.

"Mrs. Gigliardi," he said, turning to Mamma again. She sat straight as a rod, her hands folded on her knees, her gaze fixed on the floor. "I can understand that this is very sudden. Your daughter brings home a man she is about to marry, a man she has not known very long, a man who is, er, quite a few years younger. I can just imagine what it looks like to you."

Mamma stirred but still averted her eyes.

"I understand that you may be suspicious of me and my motives," he continued. Drops of perspiration formed on his forehead. "After all, you don't know me from Adam. But I can assure you that, despite the brevity of this relationship, I love Megan very much and I can't imagine *not* being with her. I promise you that I will do whatever I can to make her happy, and that I will never give up trying."

Mamma's glance traveled from the floor to the cake stand on the table. She smoothed her skirt but still didn't look at either of us.

I put my coffee cup on the table and cleared my throat.

"Mamma," I said, in a cheerful, upbeat voice. "This is what Brent and I would like to do: We would like to get married in Florida sometime within a couple of weeks. I, um, *we* decided to settle there."

I saw Mamma flinch but decided to continue.

"Anyway, after we get married, we would come back here to pack up my stuff and put my place up for rent. And, of course, we would like to have a wedding reception, more of a *post* wedding reception actually. What do you think?

Slowly Mamma raised her eyes from the cake stand to me.

"Francesco cater weddings," she said, after a long pause. "I ask him."

"Mamma, would you?" I responded enthusiastically, though I wasn't at all crazy about that gossiping old goat catering the reception. Still, if it made Mamma feel better...

Another silence followed and I stood up.

"Well, it's time for us to hit the road," I said.

I saw relief on Brent's face. He stood up too.

"Please excuse such a short visit, Mrs. Gigliardi. I do have a plane to catch. But it was very nice meeting you and I hope to have the pleasure of seeing you soon again."

Mamma followed us to the door.

"Before I forget; dinner tomorrow at, say, five?" I asked. "Hayley is looking forward to seeing you."

Mamma perked up.

"Yes. I bring food."

"Goodbye Mamma," I said. "See you tomorrow."

"Goodbye Mrs. Gigliardi," Brent said. "See you soon."

Out on the street Brent reached into his pocket, took out a tissue and wiped the droplets of sweat from his forehead.

"Jesus," he said. "I can only hope that it will get better from now on. I don't want to break into a sweat every time I see your mother."

"*I* have been breaking into a sweat every time I see my mother." I laughed. "But please, don't let it discourage you. You were wonderful and I'm sure Mamma was duly impressed. Of course, it may take her awhile to realize it."

"Well, at least I didn't break or spill anything. So no major disasters on the buffoonery front."

We got to the airport early and sat in the food court sipping coffee.

"Nothing like a sturdy, no–frills paper cup," Brent said. "Even if it does hold tasteless coffee."

I chuckled.

"You really don't care for the finer things in life, do you?"

"Well, in my experience, the 'finer' things in life are usually horrendously overpriced and untouchable to a clumsy klutz like me," he said. "So yes, you may safely assume that, until further notice, you should keep all that stuff out of my reach."

"Oh, Brent, and I thought you were perfect and flawless. Now I'm finding out it's not the case."

"Getting cold feet already?"

"Nope," I said. "But you'd better tell me right now what your flaws are. Let me guess – you leave your socks and underwear all over the floor, right?"

"Not exactly. But I do have the tendency to accumulate so much dirty laundry that the basket runneth over. It's only when I open my drawer and find that I have no more clean clothes that I'm finally moved to dump it all into the machine."

"What about putting your feet up on the coffee table?" I asked.

"Definitely."

I threw my arms around Brent's neck and planted a big kiss on his cheek.

"Brent, we will definitely get along," I said. "Seems like we're a perfect match."

That evening I called Joyce. I told her about Hayley's pregnancy, my reconciliation with Brent and our upcoming marriage.

"Goodness gracious, Megan, you are impossible." she laughed. "I leave you alone for a few days and look what happens."

"It *is* incredible," I agreed, "how life can dramatically change in the course of days. Hours even. And you know what? Focusing on the positive is helping me deal with Tina's passing. I know she would be happy for me."

The mention of Tina's name brought tears to my eyes.

"What about Hayley? What is she going to do?"

"It's up in the air right now," I sighed. "She's going back to Guatemala the day after tomorrow and I'm not happy about it. "

"Don't get frazzled in advance. Sometimes things look desperate and unworkable, but in the end they all fall into place."

I smiled.

"Joyce, this is exactly what you told me when I found out I was pregnant with Hayley. Remember?"

"Yes. And I was right, wasn't I?"

"Absolutely. But anyway, enough about me. How are things with you?"

Joyce hesitated for a few moments.

"Well," she finally said, "it's nothing as earth–shattering as what's happening to you, but I have a date."

"Oh," I said with mock sarcasm. "I leave you alone for a few days and look what happens."

"Seems like we both live a mile a minute," she laughed.

"It's not a bad way to live, is it? Otherwise we'd lead thoroughly boring lives. If nobody ever took risks, there would be no progress. We'd still be in the Stone Age."

"My thoughts exactly. I'd still be stuck in a terrible marriage. And you wouldn't be a glowing bride."

"Okay," I said. "So tell me."

"It's nothing major, really. Just a dinner with my boss, Tom.

You know, he owns the gallery."

"I assume he is unattached?"

"Oh, yes. He is divorced, and has a young daughter. And..."

Joyce stopped.

"And *what*?" I prompted her.

"I'm afraid I'll have to eat crow," Joyce said. "Tom is thirty-five."

I burst out laughing.

"You copycat. Can't you write your own script?"

"I know, I know. Incredible, isn't it?"

"Yes," I said, "we've already established that. Seriously though, as delighted as I am that you are moving on with your life, please be careful. I mean, take it slowly."

"Ha, you should be the one talking."

"Okay," I said. "I know I'm not the one who should be giving you advice, all things considered. After all, I rammed my way into the relationship with Brent."

"I know it may seem like I am on the rebound," Joyce said. "But hey, it's only dinner. I have no expectations beyond that."

"Well then, have a great time. And who knows, if everything goes well, you and I may form an 'old wives club'."

"Get out of here," Joyce laughed. "*You* are about to become an old wife. Me, I have no interest whatsoever in ever tying the knot again."

"That's what I thought too. And look at me now."

"Well, I suppose I'll just have to live through you vicariously," Joyce said. "So make sure that you are happy enough for both of us."

The last thing I told Joyce before I hung up was that I fully intended to live up to that challenge.

The next afternoon, after a touching memorial service for Tina in our neighborhood's small Unitarian hall, Hayley and I braced ourselves for Mamma's visit. Poor Mamma. One day she was told that her daughter was getting married after a whirlwind courtship of only several weeks. The next day she was to find out that her granddaughter was pregnant after a whirlwind courtship of only several weeks. All of a sudden I felt an unprecedented compassion for Mamma.

"You know what?" I told Hayley as we set the table for dinner. "Our current lives are stuff soap operas are made of."

"Yes," she agreed. "We should find a suitable name for it."

"How about *As the Stomach Turns*?"

We laughed, but deep down inside I felt seeds of apprehension taking root. Yesterday, when she came back from Dr. Felder's office, Hayley looked pale and thin.

"I'm about five weeks along, so it's early yet," she said. "I'm due in November."

"And what did the doctor say about you going back to Guatemala?" I asked. "Is it safe?"

"Well, he did mention that I should be eating a healthy, balanced diet, which is not always easy over there. He gave me some vitamins. In any case, I expect to be back before my first trimester is over. He will do an ultrasound then."

"And what are your plans afterwards?"

Hayley sighed. She looked so young and vulnerable. The thought that my baby would soon be a mother herself had not yet quite sunk in.

"I really don't know, Mom. All this happened so unexpectedly, Pedro and I had no chance to make any definite plans. I'd like to go back to college for that last semester, as I promised. As for Pedro, I really don't know what certification he'd need to work as a doctor here. He did go to medical school in this country – in Florida as a matter of fact – so who knows."

"Sweetheart," I said. "I have to ask. Are you truly in love with Pedro, or are you talking marriage only because you're pregnant?"

"We really *are* in love, Mom. Maybe we wouldn't marry quite so soon if I wasn't pregnant. But we'd definitely be together."

"I'm relieved to hear that," I said. "All I want is for you to be happy."

"I *am* happy, Mom," she said. "I'm still getting love and marriage and baby carriage, even though I'm going about it backwards."

Now, as we awaited Mamma's arrival, I thought of how to break the news to her gently, but I was at a total loss. Knowing Mamma, I was sure that she was still smarting from yesterday's revelation. I was afraid that Hayley's pregnancy might be too much for her to handle.

The dinner – tomato, mozzarella and basil salad followed by cannelloni – went well. Hayley talked animatedly about the places she visited in Guatemala. I knew that she was trying to hide her nervousness behind the idle chatter. From time to time Mamma interrupted with questions such as “Isn’t it dangerous?” or “When you come back home, eh?” All in all, however, the conversation went smoothly and without major glitches.

I noted that Mamma didn’t mention meeting Brent the previous afternoon, or my impending marriage. I wondered whether she had – subconsciously or not – wiped the information from her mind.

Earlier, Hayley and I had decided not to tell Mamma about the baby until after we finished eating. No sense wasting a good, home–cooked meal.

After dinner Mamma stood up to clear the table, but I caught her arm and pulled her down.

“Mamma, sit down,” I said, my heart pounding. “Hayley and I have something to tell you.”

Mamma sat and looked at me.

“What’s the matter, eh, Brad decide he don’t wanna marry you no more?” she asked.

“No, Mamma, that’s not it.” I tried to keep my voice calm and steady.

From the corner of my eye I saw Hayley’s face. She stared nervously at her empty plate and fidgeted with her fork. I reached out for her knee under the table and squeezed it.

I took a deep breath.

“Mamma,” I said, “Hayley is pregnant.”

I shut my eyes, relieved that I had been able to blurt out this news, then opened them to see Mamma staring at me in horror. Her eyes were wide, her face ashen, her mouth open. Even the announcement of my own pregnancy way back when hadn’t elicited such a frightening expression.

“Mamma, are you all right?” I asked, after more than a minute passed and not one of her muscles had twitched.

Hayley ran to the sink and came back with a glass of water. She brought it to Mamma’s lips.

“Here, Nonna, drink this.”

Mamma looked down at the glass as though contemplating its contents. Then she slowly raised her hand and knocked the glass, spilling the water on the floor. Tears streaked down Hayley's face.

I was torn between annoyance and compassion. I was angry at Mamma's reaction, but at the same time I felt a measure of empathy for the feelings this announcement must have unleashed. Mamma's beloved granddaughter, on whom she had pinned all the hopes that her own daughter didn't live up to, was now following her mother's road to perdition. And with that Mamma's dreams of a suitable husband and a respectable life for Hayley had bitten the dust.

Hayley brought paper towels over and dried the puddle. She then stacked the dishes, glasses and cutlery in the dishwasher. At least five minutes had passed since the announcement and Mamma still hadn't uttered a single word.

I was about to get up when I saw Mamma's lips move. She said something but her voice was so low, I couldn't hear it.

"What did you say?" I asked.

"I ask, who is this man?" she said and turned to Hayley. "Who?"

Hayley came back to the table and sat down.

"His name is Pedro," she said. "He is a Guatemalan doctor."

Mamma winced as though she were in pain. She closed her eyes for a few moments and when she opened them she turned to me and glared.

"You," she said in a voice so low, it was almost a whisper. "Is all *your* fault!

"Really?" I asked. I had no idea what Mamma was getting at. "And how is it *my* fault?"

"You allow her to go to South America. That's why she pregnant now."

I opened my mouth to tell Mamma what a ludicrous statement this was but Hayley jumped in.

"Nonna," she said, wiping tears from her face with a paper towel. "It's not Mom's fault. It's nobody's fault. This happened because it was *meant* to happen. I really believe that I was meant to have this child."

"What kind of nonsense is that, eh?" Mamma shouted. She then turned and pointed a finger at my face. I briefly wondered whether this was how the expression *'pointing the accusing finger'* originated.

"What kind of mother you are, eh? You no worry about your

child, you think only of your Brad!"

"Nonna!" Hayley exclaimed in outrage. Then she jumped out of the chair and ran to her room. I heard her muffled sobbing through the door.

"See?" Mamma yelled. "See what you do to your own flesh and blood, *povera bambina*? You *bad* mother!"

I chuckled. It wasn't an amused chuckle, but a sneer.

"Funny you should mention it," I said through clenched teeth. Although I was seething inside, I tried to keep my voice low. "That's exactly what Annabelle told me. So the two of you are not that different after all."

I stood up and turned on the dishwasher. Although my back was turned, I could hear Mamma breathing faster, a sure sign that her agitation level was dramatically rising.

"How can you say this to me, eh?" she screamed, her face as red as a beet. "You comparing me to that, that *strega cattiva*, the crazy witch?"

Whatever empathy I felt toward Mamma just fifteen minutes ago had dissipated. All I could think of now was my sobbing daughter and my own wounded sense of pride.

I started to walk toward my room. Before I slammed the door in Mamma's puffy face I turned to her and said:

"Yes, I *am* comparing you to Annabelle. If the broomstick fits, fly it."

Mamma's breathing accelerated.

"How dare you talk to me like that?" she screamed.

"Well," I yelled back, "sue me!"

All I heard as went to the bedroom was Mamma's fast breathing, followed a few minutes later by footsteps and the sound of my front door closing.

For the first time in my life I mustered the courage to stand up to Mamma and I didn't have an ounce of regret.

"**I** have been walking around her on eggshells my whole life," I told Brent on the phone later that night. "Finally, something just snapped."

I sat in bed propped up on three pillows, snacking on leftover cannelloni. I ate with my fingers straight out of the baking dish. I was so nervous during dinner that I hardly touched my food. Now

I was hungry.

"I guess all the pent–up frustration got the better of you," Brent said. "I hope you are feeling better now."

"Actually, I am. It was strangely liberating. There's nothing like an act of defiance, even if it comes thirty years too late."

I put the baking dish on the night table and wiped my hands and mouth with a Kleenex. I was just glad that Brent wasn't here to see it.

"I thought I'd feel bad for mouthing off to Mamma, but you know what? I don't. Come to think of it, I should have done it a long time ago. I mean, all these years and not once has she said anything positive about me. It's always been a guilt trip with her."

"Maybe she doesn't realize that she has been doing this," Brent suggested gently. "Some people need a jolt to make them see themselves the way others perceive them."

"I suppose I'm partly to blame. I should have taken a stand a long time ago, instead of coddling her. "

"Listen," Brent said. "Give her some time to chill. She'll probably sulk for a while and then she'll come around. You'll see."

I slid down into a lying position and closed my eyes.

"My biggest concern right now is Hayley," I sighed. "She is going back to Guatemala tomorrow and I'm really worried."

"I understand that. But she did say she'd be back soon, right?"

"Yes, she is planning to come back in a few weeks. As soon as Pedro gets a visa."

"So there. No need to worry. Besides, you will be coming down here in a few days. And then..."

"What?"

"Nah. Won't tell you. It's a surprise!"

"Oh, c'mon. Tell me."

"No."

"Give me a clue. Is it bigger than a breadbox?"

"Hmmm. Just barely."

"You bought me the Hope diamond?"

"Shucks. How did you manage to pry this information out of me?"

"Seriously though, what is it?"

"Megan, has anyone ever told you the definition of the word *surprise*?

"Fine, you don't have to divulge it. Just tell me the first letter."

"You're incorrigible," he laughed. "However, you will not finagle any information out of me. My lips are sealed."

I laughed too. I was just glad to end this hellish day on a happy note.

Chapter Twenty-One

I arrived in Florida three days after Hayley's departure. Brent picked me up at the airport and, on the way home, we stopped at the Manatee County Clerk's office to apply for a marriage license.

"It won't be valid for three days," Brent said. "Just make sure you keep your feet toasty warm till then."

I shook my head.

"I won't run out on you again. Of course you do realize, don't you, that if Mamma had her way this marriage wouldn't take place. She's totally against it."

"On what grounds?"

"Insanity," I laughed.

My mind wandered to Mamma and our fight on the eve of Hayley's departure. We had not spoken since then. The rift did bother me, but the more I thought about it the more I realized that, after years of quelling my own thoughts and desires and obediently swallowing every nonsense Mamma had dished out, my outburst wasn't out of place.

In Brent's house we sat down on the patio and drank lemonade from tall, palm–shaped glasses.

"Well?" I said.

"Well, what?"

"Well, where is it? My surprise?"

"I never said I'd give it to you right away," he grinned. "As a matter of fact, I think I should wait until *after* we get married."

"Surely, you jest. I want my surprise *now*!"

"Oh, okay then. You are so good at arm twisting." Brent got up and went into Sean's room.

I heard some whispers and rustling noises. A minute later

Brent came out carrying a picnic basket.

"Here," he said, placing it on my lap. "Open gently."

I put my hands around the basket and felt a movement inside. Slowly I removed the lid to see a small, soft, white bundle lying on a baby blanket. The bundle raised its head and looked straight at me. It was a Labrador puppy.

I smiled. I reached inside, brought out the pup and held it against my cheek. Its tiny floppy ears were as soft as velvet.

"Oh, Brent," I said as the puppy licked my face. "He's adorable. What a wonderful surprise this is."

"He's only six weeks old," Brent said and patted the pup's head. "I already started house training him. Hence the newspapers scattered all over Sean's floor."

"You can't know this, of course, but as a child I dreamt of having a pet. I used to beg Mamma to let me have one. Dog, cat, hamster, anything. "

"Let me guess. She said no. Right?"

"Right," I said. "Whenever I brought up the subject, she shouted, 'You crazy? They bring disease! Our neighbors back in Italy, they had goat. They all die from some horrible illness!' One day while walking through a park I saw a small, scruffy mutt lying under a bench. I went over to pet him. He was thin and dirty and I decided to take him home. Mamma was at the store so I gave the dog the leftovers from the fridge and some water. Then I carried him to the bathroom, put him in the bathtub and poured some shampoo over his coat. The dog didn't move; he just stood there covered in suds from head to paw and stared at me. The poor thing probably thought that he had died and gone to heaven. Just then Mamma came home. She must have sensed an unusual activity in the bathroom because she marched right in, saw me kneeling over a soapy creature and shouted, "'*Dio mio,* why you washing a big rat in my bathtub, eh?' I started to explain that this was a small dog and I begged to keep him. Mamma, of course, didn't want to hear my pleas. She ordered me to get the dog out of the apartment. I remember carrying him in my arms, crying all the way to the park. Back home, I could smell bleach as soon as I got out of the elevator. For the next three hours, as I lay sobbing on my bed, Mamma was on her hands and knees scrubbing and disinfecting every inch of our apartment." I paused and scratched the puppy's back. "Needless to say, I never brought another living creature into the house."

"Jesus, Megan, you're breaking my heart."

"I did briefly consider getting a dog after the divorce," I said. "But living in a small apartment in Manhattan didn't strike me as pet-friendly."

And now I sat on the patio of Brent's, and soon to be mine, home cuddling an adorable pup. Oh, if Mamma could see me now.

"What's his name?" I asked.

"That's the best part," Brent smiled. "I named him 'Paris'."

"That was very thoughtful of you, Brent," I laughed. "And how very appropriate. Just think, we'll always have Paris."

"Good thing I didn't name him 'Detroit', huh?"

"Okay, enough of this." I gently put the pup down and he scurried happily around the yard. "Let's talk about the wedding."

"Okay, let's. Four days from now, the beach, at sunset. Don't stand me up."

"I'll be there. I'll be wearing a yellow sundress, the color of the sun. It's my favorite one. Now, what about you?"

"Alas, I don't own any yellow sundresses."

"Okay, what *do* you own?" I asked.

"Let's see. The only wedding – appropriate attire would be a pair of new jeans without holes, and my favorite shirt with the likeness of Jerry Garcia on it."

"Sorry, sweetheart, but no hippie weddings, okay? Casual and informal, yes, but no beads or flowers in our hair. Please?"

"I suppose that means a suit and a tie, the most dreaded attire of all," he sighed.

"C'mon, you'll look great," I pleaded.

"Only because I love you so much. But promise me you'll never make me wear that stuff again."

The afternoon of our marriage I found Brent sitting in front of his computer with a bewildered expression on his face. He wore a button–down shirt with a tie loosely draped over his shoulder. He looked intently at some kind of a graphic. I came closer to the screen and peered at a series of twisted shapes.

"What is this?" I asked.

"I'm learning to tie my new necktie," he said sheepishly. "This is only the second time in my entire life that I have to wear one."

"You're kidding, right?" I laughed. "Please tell me you're kidding."

"Stop laughing," he said, carefully slipping the noose around his neck. "I can't focus if you laugh."

"Brent, you look like you're going to hang yourself. Honestly."

Brent's mouth twitched but he kept a straight face.

"I don't know why you're making fun of me. After all, I'm doing this for you. If *I* had my way I'd get married in my Jerry Garcia shirt. But because *you* insist on a sense of propriety for our wedding, I'm learning to tie the knot so that *we* can tie the knot."

"Brent," I giggled, "don't you ever get tired of old clichés?"

"I do," he said, still struggling with the knot. "I'll tell you what though, as soon as I tame this beast here, let's invent some new ones."

We got married at 6:38 p.m. Only Sean and a couple of curious bystanders were there to witness the brief ceremony. As the magnificent bright orange sun blazed on the horizon, Brent's neighbor, the Rev. Joshua Carter, pronounced us man and wife. We exchanged thin gold bands we had purchased just the day before and stood facing each other, clasping hands.

"Before you folks go and celebrate, let me tell you a few words," the minister said. "God gave both of you a second chance. You have been married before so you know that it's not all smooth sailing. But, when difficult times come, and they *will* come, remember *this* day and *this* place, and what brought you here in the first place. God be with you."

Brent and I turned toward each other. Our eyes were moist.

"I love you, Megan," he said, his voice breaking.

"I love you too, Brent." A single tear streamed down my face and I wiped it with my finger.

The fact that I was now a married woman hadn't yet sunk in.

"Let's remember what the minister told us," Brent whispered. "Let's never lose sight of the love that brought us together in the first place."

"I won't, ever." I promised.

Sean approached and hugged his father. Then he turned to me and gave me a wooden box. Inside, wrapped in tissue paper, was a large conch shell. I took it out and gently touched its grainy tan exterior and the smooth pink lip.

"It's beautiful, Sean." I planted a kiss on his cheek and give him a hug. "Thank you very much."

"I kept it on the top shelf, so Katie couldn't get to it," he said.

"Tell you what. I'll keep it on the top shelf too, so Paris can't get to it."

The adorable pup had been wreaking havoc in the house. Several times I found him happily scavenging in the garbage, with only his wagging tail sticking out of the trash can. Mamma would have had a fit.

After the ceremony, the three of us walked to the nearby Beachhouse Restaurant for a celebratory dinner of broiled Gulf grouper for Brent and I, and a burger for Sean. We sat on the restaurant's wooden deck and watched the darkening sky.

"It was a beautiful wedding," I told Brent later that night as I circled my shiny new wedding band around my finger. "And you know what?"

"Oh no, don't tell me the honeymoon is over before it even started!" Brent shouted.

"Silly you," I snuggled closer and gave him a long, lingering kiss. "Does *this* strike you as the end of the honeymoon phase?"

Brent chuckled.

"Okay, I take it back. And beg for more."

"All in good time. However, what I meant to tell you before you diverted my attention to more carnal matters, was that I'm glad Mamma wasn't here. I never thought I'd say it and not feel guilty, but it's true. In all probability she would throw a fit, or pout, or otherwise manage to spoil the day."

"Write her a note," Brent urged. "At least tell her you're married now, and give her this address and phone number. She has to know where you are."

Brent was right. Three days after the wedding I sat down with a pen and paper, and wrote a note.

"Dear Mamma," it said. "I just wanted to let you know that Brent and I got married last Thursday. I will be in New York at the end of the month to pack up my things and try to find a tenant for the apartment. By the way, my new name is Megan Newman." I included my new address and the phone number.

Three weeks passed and I had no word from Mamma. I began to worry that she was ill, or that some other misfortune befell her.

"Give her time," Brent said.

"Give her time," said my aunt Gioia when I called her to make sure that Mamma was fine. "You know Angelina, she is very stubborn. She sees things her way and that's that."

"Yes," I sighed, "that's that."

I didn't even see Mamma when Brent and I flew to New York to pack up my belongings. I found a tenant, a professor at Columbia recommended by Lizzie. He was ecstatic to find a furnished apartment in Manhattan, so I didn't even have to put the furniture in storage. And the rent, much more than I had expected, was the icing on the cake. As a matter of fact, the rental income more than compensated for the loss of my meager wages.

We stayed in the city for over a week, and although I called Mamma and left several messages inviting her to dinner, I didn't hear back from her.

"Maybe she is so fed up with me, she decided to disown me," I told Brent when we returned to Bradenton. I meant it as a joke, but deep down I felt a disquieting surge of anger. "I really don't understand how she can be so unreasonably obstinate."

"Give her time," Brent said.

"That's all you ever say, *'give her time.'* Can't you tell me anything else for a change?"

"Not really. That's the only answer that comes to mind."

But that night, as we lay in bed, Brent turned to me and propped himself up on his elbow.

"You know, I think maybe she is waiting for you to apologize."

"*Me*? Why should *I* apologize? I have been bending backwards my whole life to accommodate her various quirks and idiosyncrasies, and *I* should be the one apologizing because *she* finally went too far?"

"Well, she *is* your mother."

"So, just because she gave birth to me she is entitled to behave like a spoiled brat and I have to put up with it for the rest of my life?"

"Someone has to take the first step. Might as well be you."

"Really?" For the first time since we met – could it have been only three and a half months? – Brent got on my nerves. "I beg to disagree, but I believe that *she* is the one who must make the move, not me."

I realized that I was shouting but I became so agitated, I could not stop.

"If I back down now, she will never understand that her behavior and comments that evening were inappropriate and hurtful. She will never realize that she has been overbearing, and, at times, totally obnoxious. And she will go on being her difficult self and thus continue making my life, Hayley's life, the baby's life and *your* life unbearable."

"Megan," Brent looked at me with a shocked expression. "You are talking about your *mother*!"

"So?" I glared at him. "What are you going to do about it? Wash my mouth out with soap? Ground me?"

"Megan, stop it." Brent reached out to touch me, but I pushed his hand away and jumped out of bed.

"I'm sleeping in Sean's room," I shouted as I headed toward the door. "Now the honeymoon is *really* over!"

I curled up in Sean's bed and pulled his blanket over my head. But, as my rapid breathing started to subside, I began to realize that I had overreacted.

I slowly got up and tiptoed into the bedroom. Brent was sitting up in bed.

"Missed me?" I asked and slipped under the covers.

"I was just trying to figure out what happened." He looked at me with a puzzled expression. "What did I do?"

"Sweetheart," I sighed, "I flew off the handle. I suppose I still carry all this pent–up frustration inside me. It's eating me up. I know I have to do something about it but I don't know what."

"Well, there *is* one thing, but I'm not sure you're ready yet."

"What?"

"Forgiveness," he said. "It can be very liberating. The day I decided to let go of my anger toward my father for abandoning Andie and me, I felt so much better."

"Forgiveness implies that Mamma *intentionally* did something to hurt me. I know she didn't. She always had my best interests at heart, no doubt about it. She did the best she could, under the circumstances."

"Then why *don't* you take the first step?"

"I'm not sure," I sighed. "I *am* angry at the things she said to me the night before Hayley left. She yelled at me in front of my daughter and called me a bad mother. It's like the pot calling the kettle black. Even though I know that she doesn't have the intellectual capacity to see the error of her ways, or to change, I'm hoping that, at the very least, she'll realize how hurtful her words were. Whether or not she is capable of that, I really don't know."

"So, how are you adjusting over there?" Joyce asked during one of our weekly phone calls.

"Funny thing," I said. "I had always considered myself a quintessential New Yorker, thriving on the hustle, bustle and energy of the 'city that never sleeps'. I took an almost perverse pleasure in knowing that thousands of people across Manhattan were awake and ready to serve me around the clock in the unlikely event that I had a sudden craving for pizza, or needed a tube of toothpaste in the middle of the night. So, initially at least, the prospect of leaving this comfort zone for a much smaller, laid-back town like Bradenton made me a little jittery."

"And?"

"And I was pleasantly surprised to discover that I immediately took to Bradenton like a dolphin to water – ha, ha, wasn't that cute?"

"Yeah, very cute," Joyce said, with a touch of sarcasm in her voice. "Your wit never ceases to amaze me."

"So, as of now, there's no homesickness, no regrets, no hankering after midnight snacks. How *can* I miss the noise, the mess, and the jostling crowds when I'm surrounded by sandy beaches, warm Gulf breezes, palm trees and glorious year–round sunshine?"

"Sounds idyllic, Megan. I'm flying down for a visit as soon as I save some money."

"That'll be great. Actually," I sighed, "there *is* one cloud in the otherwise clear blue sky, aside from the rift with Mamma, of course. Hayley. Despite her initial resolve to come back fairly quickly she is still stuck in Guatemala, with no plans to return in the foreseeable future."

"Why? Don't tell me she actually *wants* to live there."

"No, but Pedro is having problems getting a visa. The whole process is turning out to be more complicated and time-consuming than Hayley had thought."

"Why doesn't she come home and let Pedro deal with the

paperwork himself?" Joyce asked. "It would make more sense for her to be here, close to medical facilities."

"That's exactly what I've been telling her. Plus, Brent has already started converting a large loft over the garage into living quarters for them. But," I sighed, "she doesn't want to leave Pedro. She's just hoping things will work out soon."

"Have faith. Everything *will* work out in the end."

"Joyce," I chuckled, "I had no idea you were so wise."

She laughed.

"Neither did I. 'Wise' is not what I'd call myself. I'm just a FADAD."

"Who?"

"Forty-something, Almost Divorced And Dating. It's a phrase I coined myself. Like it?"

"Joyce, I know you love being a FADAD. You are happier now than you've been in a long time. And that Tom of yours sounds like a wonderful guy."

Joyce had been dating Tom, the gallery owner, for several months and they seemed to be getting along very well. He even offered, when Joyce had to move out of her temporary lodging, the top floor of a brownstone he owned in upper Manhattan. Joyce refused, preferring to rent a small one-bedroom place in the Village.

"Whatever acronym you choose to call yourself, I'm really happy at how well you are managing," I said. "You should be an inspiration to all SUMs."

"All who?"

"Haven't you ever heard of SUMs? Still Unhappily Marrieds?"

"Oh, *those* SUMs? Not only have I heard of them, but I was their founding member."

"You know, we must talk more often," I sighed. I suddenly felt a pang of nostalgia for Joyce, for the way we used to meet back in New York. "As much as I love my husband, nothing beats a little coffee klatch between us women. Even if there's no actual coffee involved."

I did feel better when Joyce and I hung up. But an unsettling feeling in the pit of my stomach was gaining momentum. And it revolved around my daughter.

Chapter Twenty-Two

I had been awaiting Hayley's return for the past four months. And the longer I waited, the more I worried. Was she getting adequate medical care? Was she eating right? What if she didn't get back home before the birth?

Constant worry brought out character traits – *flaws* would be a better word – I never knew I had. I became snappish, irritable and irrational. I shouted at Brent for no apparent reason. Even poor Paris cowered when he saw me coming.

"Megan, relax," Brent, the paragon of patience, kept telling me. "Take deep breaths, meditate, chant, whatever. Just take it easy. *Please.*"

"Easy for *you* to say," I snapped. "*You* don't have a pregnant daughter in Guatemala."

"Megan, be reasonable. Being pregnant in Guatemala is not the end of the world. Millions of other women give birth there every day."

"None of the millions of women you cite is *my* daughter," I shouted. "You think inane comments like that are going to make me feel better?"

Brent shook his head.

"I have no idea any more what is going to make you feel better." His voice was a mixture of sadness and resignation. "No matter what I say, you shoot me down. Maybe I should just keep my mouth shut."

When Brent's attempts to make me feel better were repeatedly – and rudely – turned down, he went to the garage, shut the door and worked into the wee hours of the morning. I spent many nights sleeping alone.

"I don't think he loves me anymore," I sobbed to Joyce one evening. "I can't say I blame him. I have turned into a monster. *I* don't even like myself anymore."

"Stop it, Megan! It's not like you to be so melodramatic," she said curtly. "Just go to him and apologize."

"Of course I will. But you know what else scares me? I'm becoming like Mamma. Unreasonable, irrational, *crazy*. Maybe genetic ties are stronger than I thought."

"Megan, you *are* being unreasonable, but, unlike your mother, it's only a *temporary* lapse."

That evening I went to the garage and put my arms around Brent's neck.

"Sweetheart, I'm *so* sorry, really," I sniffled into his shoulder. "I don't know what's happening with me."

"Well, I guess all that upheaval with Hayley has really gotten to you," he sighed and patted my shoulder. "I'd like to help but I don't know how. Whatever I say, you snap at me."

"Brent, I have to ask. Do you still love me?"

The mere thought that Brent might have fallen out of love with me was making me nauseous.

"Of course I do," he smiled. "You think my feelings are so fickle that I'd stop loving you simply because you've been acting like a jackass?"

"I hope not," I said, wiping my tears on Brent's T-shirt. "After all, we did promise to stick together for better or for worse."

"True. And I want to stick around long enough to actually experience the *'better'* part."

I decided to let that comment go. Instead I put my head on Brent's shoulder and felt the wetness of my own tears on his sleeve.

"You know, I think that I have developed a new empathy for Mamma," I said. "I'm beginning to see how a frantic worry about one's children can turn even the most level-headed person into a raving lunatic."

"If this is going to bring you closer to your mother," Brent smiled, "at least my suffering has not been in vain."

Unfortunately, there was nothing either Brent or I could do to help Hayley. She refused to come home without Pedro and all the attempts to get him a visa had, so far, been futile.

"We are getting married anyway," Hayley announced on the phone. "We don't want to wait any longer."

I begged her to come home. Although Hayley and Pedro both assured me that she was getting adequate medical care, I knew, from the online research I had done, that it was probably not the case. At best, she was receiving *rudimentary* care.

Still, the pregnancy seemed to progress normally and photos sent over the internet showed a glowing Hayley with Pedro at her side. The sight of her by now sizeable bump brought tears to my eyes.

"You are probably worrying for nothing," Brent said. "She looks perfectly healthy and content."

Now, as I sat at Brent's computer e-mailing Hayley, the phone rang. I glanced at the caller ID and saw Mamma's number. A shiver went through me, although it was sweltering hot outside.

I took a deep breath.

"Hello?"

"How's Hayley?" Mamma asked. No hi, how are you, how have you been these past four months. Her voice was as flat as though we had just spoken yesterday.

I decided not to beat around the bush. My days of coddling Mamma's feelings for the fear of upsetting her were over.

"She's still in Guatemala, Mamma," I said, trying to keep my voice calm and steady. "She's five months along now. She seems to be healthy and happy. And she and Pedro are married."

I waited for a sharp intake of breath, or some other familiar manifestation of Mamma's distress, but, to my utter surprise, none came.

"Still in Guatemala?" she asked, her voice quivering just a bit. "But why? Why she no come back yet?"

"She, *they,* have had some problems getting a visa for Pedro. And she refuses to come back without him."

"*Dio mio,* I hope she be back before baby come."

"Yes, Mamma, me too. I keep telling her to come back, even if she and Pedro have to be apart for a little while. But she doesn't want to hear of it."

I heard Mamma breathing on the phone; not the heavy, hysterical heaves I had grown accustomed to, but soft, almost melodious ones. Was Mamma on tranquillizers?

"And how have you been?" I couldn't talk to Mamma after a

four-month silence and not ask about her well–being.

"I been fine," she said. "Nothing new."

I waited for her to inquire about *my* life, which, I thought, was a totally reasonable expectation, given our lengthy estrangement. But no questions came.

"That's good to hear," I said, after an awkward silence. "Everything is fine here too. Brent and I are very happy and I have adjusted to Florida without any problem."

For a second I wondered whether I sounded like I was boasting. If I did, I hoped Mamma wouldn't catch on. I certainly didn't want to alienate her further.

"Good," she finally said after what seemed like an endless silence. "Let me know about Hayley. I worry about *povera bambina.*"

"Will do," I said.

After Mamma hung up I sat by the computer wondering what had happened to her. She sounded so calm and subdued, so totally unlike the Mamma I knew, I began to worry that she was ill. No, I thought to myself. I can't worry about Hayley *and* Mamma. I just don't have the tenacity to carry two burdens on my shoulders.

I did, however, make a mental note to call Mamma once a week with the news of Hayley. Hopefully, the news would be all good.

To hear her tell it, Hayley seemed to be doing relatively well. She and Pedro lived with his parents and three siblings in a house on the outskirts of Guatemala City. The food, she said, was simple but adequate, and she was seeing an obstetrician who was Pedro's med school buddy.

"It's not exactly like back home, but it'll do," she told me. "As long as the pregnancy progresses without any complications, everything will be fine."

Was she trying to reassure me, or herself?

"When are you coming back, honey?" I asked. "Don't wait too long because it may not be safe to travel."

"I'm giving it another two weeks, Mom. If Pedro doesn't get a visa by then, I'll come alone."

Three days before she was due to fly back she called again. The moment I picked up the phone I *knew* that something was wrong.

"Mom," Hayley shouted over the crackling line, "I have a really bad case of food poisoning."

"Oh, my God, what happened?"

"Pedro and I went to visit his relatives in the countryside. We had lunch there. By the time we got back to the city at night I was throwing up all over. I can't keep anything down so my doctor said I should go to the hospital for a couple of days to be rehydrated."

I felt the telltale symptoms of an anxiety attack coming on. My chest felt tight and I couldn't breathe. I shut my eyes and tried to focus on Hayley.

"Sweetheart, can I do anything? Do you need any special medication? Or do you want me to fly over?"

I tried to keep my voice calm even though I was fighting off a wave of dizziness.

"That's okay, Mom. I'm sure I'll be better by the weekend. Pedro will try to change my flight for next week."

"Just make sure you recover completely before flying," I urged. "And please call tomorrow to let us know how you are doing."

"I'll try. It may not be possible from the hospital, but I'll tell Pedro to call."

"Take care of yourself. Please."

"Mom, I have to run. I mean, literally *run*. For the bathroom..."

I hung up the phone and ran to the bedroom. When Brent came home half an hour later he found me curled up on the bedspread, my eyes tightly shut, breathing erratically. My face was streaked with tears.

"Megan, what happened?" he asked, alarmed. "Hayley?"

"She has food poisoning. She is in the hospital."

My chest felt as though it was crushed by a heavy object.

"I can't breathe," I croaked. "I'm choking."

"You must be hyperventilating. Stress can cause this."

Brent ran into the kitchen and came back with a brown paper bag and a glass of water.

"Try to sit up and breathe into the bag," he said. "It'll increase the amount of carbon dioxide in your blood and make you feel better."

He helped me sit up and supported my back while I took slow, deep breaths.

"Feel better?" he asked.

"A little," I gasped.

He brought the glass to my lips.

"Drink this slowly," he said, still supporting my back.

I took small sips of the ice cold water.

"Megan, love, you *must* find some kind of antidote to stress," Brent implored. "You just can't go on like this."

"I know." I snuggled against Brent's chest and shut my eyes.

It was three days before Hayley called again. She was out of the hospital, feeling better but still weak. She had lost six pounds and, while at the hospital, started to have early contractions. She sounded tired and beat.

"The doctor says I shouldn't travel just yet," she said. "I might go into premature labor."

"That's it!" I shouted to Brent after Hayley and I hung up. "I'm going over there. I'll get crazy if I don't."

Brent snickered.

"*Get* crazy?"

"I'm in no mood for jokes," I snapped.

"Yes, you haven't been in the mood for *anything* fun lately."

"Listen," I said curtly, "I don't need any complaining or whining from you right now. Can't you see how frazzled I am?"

Brent opened his mouth as if to say something, but instead he shook his head in resignation and turned away.

"Come, Paris," he called and the puppy pranced. "You and I are going to spend some time in the doghouse."

With that Brent left the house, followed by Paris. I immediately felt a pang of regret.

I was making arrangements to fly to Guatemala when Hayley phoned again the next day.

"Mom, I'm feeling better, so I'm coming home tomorrow," she said. "I 'm flying into Miami."

Finally!

"That's great honey, but are you sure?" I was torn between joy and apprehension. "What about the contractions?"

"They stopped. I figure this is my last chance to make a run for it. If I don't come home now," she stopped and hesitated, "I may have to give birth here."

"Sweetheart, are you *sure*? I mean, you're eight months pregnant. Is it safe to fly?"

"Mom, it's a short flight. I'll be fine."

"Okay, honey, it's great news," I said. "We'll leave for Miami early in the morning and meet you at the airport. By the way, I found an obstetrician for you. He can see you as soon you get here."

"Terrific. See you tomorrow then?"

"Yes, sweetheart." I couldn't stop smiling. *"Hasta la vista.*

After we hung up I called Mamma. She and I had been talking almost every week, brief, non–committal conversations focusing mainly on Hayley. Neither of us had mentioned the incident on the night of Hayley's departure.

"She is coming home tomorrow," I said. "Finally."

"Thank God. Tell her to call, eh?"

"I will. It may not be until the evening though. She arrives at 3:30 and it's about a four–hour drive home."

"Is okay. I be up, waiting."

I couldn't sleep at all that night. My excitement at seeing Hayley again was mitigated by my growing worry that something horrible was about to happen. I tried to push these thoughts out of my mind.

Chapter Twenty-Three

Brent and I stood in the arrivals area at the Miami airport. A tropical storm was nearing the east coast of Florida and I was praying that Hayley's flight wouldn't be delayed. After almost seven months of waiting, I couldn't stand to wait one more minute.

I glanced at the arrivals monitor.

"Another fifteen minutes," I told Brent.

He handed me a cup of coffee he had just bought at a nearby stand.

"Drink this," he said. "Hopefully it will calm your nerves."

"*Caffeine* will calm my nerves?" I asked, turning to him.

"You're right, bad idea. What was I thinking? Drink this and you'll be all over the walls. As though you weren't already."

"Brent, I *know* I haven't been easy to live with these past few months," I said. "For most of our brief marriage I've had terrible mood swings and I've made your life miserable. I promise that as soon as we get Hayley home safely, I'll make it up to you. I won't ever put you through the wringer again."

Brent looked at me with sadness in his eyes.

"To tell you the truth, Megan, I started to have my doubts," he said softly. "I didn't stop loving you, but I did, at times, wonder what I got myself into. And I couldn't even talk to you about it. I mean, you've been ..."

"A bitch?"

The mere thought that Brent might have regretted marrying me sent shivers down my spine.

"Yes, you took the words right out of my mouth."

"I know, Brent," I sighed. "But that's over and done with. I promise."

There was a moment's silence. My heartbeat thundered and my throat constricted, cutting the flow of air into my lungs. I gasped. Did Brent consider *ending* our marriage?

Finally he turned toward me and grinned.

"All right. I'm not an unreasonable person so I'll allow myself to be placated."

Relieved, I smiled and stretched out my hand.

"Truce?" I asked.

"Truce," he said and shook my hand. "I've always been a firm believer in making love, not war. So," he winked, "I'm looking forward to celebrating the ceasefire the minute we get back home."

The monitor showed that Hayley's plane had landed and we waded through the jostling crowd to move closer to the railing.

"There she is!" I shouted.

Hayley came out of customs, pushing a trolley laden with two bags. Despite her ordeal she looked lovely. Her hair was shorter, her skin tanned.

"Mom!"

We ran into each other's arms and embraced. I held her tightly and didn't want to let go.

"Goodness," I said, patting her stomach. "I'm certainly not used to having *that* come between us."

Brent came over and gave Hayley a hug.

"Welcome back," he said, grinning. "I'm sure glad you're home. Maybe *now* your mother will go back to being her old, lovable self."

"Brent, please be on your best behavior in front of the child."

Laughing, we came out of the terminal and headed toward the car.

"So how was your flight?" I asked. "And how are you feeling?"

"Well, I had contractions the whole night, some of them pretty strong. But this morning I felt fine so I decided to bite the bullet and fly. And here I am." She pushed the bangs out of her eyes. "I'm *so* looking forward to life's little comforts like unlimited hot water and air–conditioning. And, oh yes, water straight from the tap."

We piled up into Brent's SUV and started the long drive home. I told Hayley about the attic above the garage that Brent renovated for her, Pedro and the baby.

"It's two rooms, a kitchenette and a bathroom." I said. "It's not very big but it'll do just fine for now. And, by the way, Sean is looking forward to finally meeting you."

I didn't hear any response, so I turned and saw that Hayley had fallen asleep in the back seat.

"She is sleeping," I whispered to Brent and yawned. "Mind if I take a little catnap myself?"

I fell asleep before hearing Brent's answer.

I heard a strange, anguished noise and felt insistent poking on my left arm. Groggy and disoriented, I opened my eyes and saw Brent's panic–stricken face staring at me.

"Wake up," he said, his voice sharp with urgency. "It's Hayley."

I turned around and saw Hayley's frightened expression.

"Mom," she said, her breathing heavy. "The seat is completely drenched. I think my waters broke."

"Brent, pull over," I said as calmly as I could, although my heart rate started to accelerate.

Brent's face was a pale shade of grey.

"I can't here. I'll pull over as soon as I find a spot."

I reached back and took Hayley's hand.

"Honey, we'll pull over as soon as we can. It'll be okay."

I didn't know what else to say. My mind drew a blank.

"There's a rest area fifteen miles down the road," Brent announced. I saw droplets of sweat forming on his forehead. "But shouldn't we go straight to a hospital?"

"Where are we?" I asked. "Where is the nearest town?"

"We're on I-75 heading west. I hate to tell you, but this is a pretty desolate stretch of the highway. No major towns until Naples. But that's about an hour's drive."

"Oh, God!"

The sound coming from the back seat was so gut-wrenching, it took Brent and me by surprise. We both turned around at the same time to see Hayley, her face contorted in pain.

"I just had a contraction," she moaned.

I climbed into the back seat.

"Lie down, honey."

I touched the upholstery and felt the wetness.

"Brent," I shouted, without really meaning to. "Do we have any clean blankets in the car?"

"Um, no, only Paris's cover."

"Mom," Hayley whispered. "I have some towels in my brown bag."

My hands shook so much, I struggled with the zipper. After a few tries I finally managed to open the bag and fish out two beach towels and some T-shirts.

"Here." I spread one towel on the seat. "Lie down, Hayley."

I tried to gently push her down, but Hayley sat in the middle of the seat, her eyes closed, her head bowed, and both hands tightly gripping the seat's edge.

"Oooooh!" she yelled.

"Another contraction?" I asked quietly, although I already knew the answer.

"Yes," she breathed heavily.

I felt a familiar wave of dizziness coming on.

"Brent, what are we going to do?" I asked, my throat so dry I almost couldn't talk.

"I'll pull over as soon as I can. In about five miles."

"But then what? I think she's in labor."

"What?" he exclaimed. "You mean, the baby is coming *now?*"

Before I could answer, Hayley was in pain again. She rocked back and forth, her eyes glazed over, her skin damp.

"Yes," I said. "*Now.*"

"But, how's it possible? I mean, so quickly?"

"She's had three contractions on top of each other."

I put my arms around Hayley and kissed her forehead. Her skin was hot and clammy.

"Shhhh," I said. "It'll be all right. Just breathe deeply."

"I'm calling 911," Brent said and pulled out his cell phone. "I'll tell them to meet us at the rest area. Of course, given the distances here it may be a while before they arrive."

As Brent spoke to the dispatcher Hayley had another powerful contraction. She cried out and squeezed my hand so hard I felt as though my bones would break.

"How often?" Brent shouted. "They want to know the frequency of contractions."

"I'm not sure. Maybe two or three minutes."

Brent relayed this information to the dispatcher.

"We're here," he said. "The rest area. The paramedics are on their way. I'll stay on the phone until they get here."

Brent stopped the car. The area was deserted and there was a grassy patch under a palm tree. I turned to Hayley.

"Honey, let's spread the towel on the grass under that tree. You'll be more comfortable there."

Brent and I helped Hayley out of the car and laid her, gently, on the towel. As soon as we positioned her she clutched her stomach and wailed.

"Mom!" she yelled. "This hurts so much. I can't stand it any longer."

I knelt next to her and wiped the perspiration from her face with the towel's edge.

"Yes, honey, I know. Please be brave."

I knew how silly, how utterly ineffective, my words were, but I couldn't think of anything more comforting to say. "Please God," I silently prayed. "Stay with us. Stay with Hayley. *Please*."

I turned and looked at Brent. He paced nervously, cell phone glued to his ear.

How long had it been since Hayley's water broke? Half an hour? Longer? I totally lost any notion of time. All I was aware of, all I cared about, was my daughter spread out on a towel under a tree.

"Ooooooh," she screamed.

"Breathe, honey," I said and squeezed her hand. "Inhale, exhale, one, two, three, four."

Hayley turned her tear-streaked face toward me.

"Mom," she moaned, "I just want to die."

"Shhhh, honey, you don't mean it. It's the pain talking."

"When this is over and done with," she said, breathing heavily, "I don't ever want to have another baby."

"Honey," I smiled. "All women say that. And then they go on to have more children."

I thought about the day Hayley was born. The drug-induced sleep, the comet dream...

"OH, GOD!"

Hayley was now pulling on my arm, her nails embedded in my flesh. I winced from the pain but didn't budge.

"Mom, I feel like I have to push," she panted. "What should I do?"

"Breathe, honey, rapid, shallow breathing."

I turned around to look for Brent. He stood a few yards away, watching wide-eyed.

"Brent, the baby is coming! Where are the paramedics?"

He relayed the information to the cell phone.

"About ten miles away," he said.

"But what should I do? She is ready to push!"

Again, Brent spoke with the dispatcher. He listened and nodded his head.

"We need something to disinfect and cut the cord," he shouted back, as though giving instructions for a home improvement project. "What do we have?"

"Look in the first-aid kit, in the glove compartment. And get another towel from the car, just in case."

Brent ran to the car, rummaged through the glove compartment and took out the kit.

"There are clippers here and a disinfectant and ..."

He listened to the phone.

"They say to disinfect our hands and the clippers."

He poured the liquid on my hands and then on his. I felt like a surgeon scrubbing for an op.

"Mom, I'm pushing, "Hayley yelled. "I can't hold it any more."

If I had all the freedom in the world, freedom to do whatever I wanted to at that particular moment, I would faint. As it was, I knelt between Hayley's legs, removed her jeans and underwear, and saw the baby's head crowning. I felt very light-headed.

"Good grief, Brent," I screamed, "the baby's head is almost out!"

Brent shouted into the phone.

"The baby's head is almost out!"

He came closer and peered.

"I can actually see it," he told the dispatcher. "It's a baby!"

Hayley shut her eyes, grabbed the edge of the towel, held her breath, and pushed. The baby's head inched outward.

"They say to take the head, turn it sideways very gently, and, with the next push, try to pull it out."

I wiped my forehead on my sleeve.

Half a minute passed, maybe less, and Hayley let out another cry.

"I'm pushing again," she said in croaky voice. She inhaled, held her breath, and raised her head and shoulders. I could now see the baby's eyes and nose.

Brent hovered over my shoulder.

"Turn the head," he said with urgency in his voice. "Gently."

I tried to steady my trembling hands.

"What if I crush the baby's head?" I shouted.

"Do it, Megan. You can do it!"

I took a deep breath and ever so gently rotated the baby's head to the right. It was soft and warm in my hands.

"Push again, honey. The baby's almost out."

In the distance I heard the wailing of the siren.

"Here it comes," Hayley whispered.

She grunted and pushed.

"They say to hold the head with one hand, and just under the shoulders with the other, and gently pull." Brent said. He was as breathless as Hayley and I. "Easy does it."

"Brent, I can't." I felt tears stinging my eyes. "What if I do it wrong? "

"Megan, this is not the time to think about 'what ifs.' Just do it, Megan, just *do* it!"

"Keep pushing," honey," I told Hayley.

I put my right hand under the baby's head and the left one on the torso, and pulled gently. The little body slipped out easily. Hayley moaned.

"It's a boy," I whispered. "You have a son."

Hayley smiled and raised her head to look at him.

"Is he okay?" she asked.

"He is beautiful. Lots of dark hair."

I felt hot tears streaming down my face. Brent came over with a fresh towel, gently wrapped it around the baby and handed him to Hayley.

"The paramedics are here," he announced, his voice breaking.

As Brent and I sat under the palm tree, paramedics cut the baby's umbilical cord, cleared the mucus, wrapped him in a clean sheet and delivered the placenta. Within twenty minutes Hayley and the baby were in the ambulance, on their way to the hospital.

Brent and I sat on the grass like battle-worn warriors. We were dirty, sweaty and exhausted.

"Well," he chuckled, "she *did* want to have the baby in America. And she got her wish."

"Yes," I laughed. "And her son can always boast that he was born under a palm tree off I-75. How many kids can say that?"

I reached out for Brent's hand.

"How about finding a hotel for the night?" I asked, relieved that Hayley and the baby were now in competent hands. "We both need a good rest."

"Terrific," he smiled. "I never slept with a grandmother before."

Chapter Twenty-Four

Dear Mamma,

As I told you on the phone, your great-grandson, Dylan Pedro Dominguez, is a healthy, beautiful baby. Despite being born a month early, he weighed in at a healthy seven pounds. He has dark eyes and dark hair, like Pedro. Of course, Brent and I haven't yet met Pedro, but yesterday he finally received his long-awaited visa. He will be arriving here next week. He will try to get his medical certification so that he can work as a doctor in this country.

Hayley and Dylan have settled in the small apartment over Brent's office. She is slowly adjusting to her new life as a mother and, lucky for her, Dylan is a calm baby. He hardly ever cries and is not at all fussy or cranky.

In January Hayley will go to Brent's alma mater, the University of South Florida. They have a campus just a few miles south of us, in Sarasota, so it will be an easy commute for her. While she's finishing her last semester I'll be taking care of Dylan. I just hope I'll still know how.

Mamma, you asked me to send pictures of the baby, but I have a better idea: why don't you come down here and meet Dylan in person? If you arrive after next week you'll be able to meet Pedro as well. All of us, and I in particular, would like that very much.

You and I have had a falling out and, for the first time in our lives, we have not spoken for months. We stubbornly let our anger and resentment toward each other stand in the way of reconciliation. I can only imagine that you were waiting for me to make the first step, as I waited for you to do the same.

Truth is, I was very angry with you, Mamma. Angry not only for the comments you made during that dinner with Hayley

– that was admittedly the last straw – but for the many times prior to that night, for years prior, when you ruled over me with guilt, criticism and disapproval. Please understand that I have carried this anger, resentment and frustration for a very long time. I have managed to bury these feelings and suppress them until one day, inevitably, they came out – actually, forced their way out –like a massive avalanche.

These past months, as I worried about Hayley, I morphed from a steady, even-tempered person into a raving and raging lunatic. I realize now that mothers can't be perfect creatures. In our sometimes desperate, and often futile, attempts to protect our children and keep them safe we can, and do, become irrational and erratic. I understand you better now, Mamma, and I know that you did the best you could, the best you knew how.

Mamma, the other day, as I thought about the rift between us, I remembered Tina. She was a very deep, insightful and spiritual person who firmly believed in – and lived by – the carpe diem principle: seizing each moment and enjoying it to the fullest. She would be aghast at the thought that people who love each other allow anger, bitterness, and unresolved conflicts to drive them apart.

Now that Hayley and Dylan are home safely, I finally have time for introspection. Free from constant worry and anguish, my mind can roam and explore thoughts and feelings that I have pushed aside for months. I realize now that I no longer need to hold on to the anger that has prevented me from fully appreciating and enjoying all the wonderful people in my life. I am saying, Mamma, that I'm not angry with you any longer. I made my peace with my past. (Brent tells me this is called "the wisdom of maturity.") And, to tell you the truth, I actually miss those wacky stories of yours. Somehow, my life is not quite the same without them.

Would you please come and visit us, Mamma? You could have Sean's room. He only comes over on weekends and I'm sure he won't mind sleeping on the sofa.

One more thing I want to say to you. I haven't said it in a long, long time, and I am so sorry I haven't: I love you, Mamma.

Megan.

Epilogue

The sheet of paper billows in the wind and I grasp it tightly. I bring it closer to my face and squint at the small, slanted handwriting.

Dear Megan,

I get your letter yesterday and I read it three times. Every time I read it I cry. All the months we don't talk I don't cry. Now I get your letter and I cry.

That fight we have before Hayley leave, I get very, very angry. I don't understand why you talk to me like this. I think you don't love me, you hate me so much, because no child can talk to her Mamma like this.

I wait for you to come to me and say you sorry. I wait and wait but you don't say it. I don't understand why.

Now I get letter and I understand better. I no angry no more. Is true, I never think that I do these things to you. I very young when your Papa die and I don't know what to do. I afraid that I be bad mother, that I don't take good care of you, that you be hurt or sick or hungry. Nobody here to teach me, to tell me what to do, how be good mother. I only know what my own Mamma tell me and what I hear at the store.

I tell Francesco this morning that I want to go to Florida. I work here thirty-nine years and I never take no vacation. He tell me that Vittoria, his wife, she has nephew who work in travel agency on Queens Boulevard. I go there tomorrow and ask for ticket to Florida. I very nervous because I never leave New York. I afraid to fly too but I want to see you, Dylan, Hayley, Brad and Pedro.

I call you when I know more.

Ti amo,

Your Mamma

P.S. I hope there no mistakes in this letter. I write this with dictionary.

I fold the letter and reach into my jeans pocket for a tissue. I dry my tears and blow my nose. Then I hear the wind whistle my name.

"Megaaaaan... Megaaaaan."

I turn around and see a figure walking briskly toward me, his path lit by a flashlight.

"I'm over here, Brent," I wave.

He comes over, kisses me on the lips and sits down.

"So there you are. I've been wondering where you went."

I hand him the letter.

"Read this."

He unfolds the paper and shines the flashlight on it. I watch his facial muscles twitch and, as he finishes reading, break into a smile. He reaches for my hand and squeezes it.

"Megan, I'm so happy for you, for your Mom. This is such a relief."

"You can't possibly know." I dab at my eyes with the crumpled tissue. "'Relief' doesn't even begin to describe my feelings."

"Okay, so tell me."

I shut my eyes and think.

"It's a jumble of emotions. But," I open my eyes and turn to him, "if I had to choose just one word to describe what I feel, it would be 'light–hearted.' It's like whatever burdens – anger, frustration, resentment – all the things that have been eating at me and building up in me all these years, are suddenly gone. Evaporated. I feel so light I could skip all the way home."

We stand up, dust off the sand and start to walk back.

"What a great ending to a tumultuous eleven months," Brent says. "And to think that we only survived because of *my* saint–like patience. Gandhi himself would be proud of me."

"Actually, it's a great ending to a tumultuous forty–four years," I sigh. "And please remember, that Gandhi never boasted."

I stop and turn to Brent.

"You know what I just realized? As much as she used to annoy and irritate the hell out of me, at least I knew what to expect. Mamma was Mamma. Now, well, she sounds so *normal*, so subdued. I never, *ever,* thought I'd say this, but, I don't want a *normal* mother. I'll miss her quirkiness."

"Sweetheart, I'm sure she couldn't have changed *that* much. People her age can't alter their personalities just like that. I'm sure that quirkiness, as you call it, is still very deeply ingrained in her psyche."

"I hope so. I mean, I'd like Dylan to grow up hearing her crazy stories. God, *what* am I saying? I must be losing my mind."

Brent laughs and pulls me close to him. We are almost at the beach's edge when he suddenly stops.

"Look," he says, pointing to the sky.

Even before I raise my eyes I know what he is showing me. I slowly look up and smile. Polaris.

"Shall we follow it home?" he asks.

"Yes," I say, and start to skip.

THE END